THE
MALEFICENT
MAID

Jacqueline Beard

The Lawrence Harpham Mysteries are published
by Dornica Press

The author can be contacted on her website
https://jacquelinebeardwriter.com/

While there, why not sign up for her FREE newsletter.

ISBN: 1-83-829556-9

ISBN: 978-1-83-829556-1

First Printing 2021

Dornica Press

Also, by this author:

Lawrence Harpham Murder Mysteries:

The Fressingfield Witch
The Ripper Deception
The Scole Confession
The Felsham Affair
The Moving Stone

Short Stories featuring Lawrence Harpham:

The Montpellier Mystery

The Constance Maxwell Dreamwalker Mysteries

The Cornish Widow
The Croydon Enigma

Box Set (Kindle only) containing
The Fressingfield Witch, The Ripper Deception &
The Scole Confession

Novels:

Vote for Murder

PROLOGUE

31 May 1902

Home again, back to the same hellhole I fled from as a boy. Not quite the exact location, for my father dragged the sorry remains of his family thirteen miles west to Peasenhall the week before I left for Devon. I didn't go with him. Our most recent altercation provided the motivation I needed to leave my roots forever, or so I thought. But life isn't like that, and here I am back again, tail between my legs, skulking towards the only family I have ever known, like a mangy cur cowering before his master.

Running away to sea should have been the making of me. And for a long time, I thrived on board the ship, co-existing with hardened sea dogs; tattooed, fearless men, singing shanties and labouring hard as they travelled the oceans. Some, like me, were running away. Others, much older, were press-ganged as youths and dragged from the docks kicking and screaming for their

1

mothers. They could have served their time and returned to Blighty, but they joined the Royal Navy instead. The life of a sailor, however rough, lures like a siren at the dread of living back on land. I never thought to return to Suffolk, but I had no choice. I will never again sail across the blue, and something deep inside me withers at the prospect.

Land living works for some, but not for me. Not because I'm afraid of good, honest toil, but because no one will give me a chance. They didn't before and they certainly won't now, disfigured as I am. My face is a horror show of scarred flesh, my torso a pitted hide of flailed skin. Injuries mark every visible part of my body, and I wear my shame as they intended I should. I don't know which is worse – the scars in my mind or my maimed and broken flesh. It wasn't always this way, though memories of happier times dwell so far in the past that I can barely recall them. But once in a while, Mother enters my dreams and strokes my hair like she did when I was small. And on those rare occasions, I wake up smiling until I remember what happened to me. Until it all comes crashing down again.

I often think of my early school days, which my father considered a waste of time – strange because he enjoyed a rudimentary education and seemed to value his ability to read and write. But I was the eldest boy, and Mother wanted me to go, so I did. And I liked it. I was clever with a quick brain, though my intelligence has done me no favours in life. Better to be witless and happy than bright and frustrated, teased, and tormented. But the education I gained between the ages of six and eleven when my father hauled me out of school to labour at the farm was enough that I could read, write, and do my sums. I didn't want to leave school and I hated leaving my friends behind to continue without me. Both Cyril and Georgie finished their education in Yoxford while I picked stones in the field, then graduated to handling cattle. I didn't mind the hard work, but it was monotonous, and I longed to learn.

My father knocked that longing out of me before I reached my twelfth birthday. By then, there were four of us – Phoebe, Louisa, Mark, and I, all sharing a bed, boys at the top, girls at the tail. Mother and Father slept downstairs next to the parlour, which is why it took us a while to notice the bruises. Phoebe saw them first and asked me if Mother had fallen over. I didn't know, but I sneaked a look while she was serving the evening meal, and sure enough, her neck was black and blue. But I couldn't see the extent of the bruising until Mother unbuttoned her collar in a fit of the vapours. At first, I assumed she may have been careless, and thought nothing of it. But the bruises soon reappeared. And that's when I realised my father was more often drunk than not. When he was sober, he was quiet and withdrawn. But as the day went on and the beer jug emptied, Father was brutish, snarling, spitting and angry, all of it directed at his wife.

She bore it as only a mother can, downtrodden and fearful of losing her children – tolerating pain and humiliation to keep her family together. But it couldn't last. Father's outbursts grew worse, and eventually, he lost his job. The few pennies I earned were not enough to keep the house, and Mark was only four, so my mother couldn't work. Phoebe left school, Louisa followed, and the three of us worked long hours to put food on the table. But as hard as we tried, we couldn't support a family of six. Mother, Father and Mark went into the workhouse at Bulcamp, soon followed by Louisa. Only Phoebe and I remained, but we couldn't pay the rent, and they took the cottage away. Kindly Mrs Grey took Phoebe into service, but there was nothing for me until Cyril persuaded his uncle to let me stay in the barn, and Georgie kept me supplied with food during the long, cold winter. My old school friends rallied my spirits when I was at my lowest ebb. I can never repay their kindness.

Several months without alcohol left Father a step closer to the man he used to be. He discharged himself from the workhouse one frosty February morning and started the humiliating climb back to prosperity. First, he approached his previous employer, who wouldn't give him the time of day. But undeterred, he went from farm to farm until he secured work in Sibton with the benefit of a tied cottage. We came home – all but Phoebe, who had settled with her mistress and was in no rush to risk living in her father's house again. She was right to be cautious. Father held himself together for six months, but his willpower was weak, and he reverted to his old ways.

One day, Mother didn't get up. Father said she was poorly, and we should leave her alone. But when the fireplace was cold the next day, I waited for Father to go to work, tapped on her door and opened it a chink. Mother moaned and tried to tell me to go away, but I went inside anyway. Mother tried to pull the blanket over her head, but I sat beside her and swept the hair from her face, finding it crusty with blood. I couldn't see properly and opened the curtain hanging limply from the tiny cottage window. A little light filtered in; not much but enough to see her bloodied mouth and two black eyes. Mother's nose was halfway across her face, and she'd broken all the fingernails on one of her hands. I held her in my arms and cried into her shoulder, promising I would make it better. She stayed silent and stared ahead as if nothing mattered anymore. I begged her to tell me if my father had done it, but she didn't reply. Mother refused to utter a single word while I was in the room, and eventually, I left. It took another three days of bed rest before she got up, by which time Father had jolted himself into sobriety for fear that he would kill her. Mother recovered, but she was never the same. As Father conquered his demons, Mother succumbed to hers. She began spending time with a friend in Badingham. I don't know what they did there, but Tilly Bartlett was like a tonic to my mother, and no matter how low she felt before leaving home, she was markedly happier when she returned. Until the day she didn't.

They found her in a ditch by the side of the road about sixty yards from the Bowling Green Inn. And it was there that the inquest was later held. Mother had been socialising alone, imbibing two glasses of stout before leaving the establishment, her departure encouraged by the landlord. Tilly gave evidence at the inquest, telling the jury that my mother had arrived at her house in a very depressed condition, complaining of family matters and saying that her troubles were more than she could bear. But Tilly was adamant that Mother never had or ever would take her own life. Mother drowned in the ditch with a verdict of accidental death, and they expected us to accept this because there were no marks upon her. But I wasn't sure. For all her weakness, I loved my mother, and I stood by her graveside with a heart as weary as ever it could be. Father prospered for a while after Mother's death and seemed undeterred by the inconvenience of losing her. The low spirits that sent her to an early grave saddened us, but not Father, which struck me as a good reason not to trust him. After all, he knew she went to Tilly's house and could easily have intercepted her. And sure enough, within weeks of her death, he took up with a woman half her age, albeit for only a few months.

Without Mother, all structure left our lives. Father and I worked during the day, and Louisa went back to school for a while, but nobody cared for Mark, and before long, the authorities summoned my father for abandonment when they found Mark wandering the streets. Father took the criticism badly and slid back into his old ways and, with Mother gone and his pent-up cruelty simmering beneath every drunken rage, it wasn't long before I took up the mantle of whipping boy. I was only thirteen and a scrawny, anxious thirteen at that. Timid, slight, and underfed, I was smaller than Georgie and a full head shorter than Cyril. And when Father summoned me into the yard at eight o'clock one autumn evening, I didn't hesitate to obey him. I walked behind him as we went outside, trying to stand downwind of his acrid breath. Father swayed as he walked to the yard, and when we arrived and were safely away from prying eyes, he asked if Mark had gone to school earlier that day. I said I didn't know, and his lip curled. "I left you in charge," he snarled, fists balled, knuckles white and angry.

I shook my head, puzzled. We'd made no such arrangement, and I didn't hesitate to tell him. The words had barely left my mouth when he punched me squarely in the face, and my nose crunched

5

as blood spurted from the wound. The force of the blow sent me reeling across the yard. I still remember lying there, all these years later, flat on my back, hand clutching my cheek and trying to stem the blood. I waited for Father to say something, but he didn't. Polishing his knuckles, he strode back to the house, straight-backed and steadier than he came.

I crept into the byre and cried like a baby, understanding for the first time the horror of my mother's life. And I trembled as I relived the moment, for it was apparent that releasing his aggression made Father feel better. He visibly relaxed, and I knew without a doubt that it would happen again. It did, night after night, month after month, year on year. He left too many bruises in the early days, and someone must have noticed. My father stopped hitting me in the face and adopted a new method. Now, he focused on my body, kicking, slapping, using a wooden paddle – anything that my clothes would hide. And from time to time, when the mood took him, he jabbed rabbit punches to the back of my head. I didn't retaliate because I couldn't. He was big, and I was little more than a child, but inevitably, that changed. I was fifteen when he beat me for the last time. Something snapped, and instead of resigning myself to his fists, I snatched his paddle and hit him over the head. He fell to the ground like a sack of flour, and I kicked him until my energy failed. Father never raised his fists after that night, and we parted ways within a few weeks.

I lied when I joined the navy. I found an old down-and-out on the Plymouth docks and persuaded him to act as my legal guardian. And that's how I joined the ranks of the Royal Navy, aged fifteen as a boy second class. It was touch and go, as I was on the borderline of their height and weight requirements. But fortune smiled on me that day, and I signed up for twelve good years of service. And after that, for twelve more. But I didn't complete my second term, and I tremble now at the thought of the trauma that ended my naval service – an unimaginable horror that haunts my dreams to this day. It is why I found myself back in Peasenhall, where I first encountered Rose Harsent.

CHAPTER ONE

Back at The Butter Market

Monday, January 19, 1903

Lawrence was sitting at his office desk in The Butter Market and cleaning his nails with an ivory envelope slitter when the door clanged open, and a little girl burst through.

"Daddy, Daddy. There's a giant pig in the middle of the road, and it's eating Mr Fawcett's turnips."

Lawrence looked up and beamed, then picked up the child and spun her around.

"Good morning, little flower," he said.

"Come and see the pig."

"Where's Mama?"

"Outside," said the little girl, worming out of his grasp. "Come and see."

Lawrence sighed good-naturedly and followed her outside. Halfway down the street, a ruddy-faced man was chasing a large, white pig who was several yards ahead. The remains of his fruit and vegetable display lay scattered in a half-eaten, half-trampled pile. Lawrence placed his hands over Daisy's ears at the sound of the man's furious cries and unsavoury language.

"Come inside. It's too cold to stand around," said Lawrence, but as Daisy tugged his arm, he noticed Violet crouching by the display. She was trying to recover the few intact products from the man's stall.

"I wouldn't bother," said Lawrence, approaching her.

Violet stood and brushed herself down. "Poor man," she said. "But you're right. I can't do much to help."

"Where did it come from?"

"The pig?"

Lawrence nodded.

"I don't know. It just appeared while we were walking to school. It must have escaped."

"It's a nice pig," said Daisy solemnly.

"But very naughty," said Lawrence, tousling her hair.

Violet pulled up her cuff and looked at her wristwatch. "Come along now," she said. "It's time for school. I'll be back in a moment."

She smiled at Lawrence, who returned to his office, light-hearted at the sight of his daughter, and pleased that at long last, Violet was wearing the watch he had bought her for Christmas.

He settled on his chair, pulled out a sheaf of papers and was about to read them when their new cleaner, Cynthia Dixon, emerged from the rear of the building carrying a tray.

"Here you are," she said, placing a cup of tar-like coffee with floating speckles beside his inkwell.

Lawrence grimaced but thanked her all the same.

"Here's Miss Violet's drink," she continued, settling the tray on Violet's desk with more stability than she subsequently managed when transferring the cup. It wobbled, tipped over and coated the ledger.

"Oh, dear God!" exclaimed Lawrence, leaping up and grabbing the book by its spine. He shook it vigorously, and droplets splashed to the floor.

"I'm sorry, I'm sorry," said Cynthia, her eyes darting around the room as she searched for something to clean the mess. Seeing nothing, she took the end of her apron and flopped it across the sodden desk. The colour changed from white to sludge brown in seconds, but when she gathered it back into her lap, screwing it into a loose ball, coffee trickled everywhere, making an even bigger mess.

Lawrence stared at her as if he couldn't comprehend her thought process. "There's a cloth in the sink," he muttered. "I'll get it. You go home and change."

"Yes. I will. Thank you. I'll do it at once," said Cynthia, red-faced and flustered. She left the office without her coat, clutching the apron to her chest and huffing out plumes of cold air as she crossed the freezing street.

Lawrence returned with a cloth and had almost finished wiping down the desk when Violet arrived.

"What have you done?" she asked, hanging her coat on the stand.

"Not me. Clumsy Cynthia strikes again."

"Don't worry. The desk is old. A few more marks won't hurt."

Lawrence nodded to the badly stained ledger, propped up by the fireplace.

"Oh, no. Is it as damaged on the inside?"

"I'm afraid so. She'll have to go."

"But good cleaners are so hard to come by."

"I wouldn't know. We haven't had one since Annie left."

Lawrence returned to the kitchen and wrung out the cloth. When he returned, Violet was sitting at the desk looking mournfully at the ledger, now lying open and still liberally coated with coffee.

"We'll need to get another one," she said. "I wonder if Annie misses us as much as we miss her."

"She probably doesn't give us a second thought now she's happily married," said Lawrence.

"True. We always knew Robert would make an honest woman of her one day. I just wish she had settled here."

"Talking of marriage…"

Violet snapped her head up. "Don't, Lawrence," she said.

"It's been more than three years. Surely I've proved myself by now."

"We're in the office. Must we go over old ground? Can't you just accept the way things are? We're all happy, aren't we?"

"I'd be happier if you would marry me."

"So, you say. But without Daisy, you wouldn't have even considered it."

"I would. I was. It's just…"

"It's always something, Lawrence. But I faced all the difficulties alone, and I think too well of myself to marry a man for the sake of propriety."

"That's unfair. I keep asking you because I want us to live together, not just meet at work. Daisy deserves a normal family life, and it wouldn't do you any harm with the old tabbies at the Primrose League."

"And that is precisely my point," said Violet, crossing her arms. "You've as good as said it's for Daisy and the sake of appearances. It's not enough, Lawrence. And I don't want to talk about it any further. I'm happy in my cottage, and you have that lovely big house on Angel Hill to keep you occupied. Anyway, I have had nothing to do with the Primrose League since Maisie Norton swapped our seating cards at last year's spring committee meeting, thinking she was too good to sit with an unmarried mother. You know that I resigned, and I'm spending more time with Millicent Fawcett's girls now."

10

Lawrence snorted. "Girls? They're all over forty if they're a day." He narrowed his eyes. "Isn't she something to do with the suffrage movement?"

"Yes," said Violet. "She is an important figure in the National Union of Women's Suffrage Societies, as you very well know."

"Women and politics. Is this wise? What do they hope to achieve?"

"The vote for women," said Violet. "And don't pretend you don't sympathise. You've often said that I exercise better judgement than most men."

"You do," said Lawrence, "and a vote for women is long overdue. But for the sake of our business, don't get too publicly involved."

"I wish you hadn't said that. I feel very strongly about the vote, but I'm eternally grateful that you returned my share of the business. I didn't expect it, and I certainly didn't deserve it, but I would appreciate it if you didn't use my gratitude to control my behaviour."

"You've more than earned your share of the business, Violet. And I'm not trying to stop you from staying true to your beliefs, but we must be careful not to upset the good people of Bury. Few men are as tolerant as me. Anyway, if I can't persuade you to marry me, can we at least wade through some of these cases? My diary is empty. How about yours?"

"All finished," said Violet. "We found Mrs Brown's handbag in the smithy where she'd left it. It would still be there now if I hadn't retraced her movements for most of December. Old Walter saw the bag but didn't care to move it, much less tell anybody. There was a good layer of dust by the time I got there. Anyway, we'll have a small fee in the coffers by the end of the week, and then we are on our beam ends."

"Oh, come now."

"Well, not you, with most of your inheritance still in the bank. But the business must support itself for my sake."

"I can always help."

"I wouldn't hear of it. If we can't make ends meet, then I will get another job."

Lawrence's eyes widened. "You wouldn't?"

"Of course, I would. I won't be a kept woman."

"Does Daisy have everything she needs?"

"More than enough. You have been very generous. Daisy wants for nothing."

"Well, best we find a case then," said Lawrence, splitting the papers and passing one half over to Violet.

They read in silence for ten minutes until Violet looked up. "This one," she said, placing a letter on Lawrence's desk.

"I can't read that tiny writing. Oh dear, perhaps I need glasses."

Violet reached for the letter. "It's from a young lady by the name of Gracie Francis," she said. "Gracie is getting married to a young man of good social standing. He is concerned about her background."

"That sounds ominous," said Lawrence. "Tell her to enjoy spinsterhood and save herself some money."

"She loves him," said Violet. "Otherwise, I would. Anyway, her intended comes from the same village as Gracie's great-grandmother Elizabeth Everett."

"Right. So far, so good."

"Not really. Gracie's great-aunt and great-grandmother died in suspicious circumstances, both poisoned to death. They never found the culprit. The rumours have long since died away, but her young man comes from good stock and doesn't want his family name tainted. Gracie would like us to find out who killed her grandmother. And if not that, then to at least rule out any of the immediate family."

"Can't be done," said Lawrence firmly. "Great-grandmother, you say? How many decades ago is that?"

"Several."

"Meaning?"

"1847."

"Impossible. It would be a waste of our time. We've never attempted to solve a crime that old. All the witnesses will be long dead."

"Not all."

Lawrence raised an eyebrow. "Or senile?"

"Mind your manners – you'll be old yourself one day. Anyway, the granddaughter of one of the murdered women is in her late eighties and living in Bunwell. According to Gracie, she's as sharp as a tack and with an excellent memory."

"But what could she reasonably recall?"

"She wasn't a child in arms, Lawrence. If she's in her late eighties now, she would have been in her late twenties or early thirties when the murders occurred and mature enough to understand."

"I still think it's a waste of time," grumbled Lawrence. "If they couldn't solve it over fifty years ago, what chance have we got now? It sounds like one for Bobby Bradford."

Violet got to her feet and walked towards the window, staring silently outside for a moment before speaking.

"We must take anything we can," she said. "Gracie will pay a fee whether or not we succeed, and I will do everything in my power to help her. But don't make light of Robert Bradford. I can't help thinking that you could walk away from detective work at the drop of a hat, but this business is important to me. I want to make my own way in the world, and since Mr Bradford set up his agency, cases have been few and far between."

"I'm surprised at you," said Lawrence, pushing his chair back and staring at Violet through misty eyes. "This business means everything to me, not just because you're here, but because it keeps me occupied and interested in life. So much has happened to us, so many tragedies, and our work is the glue that binds us together. I would never wish it away, and just because I jest about Bradford doesn't mean I can't see the danger."

"I'm sorry. I didn't mean to upset you. But Bradford is worth worrying about. He seems so pleasant, but since his arrival in Bury, he's everywhere. And he's widely respected and getting enquiries that would ordinarily come our way. We could do with another notable case, but they don't come along very often."

"Don't fret," said Lawrence. "I will don my smartest suit and attend some of the ghastly town events to track down business if that is what it takes. It certainly hasn't done Bradford any harm. Now, let me see if I can find something to investigate in the remains of your reject pile."

Lawrence walked towards the back of the office, glancing at the wooden board at the rear on which he'd pinned a calendar. "Oh," he said, before turning, sitting heavily on his chair, and opening his bottom drawer. He removed a half-empty bottle and a tumbler, sloshed it half full of amber liquid, then knocked it back in one deep swallow. Lawrence wiped his mouth and replaced the bottle in the drawer.

"No, thank you," said Violet.

"I'm sorry. I didn't think you liked whisky."

"It would have been nice if you'd asked."

"Do you want one?"

"No. Are you going to tell me why you felt the sudden urge to take a drink?"

Lawrence nodded towards the printed calendar upon which Violet had written all the important dates as she did at the start of every year.

"Oh, I see. Oh, dear. I wonder where Francis is now?"

"With the devil for all I care," snapped Lawrence.

"Come now," said Violet sympathetically. She rose, moved her chair close to Lawrence and took his hand. "It's time to forgive and forget," said Violet. "If I can, so should you."

Lawrence snatched his hand away. "Please don't. It's too confusing. And I can't forgive Francis for what he did to Catherine and Lily. Don't ask it of me, or I will disappoint you yet again."

Violet's eyes filled with tears. "You didn't disappoint me before. None of this is your fault."

"I wasn't there for Catherine, and I wasn't there for you. You comforted me, and I took advantage. No wonder you couldn't tell me about Daisy."

"Oh, Lawrence. So much of what happened is beyond your control, yet you insist on punishing yourself after all this time. You didn't take advantage. The night you came to me in Overstrand meant more than you could ever know. I wouldn't have allowed it to happen if I didn't want it to. I'm not a weak woman, and you certainly didn't make me. But for Loveday Graham, I would have told you about my condition sooner. I didn't hide it to hurt you. I did it to free you to marry the woman I thought you loved."

"And if I hadn't given in to my baser instincts with Loveday, we'd be married by now. So, I have failed you, and unlike you, I am weak. But in some ways, I don't care. I cannot rise above my emotions as you do, and I will never forgive Francis. If our paths cross again, I will kill him."

Violet reached for Lawrence's hand again but hesitated at the sight of his expression. Lawrence stared, steely-eyed, into the distance, his mind in another place, another time.

"What about Michael?" asked Violet.

Lawrence turned to face her. "What about him?"

"Today will be just as difficult for him."

"Why? It's been three years. He's had plenty of time to get used to it."

"So have you, but it's still painful."

Lawrence nodded. "You're right. We should call on him."

"At the church?"

"No. At Netherwood. He's moved in. Didn't I tell you?"

CHAPTER TWO

Return to Netherwood

"This has seen better days," said Lawrence nodding towards the slate sign on the pillar at the entrance to Francis Farrow's large home in Bury St Edmunds.

Violet shuddered. "It's covered in spiderwebs. I dread to think how long it's been since we were last here."

"Too many years to count. I can't bear to think about it."

Lawrence's voice wobbled as he stared down the driveway. Violet slipped her hand in his. He tensed but did not pull away.

"They were happy times for the most," she said.

Lawrence glanced towards her. He tried to speak, but the words wouldn't form.

"We don't have to go inside."

"I owe it to Michael," he said gruffly.

"Come on, then."

They crunched their way down the gravelled drive, passing the coach house on the way. Lawrence visibly blanched as he stole a sideways look to see if the Arnold Benz automobile, Francis Farrow's pride and joy, was still there. It was and Lawrence stifled a groan as he saw it mouldering unused and unloved in the open building.

Violet squeezed his hand. "Try not to think about it," she said.

They stood on the doorstep for a moment before Violet pressed the bell. A muffled tone rang inside, but nobody arrived to greet them.

"Perhaps he's out?" said Violet. "Did you tell Michael we were coming?"

"No. I assumed he'd be here. Michael has only had the keys for a few days and shouldn't have gone far."

"I'll try again."

Violet pushed the bell, and they waited another minute before Lawrence became impatient and pushed the door. It swung open, and they walked into the familiar hallway.

"Someone must be in," said Lawrence, cocking his head at a faint tapping sound at the top of the stairs. He glanced at Violet, and she nodded, then he bounded up the stairs two at a time. Violet watched from below before hearing a sudden scream from the upper level. Startled, she ran to join Lawrence, arriving in time to see a young woman crouching against the banister by his feet.

"Don't be afraid. We're friends of Michael's. Who are you?" asked Lawrence.

"Don't hurt me."

The girl, still sitting on her haunches, looked frantically from side to side. She was holding a cloth in one hand and a brush in the other, both objects tightly pressed to her chest as if in defence.

Violet tiptoed past Lawrence and knelt beside the girl.

"Are you working for Michael?" she asked.

The girl nodded dumbly towards Violet, her eyes round and anxious. She was slight and as pale as Violet's lace collar, but the tiny crow's feet around her eyes suggested she was older than she looked.

"What's your name?" asked Violet.

"Aurora," whispered the woman.

"Where's Michael?"

"Outside."

"We're here to visit him. Michael's not expecting us, but he'll be glad we're here."

"I see. What must you think of me? I was daydreaming, and you took me unawares." Aurora flashed an uncertain smile as she rose to her feet.

Lawrence watched with concern, knowing that he had frightened her but wondering why her reaction was so extreme. Aurora was a bag of nerves, and Michael should have known better than to let someone of her obviously tender disposition work alone in the large, unkempt house.

"We're sorry to have disturbed you. Are you feeling better?" asked Violet.

"Perfectly well, thank you," said Aurora, looking far from convinced.

"Then we'll leave you to it," said Lawrence, as they headed downstairs to search for Michael.

They didn't have to go far. By the time Lawrence reached the foot of the staircase, Michael was walking along the passageway.

"Lawrence, Violet. How lovely to see you?" he said, raising the ghost of a smile.

"How are you?" asked Violet.

"I have good days and bad," said Michael, honestly, running a hand through his once fair hair now peppered with grey. His dark shadowed eyes seemed distant and world-weary.

"Come into the drawing room," he continued. "I can't offer you much in the way of refreshments, but it's good of you to come."

They followed him through and waited while he removed a couple of dust sheets from the sofa and nearby chair.

"It must feel strange to be back," said Lawrence grimly. "How did you get hold of the keys?"

"Sit down," said Michael, "and I'll tell you all about it."

#
"I got them from Albert," said Michael lowering himself onto the chair. Violet and Lawrence sat on opposite ends of the sofa, with enough space to fit another person between them.

"Dear Albert," said Violet. "How is he?"

"Getting on a bit. Albert suffers from arthritis now, and he misses Netherwood. He sends his regards to you both."

"Is he managing?" asked Lawrence.

"Healthwise or financially?"

"Both."

"Yes. As far as I can tell."

"I can always make another payment."

"No. Don't do that, Lawrence. You've been more than generous. I wish I could tell Albert how kind you have been, but it would break his heart to know that Francis abandoned him with no thought to his future."

"I can afford it," said Lawrence. "And Albert deserves a reward for his loyalty and long service."

"I know," said Michael, "but his sense of loyalty is the reason that it's taken me three years to get the keys out of him. He thinks he owes it to Francis to keep the place secure."

"How did you change his mind?"

"I told him that Netherwood was falling into disrepair, and I couldn't get it fixed without getting inside."

"You weren't exaggerating," said Lawrence. "Netherwood looks as if it's been abandoned for decades. And as for the Arnold Benz, I can't bear the thought of a fine old car like that left to rot outside. I'm happy to take it off your hands."

"If I had the legal right, I'd let you. After all our trouble getting it back from Sussex, it deserves better than to sit there rusting, but it's not mine to give. Anyway, why do you need another car when you've already got one?"

"It would be less embarrassing to be a passenger in the Arnold Benz," said Violet. "It's painted a pleasant black and gold, unlike Lawrence's lurid lemon Wolseley."

"It can't be that bad," said Michael.

"Wait until you see it," Violet replied. "I advise you to wear dark glasses on first sight of the yellow peril."

"Most amusing," scowled Lawrence. "Presumably, Albert hasn't heard from your brother if he has given you the key at last?"

Michael shook his head. "No. Not a word in all these years."

"And you?"

"Still nothing since that first telegram. But Frank Podmore has come across him."

"How do you know that?"

"Isabel told me."

"She barely knows you. Why didn't she mention it to me?"

"Because she knows how much it still hurts."

"I thought better of Isabel than to keep company with Podmore. She has friends in low places."

"They both live in Hampstead," said Michael. "And Podmore's influence is much reduced since the demise of Arthur and Frederick Myers. He has troubles of his own now."

"Good," said Lawrence. "But that doesn't explain how he knows where Francis is living."

"They met abroad. Isabel ran into Podmore a few weeks ago, and oddly enough, they started talking about you. Isabel mentioned Bury St Edmunds, and Podmore asked if she knew Francis. Isabel said no, but that you were an acquaintance. Then Podmore said that he'd run into Francis during a trip to Mexico."

"Mexico. What the blazes is Francis doing there?"

"I don't know. But he was one of several Englishmen living in the same town, and Podmore said they were a funny bunch. Considering his interest in all things psychic, it was an odd remark for a man who spends his life around oddities. It made me wonder what they were up to."

"Well, I hope Francis rots there. And tell Isabel she'd be wise not to spend too much time with Podmore."

"I will, next time I return to London."

"Does the house still belong to Francis?" asked Violet.

Michael nodded. "Yes. He's transported all the valuables, of course. And I doubt he's ever coming back. But this was my father's house, and I can't bear to leave it in its current state."

"It will cost you a fortune to restore it," said Lawrence getting to his feet and swiping a layer of dust from the windowsill with his finger.

"He's left some valuable paintings in the cellar," said Michael, "and there are one or two pieces of silver in the sideboard that Francis overlooked."

"But if the car's not yours to sell, then neither is the artwork."

Michael shook his head. "I don't know what else to do. The house will fall around my ears if I don't do something."

"But Francis could march back in tomorrow, and you would lose all the fruits of your labour."

"I'll take my chances," said Michael. "I've made up my mind. It's my family home, and I'm going to stay here until Francis returns. And if he doesn't, then I'll live here for good."

"Is that why you've employed a cleaner?" asked Violet.

"Oh. Have you met Aurora?"

"Yes. We frightened her. She screamed blue murder when she saw Lawrence."

"I have that effect on women," said Lawrence, his eyes momentarily sparkling.

"She's very timid," said Michael. "I'm quite concerned about her."

"Where did she come from?"

"An advertisement in the *Bury Free Press*. But she brought good references."

"Be careful," said Violet. "Aurora seems very troubled."

"I'll try to talk to her," said Michael. "I might be able to help."

"Then don't get too involved. I'd advise against it altogether if you weren't a priest. But at least, you won't be compromising her position. I take it she's not staying here?"

"No, of course not. But you're right. Aurora applied for several jobs, some of them far better paid than mine. But she chose to work here because I am a man of God, and she said she felt safe."

"Good. Well, I hope you can help Aurora. And talking of help," said Violet.

"Yes."

"Lawrence and I are taking on a case. It's an old one, and it will save time to use the bishop's transcripts at the diocese office in Bury. Can you get us in?"

"Yes," said Michael slowly, "but it will be easier if I join you."

"You can go with Violet," said Lawrence. "No need for three."

"He doesn't think the case is worth pursuing," said Violet.

"Why?"

"Don't ask. I'll tell you about it when we look at the records. That's assuming you can spare the time?"

Michael nodded. "I'd be glad to. I'm finding Netherwood difficult," he said, nodding towards the door.

"I'm not surprised," said Violet.

"How far have you got?" asked Lawrence, who, having left fingermarks on the window, was now pointlessly poking the long-dead ashes in the fireplace.

"Not very far at all," said Michael. "I can't find half the keys. The study is locked, as are two of the bedrooms and the whole of the top floor. I can't break the doors down and can only hope to locate a few spare keys as I tidy. As for the cleaning, well you can see for yourselves. Aurora has just started on the hall and landing for appearance's sake, but there's a long way to go. I'm thinking of extending my leave of absence."

"Will the archbishop agree?"

"Who knows," said Michael. "I'm not sure whether I care anymore. I'm beginning to lose my faith."

"Oh, Michael." Violet stood and wrapped him in a bear hug. "Surely you don't mean that?"

"Not really," he said, wincing as if in pain. He stared at the floor, not meeting Violet's gaze, eyes downcast and heavy.

"It will pass, Michael. Truly it will."

"I know."

They stood quietly for a moment, all three contemplating the downward spiral of the once happy house.

"You're doing the right thing," said Lawrence, clapping Michael on the back. "God knows, I wish your brother nothing but pain, but you've kept the scandal away from Netherwood, away from all of us."

"It wasn't easy," said Michael. "Things would have been less conspicuous if he hadn't tried to kill you. But we managed between us, didn't we? They've stopped asking about him now, even the Freemasons. And if they do, I tell them that Francis is so happy abroad that he may never return. It keeps them at bay." Michael smiled sadly.

"We ought to go," said Lawrence. "You have enough to do."

"When shall we meet at the diocese office?"

"I'll let you know," said Violet. "I need to speak to someone first. Tomorrow, perhaps"

"Till then," said Michael, gesturing towards the door. They followed him along the dusty corridor and into the hallway, where they said their goodbyes. As they closed the door, Lawrence glanced upstairs. Aurora was still clutching the banister, her face ghostly white. He waited until they reached the bottom of the driveway before turning to Violet.

"That woman is trouble," he said.

CHAPTER THREE

Gibraltar Ahoy

September 1901

It was a balmy September, and conditions were good, at least on deck. Below the waterline was a different matter. Our quarters were muggy, though bearable, unlike July, where we toiled sweating, thirsty and battling heat rash as the Mediterranean temperature soared. The ship moored off Gibraltar, where we would remain for six months, making the most of our time ashore. Even the most hardened officers relaxed in the sun. Life was good, and I remember thanking God that I'd chosen a career at sea.

We worked hard during the day, but night-time brought freedom from the grind of our daily tasks, and when not ashore, usually when funds were running low, we stayed below deck drinking and playing cards or dice, as the case may be. We were old hands, and the four of us berthed together in HMS *Devastation* and had left the ill-fated HMS *Thunderer* in Blighty. We transferred only a few months before our journey to the Mediterranean, but it wasn't the first time we had to fit in with an old crew, and we didn't expect any problems. And there weren't any at first. Of course, the occasional tensions arose, especially when the sun was high, but life was good, and it stayed good until that fateful Friday night.

If I had to choose someone to avoid in the mess, it would have been Sludge Green, a heavily tattooed, squat-nosed man with a ginger beard and a scar above his eyebrow. He sported a tattoo of King Neptune over one bulging bicep and a shellback turtle with a fearsome expression on the other. Sludge was not his real name, and I never learned what it was. Even the junior officers referred to him by his nickname and viewed him with wary suspicion, for he was not a man to cross. Sludge had a temper that did not respect rank or seniority, and they had given him more last chances than any man ought to have. But his peers held him in high regard, and he had helped many a man get out of a tricky situation onshore if it gave him an excuse for thuggery.

At first, we were on nodding terms, but the more I witnessed his unpredictability, the more I avoided him. Then one night, when most sailors were in port, a dozen of us stayed in the mess. I was there, with Mickey Jones, who I knew well, while the rest of the men clustered around Sludge like vultures around carrion. They were playing dice – crow and anchor, if I remember rightly, and getting drunker and rowdier by the minute. Tempers frayed as they bet the few coins that they hadn't squandered onshore, and sensing the mood, I decided to go to my cabin. But one man asked Mickey if he wanted to play, and because Mickey had a few on board, he wasn't thinking straight and joined in. I didn't want to leave him alone, and against my better judgement, I sat beside him and played along.

I was lucky at dice. No reason for it, but I always had been, and before long, my pile of coins was growing as fast as the others depleted. Sludge scowled at me as I scraped another few coins across the table and stacked a third pile. Mickey, in his cups, couldn't feel the atmosphere change, but it grew hushed and tense. I decided to leave with or without him and stood to go, but Norm Diggins, Sludge's lead henchman, who was always by his side, placed a meaty hand on my shoulder and pushed me back down.

"You wouldn't leave without giving us a chance to earn our money back, now, would you?" he warned. I glanced around. The mess door was open, and the duty officer would be within shouting distance, no doubt. So, I let them have their way and carried on. I lost the next round, and the tension eased, but the dice fell lucky again, and more coins changed hands. Then I heard a smashing sound behind me and turned to see a puddle of ale and glass shards by the side of my seat. Norm Diggins grunted and swept the glass to one side with his foot before dropping a towel over the spilt beer. I turned back to resume the game, but when I looked down, all three piles of coins had disappeared, and Sludge was sitting, arms crossed, smirking beneath his beard. I should have walked away. I nearly did. But for some inexplicable reason, Sludge reminded me of my father and all the times I'd lain helplessly while he beat me to a pulp. My temper flared red and angry, and I stood, leaned across, and punched Sludge full in the face. As he flailed backwards and an incisor exploded from his jaw, a pair of rough hands grabbed me from behind and held me in a bear hug.

"Shall I finish him, Sludge?" growled Diggins through a plume of rancid breath.

Sludge wiped his bloody mouth on the back of his hand and held the bridge of his nose, clicking it into place with a grimace.

"Hold your horses," he said, just as Sub-lieutenant Johnson opened the mess door and glanced inside. I couldn't tell whether he saw me, but he was afraid of Sludge and likely turned a blind eye. Diggins dropped my arms, and Sludge stared defiantly at the young officer. "Everything alright, chaps?" Johnson asked nonchalantly.

Diggins replied. "Fine, isn't it Mullings?" I nodded. No good ever came from involving the officers in disputes, and Johnson left as quickly as he came.

I turned to leave and Mickey, whose eyes never left the table throughout the encounter, got to his feet.

"Stay," said Sludge, and he sat down again, eyes downcast. I walked away, relieved at having got away with humiliating Sludge so lightly, hoping that my retaliation would be enough to keep Sludge and his henchmen at bay. I should have known better. What followed next was worse than anything I could ever have imagined.

CHAPTER FOUR

A Village Scandal

Tuesday, January 20, 1903

Lawrence shuffled through the remaining cases in despair, wondering which of three humiliating, low-paying jobs he would have to take to keep Violet happy. If it were up to him, he'd take the week off and go shopping. His best pair of boots were leaking, and though Lawrence could easily afford another, time was precious. Not that he was resentful, but the effort involved in keeping Harpham & Smith private investigators afloat was time-consuming and costly, especially now they had a rival. Lawrence sighed, opened the drawer, and gazed fondly at his bottle of Scotch, wondering if there was enough time for a quick nip before Violet returned. But no sooner had he reached for a glass than the door opened, and Violet appeared. She was just removing her hat and coat when the bell jangled again to reveal a sombre-looking pair of elderly men.

"Lawrence Harpham, I presume?" asked the slightly taller of the two, reaching for Lawrence's hand.

"Yes. How can I help?"

"By giving me your time. A lot of it and with the utmost urgency."

Violet frowned, but Lawrence jumped to his feet and pulled two wooden chairs in front of his desk. "I'm free now," he said. "Tell me what you want."

"I'm Abraham Goddard, and this is my brother, Samuel. We are Methodist ministers."

"Pleased to meet you. This is Violet, my partner."

Both Goddards offered their hands in greeting. Then Violet sat down at her desk, watching from a distance while Lawrence spoke.

"Are you collecting funds?" he asked suddenly.

The two men exchanged glances. "No. Why do you ask?"

"The last minister who came to my office was collecting for widows and orphans at Christmas."

"Very commendable," said Samuel Goddard. "But we're here for another reason."

Lawrence steepled his hands. "What is it?"

"To save a man from censure by public opinion."

"I see." Lawrence's neutral expression belied his interest. Minutes earlier, he was on the verge of accepting a case of pet napping. But the men sitting tensely to his front seemed so serious and resolute that his sixth sense bristled, and he knew their offering would be more fulfilling.

"We come from Peasenhall," said Abraham Goddard.

"Isn't that where…?"

"Yes."

"And isn't the trial about to start?"

The Goddards nodded. "Tomorrow," said Abraham. "Now, you've been reading the newspapers, and you must know as much as any man, but I'll start from the beginning and tell you what we want you to do."

"Please go ahead," said Lawrence, leaning back in his chair.

"Shall I take notes?" asked Violet, reaching for her fountain pen.

"Absolutely."

"Carry on," said Samuel Goddard, nodding to his brother, who cleared his throat with a series of coughs.

"Now, young Rose Harsent died in May, as you are well aware," said Goddard.

Lawrence nodded. "Remind me how."

"She was stabbed in the chest, and her throat was cut. I won't go into further detail in front of the lady." Samuel looked at Violet and raised a half-smile. "Now, Miss Harsent was friendly with several young men and in the family way when she died. But they haven't identified the father of her child, though they found an assignation note after her murder. Apparently, someone came to see her that night."

"Who?"

"We don't know. Furthermore, nobody knew she was with child until after the autopsy, and the identity of her killer is a mystery."

"William Gardiner perhaps?" asked Lawrence.

Abraham Goddard slammed the desk with the flat of his hand, and Lawrence jerked back in surprise.

"That kind of remark is precisely the reason we're here," said Goddard, scratching his long white sideburns with the air of a man trying to keep a lid on his temper. He closed his eyes and exhaled loudly. "William Gardiner is a good man, one of us, you know, God-fearing and keen to spread the word. He has rapidly risen through the Methodist ranks due in no small part to his loyalty and commitment. Now, why do you say he killed Miss Harsent?"

"Because he's on trial for murder?"

"But why was he accused?"

Lawrence looked at Violet as if searching for inspiration. "Presumably, the evidence led that way?"

"It did not," said Abraham Goddard.

"The newspapers seemed to think so."

"They'll print anything to sell copies," said Samuel. "All the evidence is circumstantial, which is partly why William Gardiner escaped conviction at the first trial."

"And," continued Abraham, "we expect the same result from the second."

"Then how can I help you?" asked Lawrence. "Isn't that what you want?"

"Gardiner is blameless. The scandal that dogs him will never go away unless you find the killer and remove the stain on our church."

"People will forget in time," said Lawrence.

"That's not good enough," thundered Abraham. "We are tearing ourselves apart over this. And why should William Gardiner live under suspicion for the rest of his life? It needs sorting out, I tell you. You must find the killer."

"But the police have made their best case. If that isn't good enough, I don't know what I can do. And you're jumping the gun a bit. The second trial hasn't started yet."

"We need your help one way or the other," said Samuel. "If Gardiner is convicted, you must find the murderer, and if they acquit him again, you must clear his name. Unless you would rather we pay a visit to the gentleman detective on the other side of the road. Our solicitor recommended your services, but I doubt he knew there were two investigators in Bury."

"No need for that," said Lawrence firmly. "I hear Mr Bradford is currently indisposed. I, however, am not and can offer my help. But first, tell me, why are the police so certain that Mr Gardiner is guilty with only circumstantial evidence against him?"

The two brothers exchanged glances. Samuel pushed his glasses further up his nose, while Abraham lowered his head and shuffled his feet. After a few seconds of silence, he looked up and spoke again. "Because of the scandal," he said.

#

"I take it you are referring to allegations of impropriety by William Gardiner?" asked Lawrence.

Abraham Goddard nodded.

"Remind me what they were."

"Two young busybodies with nothing better to do followed him to the chapel and listened outside the door. Then they tattled to the villagers, and word spread about an illicit meeting between Gardiner and Rose Harsent."

"Was there any truth in it?"

"I don't believe so."

"You seem uncertain."

"I am nothing of the kind."

"Nor I," said Samuel, tapping his hand on his knee. "In any case, we held our own trial to establish the truth of the matter."

"Who did?" asked Lawrence.

"The members of the Methodist sect. The allegations didn't just damage Gardiner. They caused great harm to the chapel, detracting from all our good works."

"So, you asked Gardiner to testify before you?"

"Just so," said Abraham. "Together with the two young men who accused him."

"Their names?"

"Alfonso Skinner and Billy Wright."

"Did they remain steadfast in their story?"

"Yes," growled Abraham Goddard. "While refusing to apologise for their accusations."

"Why should they say sorry if they were telling the truth?"

"They were not. At best, those two troublemakers misconstrued an innocent man's actions."

"And what exactly did they accuse him of?"

Goddard sighed. "Impropriety with Miss Harsent, and I won't repeat what they said." Once again, he nodded unsubtly towards Violet, who waited until he turned back to Lawrence before raising her eyes heavenward. Lawrence shot her a warning glare. Violet, always the epitome of polite womanhood, had become less tolerant since her recent exposure to the suffrage movement. An unguarded eye-roll like the one she had just unwisely displayed could cause sufficient offence for the Goddards to cross the road to Bobby Bradford's office. And Violet would be the first to complain if they lost the business. Lawrence made a mental note to discuss it with her later.

"So, the young men claimed they saw or heard something, and Gardiner denied it."

"Not quite," said Samuel Goddard. "They saw nothing once Gardiner was inside. It's more about what they heard."

"Or did not," snapped Abraham.

"And will they testify in court?"

"Yes. Tomorrow."

"Presumably, your Methodist elders found Gardiner innocent of any impropriety?"

"Certainly."

"And after that, he kept his distance from the young lady?"

"I never saw them together except in church," said Abraham.

"Although others said otherwise."

"Only Henry Rouse," snapped Abraham to his brother. "And I wouldn't trust him to tell the time."

"So, the accusations dogged Gardiner until the day Rose Harsent died?"

"Yes. And if you ask me, it's the sole reason that the inspector arrested him."

Lawrence put his hand on his chin and drummed the desktop for a moment while he thought.

"Are Skinner and Wright of good character?"

"They are gainfully employed," said Samuel.

"Troublemakers," snarled his brother.

"Can you believe any of it?"

"Only that Miss Harsent and Mr Gardiner were in the chapel together. He was teaching her to play the organ. His actions were unwise but not improper," said Samuel. "And it wasn't just innocent tittle-tattle. Poor Mrs Gardiner took so poorly when she heard the rumours that she lost a baby. Her milk dried up after the shock of it, and the poor child died."

"So, are you saying that Bill Wright is an inveterate snoop and storyteller?"

"Not necessarily," said Samuel.

"What? You deny it?"

"It depends whether you are talking about Rose Harsent or the other matter. If the latter, he is not the only one."

"Stop muddying the waters," growled Abraham.

Lawrence frowned, and Violet stopped writing. "Hold on," he said. "Are we talking at cross-purposes?"

"No," said Abraham Goddard, glaring at Samuel. "My brother is referring to an entirely separate matter with no bearing on this case. He wouldn't have mentioned it but for Wright's involvement, and I don't believe a word of it, anyway."

"Nevertheless, I would like to know more."

"It will only detract from our efforts to save Gardiner."

"Let me be the judge of that."

Abraham Goddard shook his head and scowled at his brother. "You tell him as you seem to know so much about it."

"Bill Wright claims someone is following him," said Samuel dramatically.

"Who?"

"He doesn't know."

"When?"

"At night. Under cover of darkness."

"So he says."

"He's not the only one," said Samuel, dismissing Abraham with a wave of his hand.

"Who else then?"

"Skinner and Frederick Davies."

"Reprobates the pair of them," said Abraham. "I don't know why you fall for it."

"Because the same thing happened to Ellen Blowers last week. She left her house in Church Street to visit her elderly aunt and swore she heard footsteps behind her."

"Probably her imagination," said Abraham.

"Only it wasn't. Ellen didn't want to leave, but she had no choice, and on the walk back, somebody grabbed her by the shoulders. She struggled free and ran all the way home, but who knows what might have happened if she hadn't been young and fit."

"I know nothing about this. Why didn't you tell me?"

"I only heard it myself last night."

"But does it have anything to do with Rose Harsent?" asked Lawrence.

"No," said Samuel. "These events are more recent. Wright first mentioned it in December."

"Wright is probably the culprit," said Abraham.

"Thank you," said Lawrence. "I think we can safely ignore this story for now, but I will make a note just in case. Now, Rose Harsent's trial starts tomorrow, you say?"

"Yes," said Abraham.

"And you would like me to come when?"

"Tomorrow."

"That soon?"

"Yes."

"Regardless of the result?"

"Quite."

"I haven't told you my fee yet."

Abraham Goddard reached into his coat pocket and removed a leather purse, then placed a handful of coins in the centre of Lawrence's desk. "I am responsible for appointing an independent investigator to report to Peasenhall as soon as possible, and I've heard good things about you. I can see you are a straight-talking man. Save our church from further embarrassment, and we'll pay every penny of your charges. Now, what about it? Will you come?"

Lawrence nodded. "I'll be there first thing," he said.

The two men stood and shook Lawrence's hand, then tipped their hats to Violet as they left.

"Are you sure about this case?" she asked when the door closed.

"Oh yes," said Lawrence. "This is much more like it."

"But what about the Tibenham investigation?"

"You were going to investigate that one with Michael. There's no need for me to tag along."

"I know, but it's so much easier when we're working together."

"Perhaps you don't need to go there in person?"

"To Tibenham? I don't know. I must speak to the grandmother at some stage, no doubt."

"But you'll begin in Bury."

"I expect so."

"No matter then," said Lawrence dismissively. "I'll take the motor, and I'll drive you anywhere within a reasonable distance of Peasenhall."

"But will you stay there?"

"Probably for a night or two. I'll see how it goes."

"Then offering to drive me won't work. I'm sure Michael will accompany me, and I'll give your love to Daisy."

Lawrence's face fell. "Yes, do. It's so long since I've been away from Bury, I forgot what I'd be missing. You'll manage for a day or two, won't you?"

Violet shook her head. "I managed for years without you, and it's not as if Daisy spends frequent nights at your house."

"I wish she would."

"One roof over her head is enough."

"Whatever you think best, Violet. But give her a hug from Daddy." Lawrence smiled weakly, cleared his desk, and took his hat from the stand.

"Are you going now?"

He nodded.

"See you soon."

CHAPTER FIVE

Gracie's Dilemma

Wednesday, January 21, 1903

Violet took a large key from the front of her bag and let herself into Lawrence's handsome Georgian house on Angel Hill. Quite why he had felt the need to purchase a three-storey home, having spent a decade living in two crowded rooms, she would never understand. And it wasn't his first purchase either. Over the last few years, he had moved twice, each time to a larger property. Both times he had sought her approval, asking advice on decor and domestic matters, hoping, she supposed, that he could tempt her to join him. Lawrence had made two serious marriage proposals since the incident with Francis and had dropped the idea of matrimony into their conversations on multiple occasions. Once, during an uncharacteristically dark moment when a drain had burst near her cottage and stinking sewage flooded her living room, she contemplated saying yes. But Violet could not forget Lawrence's dalliance with Loveday Graham. She wasn't jealous and knew he cared nothing for Loveday now, but she was equally sure that marriage would never have crossed his mind but for Daisy.

Lawrence was a wonderful father, as Violet knew he would be. He couldn't do enough for their daughter, who saw him almost every day. Occasionally, Violet thought back to her lonely years in Swaffham and regretted not telling Lawrence sooner. In trying to do the right thing, she had deprived him of Daisy's formative years, and, on reflection, she wasn't proud of her actions.

The lock clicked, and the door swung open. Violet entered the hallway, removed her hat and coat, and placed them on the coat stand. Ignoring the double doors to the living room, she turned right into a short corridor leading to the kitchen. Violet couldn't remember which days Lawrence's housekeeper, Mrs Dade, worked, and she didn't want to put the fear of God into the poor woman, who would understandably presume that she was alone in the house. So, she proceeded to the kitchen to check, finding it empty but with Mrs Dade's apron lying rumpled on the side. The wicker basket generally kept by the range was missing, and Violet supposed that the housekeeper must be out shopping. Violet glanced at her watch. She had wired Grace Francis, asking if she could telephone rather than meet to avoid unnecessary travel. Now Violet had Daisy to consider, she couldn't drop everything and take off around the country at the drop of a hat. She had received Gracie's response early this morning, giving her a number to call at ten fifteen today. It was a little before ten o'clock, and Violet had a few minutes to spare. She opened the back door and went outside, immediately regretting leaving her coat on the stand.

Violet hadn't been in Lawrence's garden for some time now. Though she regularly brought Daisy to see him, she rarely spent much time with them for fear of giving Lawrence false expectations. So, she hadn't seen the garden since the summer when it was still a work in progress. Now, in the heart of January, starkly cold and with frost on the ground, Violet had low expectations. But Lawrence's gardener had been hard at work. The expansive lawn was relatively flat despite the weather, and Lawrence had cleaned and repointed the red brick wall surrounding the garden. A row of young trees stood proudly at the rear, with flower borders laid neatly down the sides, ready for spring. It would take little effort to fill the garden with pretty flowers, providing a structured, tidy formal garden. Violet felt a pang of envy. Though she loved her somewhat chaotic cottage garden, Lawrence's would be something else again. It could be hers too if only her pride would allow it. But Violet valued herself too highly to be anybody's second choice. She walked onto a paved area running the width of the house, rubbing her shoulders as the fierce January wind penetrated her dress.

Stooping, Violet examined the small shrubs alongside, recently shaped, and tidied and wondered if Lawrence was planning box hedging. She closed her eyes and imagined the grandeur of the garden a few years hence. She could see it now, little Daisy sitting outside in the sun next to her Daddy. Suddenly an image flashed through her mind of three people reclining in deck chairs and enjoying the garden: Lawrence, Daisy, and an unknown woman. And the woman wasn't Violet. She immediately banished the unwanted tableau from her mind, rejecting the silly idea. Lawrence was no longer young. Why would he want a wife? But it left her feeling slightly queasy. Lawrence was devoted to her, and she knew it. He would marry her in an instant if she agreed, though for all the wrong reasons. But what would happen once Lawrence had given up on the idea of them being a family. Could he, would he, find someone else? And if he did, how would she feel?

Violet shivered and went inside, determined to do something more productive than speculate about the future. She passed back along the hallway, through the double doors and into Lawrence's living room. Approaching the ornate fireplace, Violet stared into the mirror above before tucking a stray hair behind her ear. Her once dark hair was streaked with white, and though her features had softened with age, she was no beauty, and she knew it. But looks had never mattered before. Intelligent and well-read, Violet had never troubled herself with cosmetics and jewellery, fashion, or millinery. She judged people on kindness, knowledge, and friendship, not caring about aesthetics. Violet stroked her prominent crow's feet and pulled the skin above her eyelids. Her face tightened, and her jawline smoothed, but the moment she released the tension, deep laughter lines creased her face. It was unfair. Lawrence, always a handsome man, had not succumbed to age in the same way. The smattering of grey in his hair was barely noticeable, and his face was largely wrinkle-free. His slender frame bore no trace of middle-aged spread, and he looked a decade younger than his age.

Violet turned from the mirror, irritated by her internal monologue. She should be thinking of the suffragists and how to help advance the vote. Matters of the flesh were nothing compared to the current political landscape, and Violet wanted to be a part of it. And as a local businesswoman, she had some influence despite the rush to judgement from those who could not accept Daisy's parentage. The best way to set an example was to be successful, which meant getting on with the job at hand. So, Violet sat down on the settee, picked up the telephone handset and turned the hand crank.

"Number, please?" asked the call girl.

"Norwich 102," said Violet.

"Connecting you now."

She heard a click, and while Violet waited, she regarded the device with wary disapproval. It would have been more sensible for Lawrence to have a telephone installed in the office if he must have one at all. But business connection rates were double residential costs, and Lawrence decided instead to have it at home. Which was all well and good, but on the rare occasions Violet needed to use it, she had to intrude on Lawrence's privacy. Still, he had readily given her his spare house key to use whenever she wished. And in having the telephone at home, he had born the full cost himself instead of charging it to the business. But Violet felt uncomfortable at yet another status symbol elevating Lawrence ever higher in the social ranking. Telephones were few and far between in Bury St Edmunds, and Lawrence's phone number was still in single digits, albeit at the higher end. Oliver & Sons, grocers were the proud owners of Bury St Edmunds number one, a good thing in her opinion, as Lawrence would be insufferable if he enjoyed that accolade.

The line connected, and a soft, well-spoken voice thanked the operator.

"Miss Francis?" asked Violet.

"Yes, Miss Smith. I'm so grateful for your help."

#

"I hope I can assist," said Violet. "I've read your letter and appreciate your predicament, but it's awfully tricky to be useful when so much time has passed by."

"I know," said the girl. "It's a lot to ask, but I don't want to lose Phillip. And he's under a lot of pressure from his family."

"Start at the beginning," said Violet, holding the earpiece a distance from her head for a moment as the line suddenly crackled.

"I will. Well, it started with my grandmother."

"Sorry to interrupt, but that's not what I mean. Tell me more about yourself and why you feel the need to solve a historical murder."

"I see. About eighteen months ago, I met a young man on the way to work. We walked the same route and bumped into each other frequently. Eventually, we became friends, then more. His father is a retired barrister called to the bar in London and practising there for most of his working life. A few years ago, he retired early due to ill health, and he now lives on the outskirts of Tibenham. I work in a typing pool, and Phillip, my intended, is a clerk to a tea merchant. We've been walking out for the best part of a year, and he invited me to meet his parents for the first time at Christmas. Well, I knew his father had a certain social standing, and I assumed they must live in a comfortable property, but when I arrived, the house was so far above my expectations that Phillip

41

had to stop me using the tradesman's entrance. His parents live in an enormous hall in the middle of a park on the edge of Tibenham. It must be worth a fortune, and I felt so uncomfortable the first evening while sitting around the dinner table that I could barely eat a thing. But I needn't have worried. Phillip had already told them I worked in a typing pool, and it didn't seem to bother them. They accepted me, and I spent a happy week, barely thinking about the differences in our backgrounds. Then one night, Mr Wild, Phillip's father, started a conversation about local history. He'd dabbled in it for years but suddenly developed a serious interest, and I stupidly mentioned that my great-grandmother came from the village and died there. He asked her name, and I told him, thinking nothing more about it. I mean, I knew a little about the poisonings, but we didn't speak of it at home for obvious reasons. The next day, Mr Wild summoned Phillip to his study, and they talked for at least an hour. Phillip came to find me looking flushed and angry, then asked me to pack. He said we were leaving for the station and would return to Norwich earlier than scheduled. We caught the train that night, and on the way back, Phillip told me that his father had complained about my antecedents and questioned the wisdom of our forthcoming marriage. Phillip was furious and said he would marry me no matter what. He remained resolute for a while, and we continued making plans to marry in the spring. But as time has gone by, Phillip's enthusiasm has waned. Plans have stalled, and he's making excuses not to move things along."

"Do you know why?"

"I think so," said Gracie, and her voice faltered. "Phillip was ill a few months after we returned from his parent's house. The doctor said it was a gastrointestinal complaint. Food poisoning, I suppose. He was in bed for a week and couldn't keep anything down. Then he got better and improved for a month or two before falling ill again."

"Do you live in the same house?"

"Of course not," Gracie answered curtly, seemingly offended.

"So, you didn't prepare his food?"

42

"I did, actually. I brought Phillip soups and stews to build him up. He's not keen on the food at his lodgings at the best of times and eats out a lot. So, I thought a few freshly cooked meals might tempt him."

"Does he think you put something in the food?"

"I don't know. He must suspect it. What else could have caused his change of heart?" asked Gracie miserably. "His father has turned him against me, and now he doubts my motives."

"But it makes no sense," said Violet. "They can't hold you accountable for events that happened before you were born."

"I know," said Gracie. "But something is bothering him. What else can it be?"

"And you think providing proof of a murderer unconnected to your family will change Phillip's mind?"

"Exactly," said Gracie. "It's frustrating that the prime suspect for the murders wasn't even a relation. That ought to be enough, but it still leaves an element of doubt."

"Who did they suspect?"

"A rather ill-tempered maid by the name of Eliza Sage," said Gracie.

"If Mr Wild is so interested in local history, he must be aware of her," said Violet.

"That's what Edward says."

"Who?"

"Edward Fisher, our typing pool clerk."

"You've told him about your troubles?"

"Well, yes. And Harry."

"Harry?"

"Harriet. Edward and Harriet are my friends. We eat lunch together most days. It isn't easy living away from family. I've got to talk to someone," said Gracie defensively.

"You mentioned your grandmother in your letter," said Violet. "Can I take it that she's still alive?"

"Yes. And I'm sure she knows a great deal, but I haven't told Grandmother anything about it yet. She's never spoken to me about the murders, and I'm not sure how to broach the subject."

"Do you think she will help?"

"I don't know. Grandmother doesn't believe in airing private matters publicly. There's as much chance of her refusing as agreeing to help."

"Oh, dear. I'll need to speak to her to have a fighting chance of making any progress. I was going to suggest you join me, but I wonder if a little subterfuge is in order?"

"Whatever it takes."

"I'm in two minds, Miss Francis. On the one hand, I'm reluctant to take advantage of an old lady, but on the other, I've found certain ruses work well when trying to glean information."

"What do you mean?"

"I've pretended to be a newspaper reporter once or twice in the past to good effect. How do you think your grandmother would respond to that?"

"Badly," said Gracie without hesitation.

Violet thought for a moment. "How about an inheritance finder?"

"How would that work? My family are not wealthy."

"They don't need to be. And anyway, it won't be true. Inheritance finders use family trees to connect relatives, which works especially well in the case of estrangement. Then they find the closest living relative to inherit the legacy. I can present myself to your grandmother, tell her someone has left a will and ask for her help to find the nearest kin. But first, I will need to make a detailed family tree to determine who was in Tibenham when the poisonings occurred. Unless you know that information already?"

"No. We don't have a family Bible or any written notes, as far as I'm aware. My mother knows more than I do, but she was born after my great-grandmother died, which doesn't help. I think your idea could work as long as my grandmother doesn't know we're acquainted. Otherwise, she will wonder why you are asking her when you could just as easily speak to my mother."

"Do they see much of each other?"

"No. Granny lives in Bunwell. It's not far from us as the crow flies, but Mother has been poorly this year, and it's been a while since they've met."

"Right. Why not speak to your mother, get as much information about your relatives as possible, then post it to me? I'll use parish record transcripts to flesh it out and find a candidate far enough removed who could have left an inheritance. Then I'll visit your grandmother and ask for help. With luck, one thing will lead to another, and she will tell me what she knows about the poisonings. If she doesn't, I'm not sure what else I can do."

"Please try. And do it quickly. I hope to be married by the end of April, and there's no time to lose."

CHAPTER SIX

A Good Starting Point

Thursday, January 22, 1903

Lawrence navigated through The Causeway and pulled up outside the Angel Inn, parking his car close to the front door. The journey has been quick despite the freezing temperatures, and as he exited the vehicle, plumes of warm air billowed from the engine. The small track was devoid of life, and the door to the inn appeared shut. Lawrence inspected his watch. It was a little after nine thirty, and the villagers should be up and about long before now. He tried the door, hoping that it would open, but it did not budge. Sighing, Lawrence approached the window and peered inside. The glass frosted instantly, and as he wiped the condensation away with his bare hands, the glass squealed and the occupant of the room looked up, clutching her chest. Seeing Lawrence, she jabbed a finger towards the door and proceeded in that direction. The door soon opened, and the woman gazed towards him.

"What do you want?"

"A room, please," said Lawrence.

"I don't know about that."

"Who does?"

"I'll fetch Charles."

Lawrence waited outside, and moments later, a young man in his late twenties appeared.

"Charles Ray, publican," he said. "And you are?"

"Lawrence Harpham, a traveller in need of a bed tonight."

"I've got one spare," said Charles Ray. "A single. Tonight only, though. I promised it to the wife's brother for the rest of the week."

"I'll take it," said Lawrence, glad to have one chore ticked off his list.

"Are you leaving that there?" asked the publican, gesturing to Lawrence's car.

"Yes, I intended to. It will be safe, I presume?"

"As safe as houses," smirked the young man.

Lawrence frowned. He detected a hint of sarcasm but wasn't sure why.

"Follow me. This way."

Lawrence trailed behind the young man carrying a small leather bag with a change of clothes, his trusty tin, and very little else. Presently, they arrived outside a tiny, dingy room on the top floor. "Come and go as you please," said Charles. "Pay when you leave. I trust you." He winked at Lawrence as he left.

"I won't remember," muttered Lawrence, placing a few coins on the side table to cover his room charge.

Lawrence deposited his bag by the bed, half wishing he had attempted to find alternative accommodation. But the outlook was pleasant even if the room was small, and he wouldn't be spending much time in it. Lawrence decided to leave the car where it was and walk into the village. But as he left the inn, he noticed a small boy pointing and laughing near the Wolseley. He waited long enough for the boy to leave, mindful of young men and mischief to vehicles, then proceeded into The Street to familiarise himself with Peasenhall.

Lawrence had already decided to conduct the investigation openly. Neither of the Goddards had asked for discretion. The trial was about to start at any moment, and he was most likely to get helpful information if he made his intentions known. So, Lawrence set off looking for shops, passing plenty but finding none with customers. When almost at the point of concluding that Peasenhall must be unpopulated, he noticed two men in the grocer's store and went inside.

"Good morning," said Lawrence, doffing his hat. "It's nice to see someone up and about."

"Don't you know what day it is?" asked the young man. "They're all at the trial."

"Of course, they are. Not you, though?"

"No. I've got to mind the shop as if anyone is going to buy anything today."

"I'm here," said the other man.

"Right, George. But only because your better half doesn't know you've left the shoes to make themselves."

"You're a shoemaker?" asked Lawrence.

"I am."

"Can you fix these until I can get into town?"

"I could. Or I could sell you a new pair. They'll be as good as any you've ever owned."

"I'm sorry," said Lawrence. "Of course, you can. But I want a pair like these."

The man nodded. "I should have some already made unless you're an odd size. Pop in when you've finished here. George Whiting. I'm a couple of doors down on the left."

"Capital," said Lawrence.

"And what can I do for you?" asked the younger man. "A pair of gloves, a nice trilby, perhaps?"

"Very funny. I'm looking for information as it goes."

"What do you want to know?"

"Whatever you can tell me about Rose Harsent."

The two men exchanged glances before simultaneously bursting into laughter. "The trial of the year is happening in Ipswich as we speak, and you're looking for information here? Go to Shire Hall and be quick about it. You'll find everything you will ever need to know in far more detail than George or I can give."

"But that would defeat the purpose," said Lawrence. "I don't want to know what they think. I want to hear points of view from those not directly involved in the trial."

"That's daft," said the young man. "Everybody who has had anything to do with the case is in court."

"Surely you can tell me something?"

"Only rumour and gossip."

"That's as good a place as any to start. Now, what's your name?"

The man narrowed his eyes. "Why are you asking? What's my name got to do with anything?"

Lawrence offered his hand. "I'm Lawrence Harpham, a private investigator."

"Alf Grice," said the young man, taking Lawrence's hand grudgingly.

"Now, that wasn't difficult, was it? As I explained, I could easily go to Ipswich and listen to all the information everyone else has heard over the last year. Better men than I have scrutinised every part of it, but someone has asked me to take another look at Rose's murder, and it makes sense to take a different approach."

"Who's asked you to do that?"

"I'd rather not say."

"And I'd rather not tattle."

"That's a first," said George Whiting, grinning from ear to ear. "Why do you think we all come here?"

"Don't talk squit. I'm not a gossip," said Alf.

"In the same way that I'm not a bootmaker."

"Haven't you got somewhere to go?"

"Alright. Keep your hair on. Come and see me when you've finished," said George, nodding to Lawrence.

"I will."

Lawrence watched as the door swung shut. "Are you sure you can't help me?" he asked as soon as they were alone.

"What's it worth?"

"I'll find someone else."

"They're all in Ipswich, as I said. If you're not going to the trial and you want to know more, you'll have to ask friends and relatives in the know. And how will you find them without help?"

"I'll ask your friend."

"He doesn't know what I know."

"Which is what?"

Alf Grice held out his hand and looked expectantly. Lawrence sighed, removed his wallet, and extracted half a crown.

Grice said nothing but raised a smirk as if surprised by the amount.

"Go on then," said Lawrence.

"What do you want to know?"

"Something worth the sum I've just paid you," snapped Lawrence, watching Grice transfer the coins into his pocket.

"I can give you a list of people to speak to," he said.

"I want more than that."

"Fred Davies didn't get anywhere with Rose. I know that for a fact."

"Remind me where he fits in."

Grice leaned across the counter and looked Lawrence in the eye. "After Constable Eli Nunn found Rose, he looked around her bedroom and found three letters, two from Gardiner and one from someone else who was meeting her that night."

"Who remains anonymous."

"Exactly. Everyone thinks it was William Gardiner, which is why they've banged him up in the jug. But they also found some verses."

"I read about that. Obscene verses, I believe."
"It depends on what you call obscene. A bit of light-hearted fun, according to the lads."
"If you're a young man, perhaps. But clearly, using language unfit for a lady."
"Rose must have thought differently. She asked for them."
"How do you know?"
"Fred told me. And he's proper sorry that he ever delivered them. The barrister tore a strip off him during the first trial. He shamed Fred and took away his good character. It's not right. Rose asked for those verses, and what's more, she asked for a leaflet about contraception."
"Yes. I read about that too. Did Davies provide it?"
Alf Grice nodded. "He did."
"When?"
"I can't remember. Some months before her death."
"Which implies that she knew she would need it. But why ask Davies unless he was the father of her child?"
"Because he liked her. He wanted to walk out with her, and she took advantage of him. She had him wrapped around her little finger, and when he got her what she wanted, she withdrew her affection."
"He might have killed her in revenge."
"He didn't," said Grice abruptly. "We're pals, Fred and me. He didn't do it. He couldn't get anywhere with Rose after he got her the leaflet. I know this for a fact. And I tell you straight, Fred Davies didn't kill Rose."
"And William Gardiner?"
"Pious Willie? What about him?"
"Did he kill her?"
Grice opened a drawer beneath the counter and extracted a pencil and paper. "I don't believe he did," he said after a moment. "He's a stupid man, too up himself to see how foolish he was while Rose played to his vanity. I mean, who goes into a building alone

with a girl young enough to be his daughter without taking a chaperone? What did he expect to happen?"

"You believe his story?"

"I don't know. Perhaps they were up to mischief, but I don't think Gardiner killed her."

"Why not?"

"It's far too risky. Gardiner was always the obvious suspect. All that scandal around the village and well known too. He was a marked man the moment Rose died."

"What about his wife and family?"

"Mrs Gardiner is in Ipswich, and they sent the children away."

"I mean, how did she deal with the scandal?"

"I don't know, but give me a second, and I'll write you a list of names."

Lawrence walked towards the window while Alf Grice scribbled on the paper. He looked outside at the almost deserted street, wondering how sensible it was to be eliciting information this way. Perhaps he could better spend his time driving to Ipswich instead of encouraging tittle-tattle. But Lawrence had to get information in ways never attempted before if he hoped to produce a different result.

"Here it is," said Grice, waving the note in the air.

Lawrence approached the counter and turned the paper to face him.

"Start with Dr Lay," said Grice. "If he agrees to speak, that is. The good doctor knows all about Rose's injuries, and he's not in court until tomorrow. I saw him by the smithy this morning, and if you're quick, you might catch him. Then you should visit Kate Pepper. Her mother, Amelia is Gardiner's next-door neighbour and knows plenty about the family." This one, "he said, pointing to the third name, "is James Crisp, brother of Rose's employer Deacon Crisp. He lives two doors down from Providence House."

"Providence House?"

"Where Rose died. You must have read it in the newspapers."

"You're right. I did."

"And this chap here is Harry Redgrift, Bill Wright's stepfather."

"The chap who claimed to see Rose and William Gardiner together?"

"Yes. And well worth speaking to. Wright and his pal Alfonso Skinner lived with Harry Redgrift. He'll know as much as any man whether they are telling the truth."

"Is that everybody?"

"No, but it's a good starting point. Many Peasenhall residents are currently in Ipswich, and you're bound to miss some opportunities. But that's your choice."

"Good," said Lawrence. "And I take it you'll be here for the next few days?"

Grice nodded. "Yes, we'll stay open while there are still a few folks left around. But what of it?"

"I'll be back to see you when I've finished with this," said Lawrence, brandishing the list. "I expect more than a piece of paper for my half a crown."

CHAPTER SEVEN

Keelhaul

September 1901

Another week passed before I finally left HMS *Devastation* for an evening on dry land. I had been on night duties, sleeping during the day and reading in my spare time. And I hadn't gone back to the mess, except at mealtimes. I wasn't afraid of Sludge, but I didn't see the point in courting trouble – a few weeks of lying low, and he might forget all about me. And once we were back at sea, there would be too many officers around for any trouble to occur. But Mickey Jones was getting cabin fever and had been nagging me for several nights. I had resisted his earlier attempts to get me on shore, preferring to save the little that remained of my money after Sludge stole my winnings. But troubles clung to Mickey like a bad

54

smell. His face was grey, his head hung low, and his eyes were dull with apathy. Mickey radiated misery and anxiety from every pore, but he did not share his burden, and I did not ask. Eventually, his constant attempts to get me to leave the ship paid off. All work and no play make a dull sort of life, and to counter the growing boredom, I gave in and agreed to a night out at Spanish Nell's.

We'd been there often. The ale was cheap, the wine flowed freely, and girls were plentiful. A night at Nell's always resulted in a sore head and usually an upset stomach from overeating, not to mention a weighty blow to the purse. But it was a release, and I would have gone more often if funds allowed. So, we arrived at Nell's at seven o'clock, and it was already full of rowdy sailors. By eight o'clock, I was replete and pleasantly merry. By nine, I was slurring yet sober enough to notice Mickey's pinched and sombre expression. He drank slowly, sip by sip as if imbibing saltwater. The conversation was stilted, and I grew tired of the silences. We sat alone, our other friends still on the ship, Mickey having said they could ill afford to join us. After twenty minutes without exchanging a word, I finished my drink and prepared to return to quarters. Mickey grimaced and seemed close to tears.

"Don't go yet," he said. "One more for the road."

"Not in here. It's too hot." I had become acclimatised to the temperature in the confines of the ship over the summer, but unnecessarily sitting beside a throng of drunken, sweaty sailors was another matter. I wanted to go elsewhere, but Mickey insisted on staying close to Nell's. He beckoned a surly girl, short, fair and with a tide mark around her neck where she needed a damned good wash, and he asked her to replenish our tankards.

She filled them from a jug, and we walked outside, depositing them on a low wooden ledge. Standing room only. It was a heady night, and the cicadas strummed their high-pitched buzzing. Salt air filled our nostrils as it did every day, and we sat watching the lapping waves. Someone yelled, and a fight broke out a few feet away, but we barely raised an eyebrow, so typical was trouble at Nell's. Mickey's apathy retreated, and he started talking about old times on HMS *Thunderer*. Another hour passed, and I was well into my cups. I remember Mickey passing me another drink, recoiling at the strange taste, then nothing. Empty. Black.

The first thing I felt when consciousness returned was the gentle swaying of the tide. I assumed I was back on board and wondered why the ship was moving, and why I was lying face down on the deck. I raised my head, but it was dark, and it took a few moments for my eyes to adjust. I was certainly on a deck, but the wooden boards felt different and did not belong to HMS *Devastation*. Much too rough. I clutched my head, temples throbbing, my pulse thrumming to a drum-like beat. Nausea gripped me, and I retched, dry heaving at first then vomiting the contents of my stomach onto the wooden planks. I rolled over and away from the pool of sick to find myself staring upwards. Above me, illuminated by the light of the moon, stood the stocky shape of Sludge Green, standing side by side with Norm Diggins. Loitering in the background, unable to meet my gaze, was my old shipmate Mickey Jones. Tendrils of fear slinked down my spine, gripping my stomach and almost making me disgrace myself by voiding the contents of my bowel. Almost, but not quite. Somehow, I held that part of my dignity intact, though I could not stop my teeth from chattering.

"Well, well. Not so cocky now," said Sludge, nudging me about the groin with the toe of his boot. I recoiled, expecting a kick, but Sludge stayed calm. Terrifyingly so. The moon was high and surprisingly bright. I stared past Sludge and towards the tall masts stretching above. There were three of them, and the empty deck and bundles of nets suggested I was on board a fishing vessel. But it was huge – a monster and probably made for commercial use. For a fleeting moment, I wondered what Sludge had done to acquire it and whether the boat's captain was part of his plan. But the moment soon passed when Norm Diggins pulled me to my feet. I hadn't noticed until then, but they'd tied my legs together, once at the ankles and again at the knees.

"Bind his hands," said Sludge, coldly, eyeing me with contempt. Norm brandished a rope, but Sludge snatched it away and handed it to Mickey.

"You do it," he commanded. "Mickey took it silently and disappeared behind me. Moments later, I felt the rope biting into my wrists.

"Now, what do you think you're doing here?" asked Sludge.

I didn't answer. It was pointless.

"I asked you a question," said Sludge, leering into my face, so close that I could feel the warmth of his breath.

I clamped my mouth shut and looked away. Sludge pulled his fist back, and I waited for the inevitable blow, but it never came. Instead, he balled his fist and rubbed it aggressively, his eyes never leaving my face.

"Never mind," he said. "I'll tell you what I'm going to do. Now, I've been a sailor all my life, and I've seen some fine old punishments during my time. But nothing compares to the old days. So, I got to thinking. What should I do to the lowlife bastard who punched me in the chops in front of my men? I know, Sludge, I said. I'll whip the cur with a cat. But Diggins says a cat o' nine tails isn't punishment enough. So, I had another think. And I nearly settled on sending you off the plank. But we're not far from land, and you'll only swim back. And you deserve something much worse than that. So, we had a little chat, me and the men, and Horace – you know old Horace, don't you? He said, what about an old punishment – something from way back in time? Ever heard of keelhauling, Sludge? he said. And I clicked my fingers and said, Oh yes. The very thing. And that's why you're here tonight."

I stared at Sludge, trying to comprehend his meaning. Whatever keelhauling was, I hadn't come across it. I had joined a modern navy. Walking the plank was a myth, and they'd abolished flogging decades before. Punishments now usually involved the loss of rations or privileges.

"I'll explain," said Sludge, seeing my bemused expression. "Norm here is going to tie you to this here line which we looped beneath the boat earlier this evening. My friend Mickey will tie this large weight to your legs, so you go down. We don't want you floating off now, do we? And then I will pull you under the boat until you reach the other side. And when you get there, I'm going to pull you back again. Is that clear?"

I stared at him in horror. The boat was enormous. If they dragged me under the water, I would probably drown. And if I didn't drown, God only knows what a hauling along the bottom would do to my flesh. I struggled against the ropes, but there were three of them and only one of me. And as they lowered me down the side, and I felt the cold brackish seawater against my skin, I cursed my false companion, Mickey Jones. The last thing I saw in my mind's eye as I slipped below the waves were the faces of Cyril and Georgie, the only loyal friends I had ever known.

CHAPTER EIGHT

New Shoes

Alf Grice had helpfully written addresses by the side of the names on his list. But instead of heading straight to Dr Lay's home, Lawrence stuck his head around the door of the shoemaker's cottage. Though cold, the weather was unpredictable, and an increase of one degree could make all the difference. The frost would inevitably turn to mush and seep into his leaky boots. New footwear must take priority over the investigation, and Lawrence was already extracting his wallet to see how much money he had left as he tapped on the cottage door. George Whiting opened it with a hearty hello and beckoned Lawrence into his workroom at the back of the house, where he proudly gestured to his wares.

Lawrence scowled at the sight of only half a dozen pairs of shoes, mentally calculating the odds of one of them fitting well enough to purchase, but luck was on his side. The first pair he tried fitted surprisingly snugly. Lawrence paced the floor, testing for snags, but the well-made shoes were comfortable.

"I'll take these," he said. "How much do I owe you?" And when Whiting replied, Lawrence beamed, hoping that the rest of the day would go as well.

"Where are you off to?" asked Whiting as if they'd known each other for years.

Lawrence looked at his list. "To see Dr Lay," he replied.

"And after?"

Lawrence showed him the piece of paper.

"Makes sense, I suppose," said Whiting.

"Good to have your approval," Lawrence said jocularly. "Should I see anyone else?"

"You've missed the drill works."

"I beg your pardon?"

"The factory where William Gardiner worked. Wright and Skinner too. It's the biggest employer for miles. I'd want to go up there if I were you."

"Why?"

"To learn how a man thinks, you must find out what drives him. In Gardiner's case, it was the fruit of his labours and the Lord's work. And some way behind were his family. Now, don't get me wrong, family matters to Gardiner, but well below work and prayer."

"It's a good point," mused Lawrence. "Can I borrow a pencil?"

Whiting produced a stub from behind his ear as if by magic, and Lawrence added a few lines to Alf Grice's note.

"That should do the trick. Now, thank you for the boots. I must fly if I'm going to catch Dr Lay before he leaves for Ipswich."

Lawrence left the property and turned right before feeling a tap on his shoulder. He turned around to see Whiting immediately behind him, grinning, and pointing in the other direction.

"Ah, thank you."

Lawrence strode up the street, waiting to feel the inevitable pinch of new shoes, but it never came. He soon arrived outside Lay's lodgings, feeling suddenly self-conscious at the worn pair of shoes he still carried in his hand. Taking a quick look left and right, he dropped them by the side of the house before knocking on the door, which opened almost immediately.

"Dr Lay, please?"

"I'm not to disturb him." A hatchet-faced lady north of forty years old gazed sorrowfully upon him as if Dr Lay's reluctance for visitors was her fault.

"I understand. Would you be kind enough to give Dr Lay my card? I'll wait for a moment in case he changes his mind."

The woman sighed, took his calling card, and disappeared into the house, returning just as quickly.

"Dr Lay can spare five minutes," she said.

"That will do nicely."

Lawrence followed her down the hallway to the rear of the house, where Dr Lay sat behind a desk in his study.

Lay stood as Lawrence entered and offered his hand. His weathered face gave the appearance of a man who had recently lived abroad, and he sported a large, bushy moustache. "To what do I owe the honour of a visit from a private detective?"

"Rose Harsent," said Lawrence bluntly. The doctor's face fell.

"If you'd told me that, I wouldn't have let you inside. Are you sure you're not a reporter?"

"No. Not at all, and I'm not acting on my own initiative. Samuel and Abraham Goddard retained my services."

"Really? They can't have much faith in the legal system?"

"The reverse, I believe. The Goddards think the court will release William Gardiner, but the scandal will dog him for the rest of his life."

"Sit down," said the doctor, nodding towards one of a pair of wooden chairs.

Lawrence did as he was asked and pulled the chair towards the desk before leaning forward. "You don't seem surprised to hear that."

"I'm not," said Lay. "Gossip put Gardiner in the dock in the first place, and I doubt it will change."

"What's your opinion on the matter?"

"That's not for me to say. I can tell you how Miss Harsent died, the nature of her injuries and her likely time of death. But I won't speculate beyond that."

"I hear you were one of the first to see the body."

"Not quite, but I arrived soon after they found her."

"Tell me what you saw?"

"I will if I can condense it into five minutes, but you won't hear anything from me that isn't already in the public domain."

"Did you give evidence during the first trial?"

"Naturally"

"Summarise it again if you would be so kind."

"Right." Lay glanced at the wall clock before crossing his arms and sitting back in his chair. "I live opposite Providence House, where Rose Harsent died, and I quickly heard the news. I proceeded directly across the road at about twenty to nine on the thirty-first of May. The young lady was lying dead on the kitchen floor. Rigor mortis had set in."

"How long had she been there?"

"Five or six hours, at a guess. Somewhere close. Anyway, my first thought was that the injuries were accidental. A lamp lay smashed beside Miss Harsent's body, and burns covered her arms and the right side of her torso. But the damaged flesh was charred and not blistered. Do you understand what that implied?"

"No. Please explain."

"Rose Harsent must have died before the flames reached her. It was the only rational explanation. She lay face down, but the damage extended to the clothing facing the floor, and her face and hair were unsinged. Miss Harsent fell over, and her gown caught fire. Do you see?"

Lawrence nodded. "So, on closer inspection, you decided it wasn't an accident. What made you change your mind?"

"I mopped up the blood, and there was a great deal of it. I had assumed it came from the broken glass. But when I examined Rose's throat, I found a deep cut running from the angle of her right jaw to the left. The wound had opened the windpipe, causing a fatal loss of blood from the jugular vein. She didn't stand a chance."

"Could she have fallen on the glass and wounded herself?"

"No. Not accidentally, and there was a stabbing wound where the left collar bone meets the breastbone, which ran up to her throat. Once I'd ruled out an accident, I naturally considered suicide. It wouldn't have been easy, but she could feasibly have stabbed herself in the neck and tried to cut her own throat before falling to the floor and dropping the lamp in the process."

"A desperate act, surely?"

"Indeed, but Miss Harsent was unmarried and at least six months pregnant. She may have seen no other way out of her predicament."

"But you don't believe that?"

"No," said Dr Lay. "I found a bruise on her right cheek and some cuts on her hand – defensive cuts. PC Nunn and I went to her room and discovered some letters, one of which was unsigned. Someone arranged to enter Providence House and meet Miss Harsent at midnight. Someone with whom we can only assume the young lady had sexual intercourse."

"And you quite naturally concluded that Rose had been murdered."

"There is no doubt about that," said Dr Lay.

"Did you suspect William Gardiner when you realised this?"

"Not at first. And whether I would have come to that conclusion in my own time, I can't say. But PC Nunn mentioned Gardiner's name almost as soon as I spoke of murder, and when he found the older letters which were proved to be written by Mr Gardiner, he was certain."

"But in terms of facts, and not circumstantial evidence, was there any proof?"

"We found a broken bottle – the one I initially thought Miss Harsent may have used to kill herself."

"Yes. What about it?"

"It was one of mine."

"Yours?"

"I mean, I had prescribed the medicine contained inside."

"For whom?"

"I couldn't tell. Blood and paraffin covered the label, obscuring the patient's name."

"Who did you think it was for?"

"Mrs Gardiner's sister."

"Really?"

"Yes. Georgiana Gardiner's sister was visiting when she became unwell. Gardiner asked me to call by, and I prescribed a linctus."

"What made you think the bottle belonged to Mrs Gardiner's sister if the label was unreadable?"

"I don't know. Just an impression, I suppose."

"And when did you know for sure?"

"About a week later. A chemist from the Home Office treated the label, removed the stain, and read the prescription below. As I suspected, it was one of mine, but I had prescribed it for Mrs Gardiner's children."

"Not her sister?"

"No."

"Do you think you would have speculated about the bottle's origin if PC Nunn had not mentioned William Gardiner?"

Dr Lay stared at the ground, ruminating. "I have often thought about this point since the first trial," he said. "And no. I doubt it. Truth to tell, the label was unreadable until they removed the stain. In hindsight, it's fair to say my guess was speculative, based on PC Nunn's suspicions."

"I appreciate your candour," said Lawrence. "Now, do you know anything else that might help?"

"Who else have you spoken to?"

"Alfred Grice and George Whiting."

"Hmmm. I doubt they know any first-hand information. I would try James Crisp if I were you. He saw the body before I did."

"Yes, he's on my list."

"Can I see it?"

Lawrence extracted the note from his pocket and passed it across the desk.

"Wright and Skinner are a pair of troublemakers," said Dr Lay, eyeing Lawrence's scribbled note beside Alfred Grice's neater lettering. I wouldn't pay too much heed to them. Especially not Wright, who has started yet another tall story."

"Another?"

"You must know that it was his eavesdropping and gossip-mongering that started the rumours about Gardiner and Rose?"

"Yes. I had heard, although I didn't know it happened more than once."

"I'm afraid so. Wright couldn't keep his nose out of other people's business and enjoyed stirring up trouble. And just when the end is in sight after the last turbulent eighteen months, he's at it again."

"Gossiping?"

"Telling tall stories. And it's causing concern among the village women. It's not right, and I will bring the matter up with his stepfather."

"Harry Redgrift?"

"You know him?"

"No. But he's on the list, and I will try to see him."

"Try to talk some sense into him when you do."

"Why? Has he been gossiping too?"

Dr Lay glanced at the clock. "I'm sorry to be rude, but I really must get on."

"Of course. I'll leave you in peace. Perhaps Mr Redgrift can tell me more."

"More nonsense if he believes his stepson. Please don't fall for it. Wright claims that someone is following him around the village and threatening his life. He's spun some cock and bull story about a man that nobody else has seen and a rock that narrowly missed his head. I wouldn't mind, but it's distressing to some of the more gullible in this village who ought to know better than to believe him."

"Ah yes. Samuel Goddard mentioned this, but Abraham was sceptical. Apparently, a young woman, Ellen, I think they said, thought someone followed her one night too."

"Ellen Blowers, you mean?"

"Yes. Is she the type to make up a story?"

"Not at all. Mrs Blowers always struck me as a sensible woman. Sharp-tongued and too fond of talking, perhaps, but essentially honest. She quarrelled with Beatrice Ray at The Angel over some missing laundry, I heard she also argued with Gardiner's wife outside her home, but Ellen Blower's never denied having a short temper."

"So, someone could have followed her?"

"I doubt it. You know what it's like at night if you're walking in the dark. It's human nature to think the worst. I expect Mrs Bowers heard a noise, remembered Wright's story, and let her imagination run wild. That's what happens when careless talk is allowed to fester. Which is why I have very little time for Bill Wright and his sidekick."

"Skinner?"

"Yes. Alfonso Skinner. He invented the ridiculous moniker currently doing the rounds."

"Dare I ask?"

"They've named the alleged follower, the Creeper, which is the depths to which these young men go to keep themselves entertained. My housekeeper referred to the Creeper the other day, and I'm afraid I gave her short shrift. Now. I must do the same to you," said Lay, reaching for his bag.

"Understood," said Lawrence. "And thank you for your time. It's been most enlightening."

CHAPTER NINE

And Thence to Bunwell

"Isn't this fun?" said Violet, watching a little girl walk by the side of the road hand in hand with her mother.

"Can I give him a carrot?" asked Daisy, more interested in the chestnut horse pulling the trap they'd boarded at Attleborough station.

"You don't have one."

Daisy's face fell.

"What about an apple?" asked Michael, reaching into his jacket pocket.

"Oh yes. The pony would love an apple."

Violet smiled. How very like Michael to have the means to keep a little girl's spirits up during a long journey. Daisy was only seven years old and still prone to boredom. She'd been content to watch the countryside from the train window, but the twenty-minute journey by pony and trap to Bunwell was a different matter. Violet had stowed one of Daisy's books in her bag, but that was the last weapon in her armoury. Daisy took the apple from Michael and polished it on her dress, then she pulled a blanket across her legs and curled into her mother.

Violet smiled, then turned to Michael. "How is your new girl working out?" she asked.

"Aurora is a hard worker," he said. "You wouldn't believe how much progress she has made in just a few days. The rooms we can access look like new."

"Have you found the missing keys yet?"

"No. And I'm not sure we ever will. I don't know what to do about it. Get the locks replaced, I suppose. But Francis will take a dim view if he ever returns."

Violet failed to suppress a shudder. "He won't, will he?"

"I doubt it," said Michael, sadly. He'd seen Francis at his worst, full of rage, having kidnapped Violet and determined to harm Lawrence. But Francis was still his brother. Time had passed, and although the incident had challenged Michael's faith, causing his recent decision to take a prolonged absence from the church, he still missed him – still felt bereft at the loss of his decade older brother, who had always been a father figure.

Violet leaned across and touched Michael's cheek. "It's for the best," she said. "And at least you have a little company during the day."

Michael shrugged. His face darkened, and for a moment, she thought he might cry. Then, as if he was reading her mind, he spoke.

"Tell me, Violet, do you ever get upset for no reason?"

"No. I'm not one for tears, even when they're justified. Why do you ask?"

"Now and then, I'll come across Aurora when she's in the middle of some task or other, and her face is blotchy and red as if

69

she'd been crying. She's distressed about something. And she never smiles. Not ever."

"Do you know anything about her?"

"A little. Aurora is a girl of few words and she barely spoke to me at first. It took a concerted effort to get her to talk, but she's grown to trust me. She said that she once belonged to an organisation and left in a hurry. She's alone now – no friends or relatives that I know of, and I suppose she's lonely."

"What sort of organisation?"

"A religious group, I suppose. Aurora is working for me because I'm a vicar. She says she finds it comforting, and I wondered if she might have left a convent. It would explain the tears. I know what it's like to question your faith."

"Yes," said Violet slowly. "Lawrence and I have seen enough to know she's upset about something. But surely she has friends? Where does Aurora live?"

"Well, that's another thing," said Michael. "She had rooms in Bury. But yesterday, she asked me if she could stay at Netherwood and work for her board instead of wages."

"Oh dear," said Violet. "How did you put her off?"

"I didn't."

"Is that wise?"

"No. But something is wrong, and it's my Christian duty to help."

"But you're compromising her position. You may be a priest, Michael. But you're still a man, a nice-looking man with prospects."

Michael smiled. "Thank you," he said.

"Seriously. You're taking an unnecessary risk. Do you know anything about Aurora? Who wrote her references?"

"I can't remember," he said, then clicked his fingers. "Yes, I do. A Mrs Sedgington of Lowndes Square, Knightsbridge."

Violet raised an eyebrow. "Have you checked them?"

"How could I?"

"By writing to her or picking up the telephone."

"She didn't leave a number. I could write, I suppose."

"But you haven't?"

"No."

"Aurora could be a thief or a murderess, for all you know, Michael. You ought to say no."

"It's too late. She'll have unpacked her possessions by the time I get back."

"Oh, Michael. Do be careful."

"I will, Violet. But she's fragile and needs protecting."

So are you, thought Violet, watching the sadness in Michael's grey eyes. Lawrence hated Francis. Violet feared him, but Michael had no such emotions to hide behind. He wore the pain of his brother's deception behind misty eyes, a thinner frame, and his hopelessness at a God who could bring such misery.

They travelled in silence, and before long, the pony trotted into a small village and pulled up by the side of a long, red brick house surrounded by a white picket fence.

Michael alighted, grabbed Daisy, and twirled her around before setting her down. Then he took Violet's hand and helped her from the trap.

"Thank you," he said, handing coins to the driver.

Violet opened her bag. "Corner Cottage," she read. "About fifty yards down North Road."

She took Daisy's hand while Michael reached for the other, and they strode up the street, swinging Daisy between them, her peals of giggles filling the air.

"Here it is," said Violet as they arrived outside a small, cream cottage standing at right angles to the road. "Now, as I've said, Mrs Leverett is elderly. She knows you are coming but has asked if you can take Daisy into the kitchen and stay with her. She's a little hard of hearing and worries that she won't be able to concentrate with a child around."

"Don't fret about us. I come prepared," said Michael, reaching into his jacket and producing a small packet before passing it to Daisy.

71

"Happy families," she squealed, opening the packet. "Mr Soot, the sweep. Look, Mama."

"Thank you," Violet mouthed as she knocked on the door before opening it. She put her finger to her lips and beckoned Michael and Daisy inside before proceeding towards the tiny parlour.

"Mrs Leverett?"

"I'm in here, dear. There's a jug of lemon barley water and some gingerbread out the back for the child."

Violet waved Michael and Daisy towards the kitchen, then entered to see an elderly lady swathed in blankets huddled in front of a mean-looking fire. The remains of a suet pudding lay on a plate by the side of her feet.

"Sit down, dear," said Mary Leverett, pointing to the only other chair.

Violet obliged. "Thank you for agreeing to see me," she said.

"I've nothing better to do," said Mary. "But what's this about an inheritance? It's a bit late to benefit me now."

#

"Oh, dear. I think we are at cross-purposes," said Violet, looking anxiously towards the elderly lady. "I'm looking for information to help one of your relatives."

There was a brief silence, then Mary Leverett smiled. "I understand," she said. "Now, who are you looking for?"

"I'm sorry, but I can't tell you," said Violet.

"Then who has died?"

"I can't tell you that either. It's confidential."

"Then how do you know I can help?"

"Because the information I have leads me to Tibenham."

"Yes?"

"And the family name Everett."

"I see. I'm not an Everett, you know."

"But you're related to them."

"Yes, I am. How much is the inheritance?"

Violet chewed her lip. Despite her evident frail health, Mary Leverett was sharp. Up to now, Violet had confined herself to obfuscation, but if her plan were to succeed, she would have to start lying and doing it well. Violet had little time to prepare, only learning the most basic facts about the case and had decided against going to the record office first. She didn't know Mary's ancestor's occupations or their status in life and how much inheritance they could realistically leave. "Not a great deal," she said, settling for the middle ground.

"I presume you make your money from earning a commission?" Violet nodded.

"Then it hardly seems worth your while."

"You're right," said Violet. "We ordinarily concentrate on the bigger estates, but it's quiet at the moment, and I live in Bury, so it should be an easy case to settle, as long as you don't mind helping."

"Very well," said Mary, accepting Violet's explanation. "What do you want to know?"

"The deceased is younger than you and a different generation," said Violet. "And to make progress, we must go back a few generations. It would help if you could tell me about your parents, their siblings and any descendants you know about."

"Half of them have moved away," said Mary. "We've lost touch with the younger ones, and as for my generation. Well, all the Pearsons and most of the Everetts are long gone. Maybe all of them, for all I know." Mary stared wistfully into the distance, recalling her younger days.

"Perhaps I could write out a family tree," said Violet, rummaging in her bag for her notebook and pen. She retrieved them and opened the leather-bound jotter that Lawrence had insisted she use for business.

"How far back do you want to go?"

"Your grandparents," said Violet firmly. Having conducted considerable family research with Lawrence in Fressingfield, she knew all too well how time-consuming it could be. And the family tree was a subterfuge for gaining information about the poisonings.

Any further back would mean a lot of work, and Violet meant to keep the details as concise as possible.

Mary reclined in her chair and lifted the blanket over her shoulders.

"Shall I stoke the fire?" asked Violet.

"Could you, dear? But don't put any more logs on."

Violet obliged and poked the pathetic embers before resuming her seat.

"My grandparents were Joseph and Susan Pearson," said Mary. They had three children. Susanna, Joseph, and Elizabeth. Joseph married Mary Lincoln, and Susanna and Elizabeth both married Everett's. Elizabeth was my mother."

"So, you were an Everett?"

"An Everett married to a Leverett." Mary cackled with laughter until a coughing fit overtook her. She spluttered, red-faced and embarrassed. Violet stood to fetch a glass of water, but Mary stopped her.

"Don't. It makes no difference. I fear I'm not long for this world."

"I'm sorry," said Violet. "I'll stop if you're unwell."

"Nothing changes," said Mary. "It will be the same tomorrow, and it's nice having visitors."

"Do let me know if I can get you anything. I may as well be useful while I'm here."

"There is something," said Mary. "Open that drawer and fetch me the tin."

Violet approached a stained wooden cupboard pock-marked with holes and did as Mary asked. She withdrew a battered tea box and passed it to Mary, who fiddled with it for a few moments, then sighed in exasperation.

"You do it," she said, holding the tin towards Violet. "My fingers don't work very well these days."

Violet pushed open the lid and peered inside. "What am I looking for?"

"A likeness," said Mary.

Violet rifled through the few pieces of paper resting upon buttons, pins and thimbles, picked out the only likely candidate and passed it to Mary."

The old woman smiled, her features softening into ageless serenity. Violet waited as she contemplated the image, transfixed at the small, faded piece of paper. Eventually, she held the drawing up and showed it to Violet. "My mother," she said.

Violet leaned forward. "She looks young," she replied.

"She must have been in her late forties then," said Mary. "It's exactly how I remember her."

"Not as an elderly lady?"

"She didn't get to be one."

"I'm sorry to hear that," said Violet, purposefully leaving a long silence, hoping Mary would fill it. She did not oblige.

"And your father?"

"He lived on for another fifty years."

"I'm glad to hear it."

"Hmmm. Well, he soon replaced my mother with a new wife a few years later. Then Susan died, and he married a third woman twenty years younger. Not that far off my age, actually, the dirty old goat."

"Men seem to need company far more than women," said Violet. "They don't live well on their own in my experience. Did you mind very much?"

Mary nodded. "Yes, I did. Perhaps it was selfish, as I had a husband and grown-up children of my own by then. I had no right to get upset, but with losing Mother the way we did, it seemed disrespectful somehow."

"I understand. I lost my father, and though I grew to love my stepfather more than I could ever have thought possible, it took time. It's only natural to resent it when someone takes the place of a loved one."

"I'm sure you mean well, but you don't understand." Mary scowled as she snapped the words out.

"I'm so sorry. I didn't mean to offend you."

"Oh, my dear. I'm the one that should be sorry. You are not to know, but my mother died in peculiar and distressing circumstances. I will never forget the manner of her death, and it has stayed with me. I have never forgotten it, and I never will. And God knows, I will join her before much longer."

Violet waited. Mary was on the verge of telling her the information she so desperately hoped to gain. But just when it looked certain that Mary would continue, another bout of coughing destroyed the moment.

"What were you saying?" asked Mary.

"I wasn't. We were talking about your mother."

"Yes. What else do you need to know?"

"Here. I've drawn out the tree so far. Susannah, Joseph and Elizabeth and their spouses. Can you give me some dates?"

"I'll try," said Mary. "Susannah was the oldest, followed by Elizabeth and Joseph. They were born around 1780 to 90. Joseph Pearson died the year before my father, about 1878, and Susannah died a few years before that. Her husband did not make old bones, and of course, my mother and Mary Pearson died in 1847."

"The same year. That's unfortunate," said Violet.

"The same day, as it happens."

"Oh, dear. Was it an accident?"

"No," said Mary, her eyes filling with tears. "It was nothing less than cold-blooded murder."

#

"Goodness me. What a terrible thing," said Violet.

"Oh, it was. And so very sad. I didn't have time to say goodbye to my mother. She died so quickly. But you don't want to hear about such awful matters."

"It might help," said Violet. "Tell me if you care to, and perhaps I can piece the tree around your story."

"I haven't spoken of this to anyone but George for years. And he gets on at me if I mention it and tells me to cheer up as if the pain will ever go away."

"George. Who's he?"

"My husband."

"Oh. I just assumed..."

"That I was a widow? No. George lives here with me normally, but he's in Norwich, with my daughter," said Mary. "I'm too ill to travel, but my husband is younger and fitter. So, he's gone off without me."

Violet flushed beetroot red. She had fallen into the trap of concluding that the elderly, frail woman was a widow, based only upon the size of the cottage, the scant fire, and the lack of another person present. But this was a poor judgement of the situation, especially for an investigator. It was a good thing that Violet was in Bunwell in the guise of an inheritance seeker, or she could be rightfully embarrassed at her lack of deductive ability.

"Which is why I appreciate the company," said Mary, saving Violet from further introspection. "I will tell you about the poisonings if you have time. Will your daughter be patient for a little while longer?"

"Yes. Daisy is a good girl and fond of her uncle Michael."

"The vicar?"

Violet nodded.

"Well. I'll tell you what I can remember, and I'm sure you'll take notes on the family. The deaths happened in the spring of 1847 at my uncle's home in Tibenham. His name was Joseph Pearson, if you remember, and he married my aunt Mary. My parents named me after her, you know. Anyway, my uncle and aunt sat down to breakfast as they did every morning with their maidservant and their lad. They were farmers and not well to do, but not poor either, if you know what I mean. My family sat at one table and the servants at another."

"Do you remember their names?"

"The servants? The boy was James, and I'll never forget the name of the spiteful little cat, Eliza Sage. A nastier piece of work you couldn't imagine. Why the Pearsons kept her, I will never know. She was rude and unhelpful. None of us liked her, but servants are hard to come by, and they tolerated far too much."

"She sounds a handful."

"She was. A hateful creature. Horrible." Mary Leverett shuddered beneath the threadbare blanket; her repulsion still evident after all the years that had passed.

"Go on."

"The family ate something or other. I can't remember what. Then Aunt Mary took tea from a kettle. Within moments, she started wheezing and couldn't catch her breath. She thought, at first, that there was something wrong with the flour."

"Perhaps she had bread and butter for breakfast?"

"Yes. That was it. Bread, butter, and cheese, I shouldn't wonder. That's what they offered us when we visited as children. Anyway, Mary was sick afterwards, but it didn't help. She huddled by the fire, worsening by the minute, and Joseph sent for the surgeon and my mother, who was also his sister, as you know. While my mother attended to Mary, she helped herself to a cup of tea. But as soon as she drank it, she was violently sick too. Joseph was beside himself and quite desperate by the time the surgeon arrived. He came from North Buckenham and set off as soon as possible, but it was close to midday by the time he got there. The surgeon could do little to help, and my aunt died first, followed by my mother soon after."

"I'm so sorry," said Violet. "Poor Elizabeth. Trying to help her brother and falling victim to the poisoner for her good deed. No wonder you cannot find peace."

"That's exactly it," said Mary. "The injustice of the murders and the fact that they will never bring the culprit to account still keeps me awake at night. They ought to be punished, but it can never be."

"Would it help if you knew who did it?"

"No. And it's forty years too late."

"Does anyone know how the poison got in the kettle?"

"No. But it was definitely in there."

"Could it have fallen in by accident?"

Mary shook her head. "No. They considered this at the inquest. The coroner said it was murder, but they couldn't convict anyone for lack of evidence."

"Was there poison in the house?"

"That's a funny sort of question to ask? How will that help with the family tree?"

"It won't. I'm just curious and intrigued by your story. I suppose my curiosity comes from having an investigative occupation."

Mary smiled. "You mean you're nosy. And I would be too if I was in your shoes."

"I confess," said Violet, holding up her hands. "It's a sad story, but an unsolved murder is always unsatisfying. A mystery with no end."

"You could say that," said Mary.

"Who do you think it was?"

"I refuse to speculate. I know who I'd wish it were if it had to be anyone – the girl Sage. She was a thoroughly unpleasant character, always causing trouble, and she didn't like her mistress very much."

"Was she charged with murder?"

"No. But only because there wasn't enough evidence."

"Did everyone dislike her?"

"Yes. Even the lad, James. My aunt was more tolerant than she had any business being. We told her to let the girl go. The family knew best and always stuck together. If my aunt had listened to us, she would have lived a normal life span."

"Do you think she kept Eliza because she was afraid that she wouldn't find another servant?"

"Partly. But my aunt was soft and thought the girl would come good in time. She never did."

"Is Eliza still alive?"

"No. She died twenty years ago. Up north somewhere."

"How do you know?"

"She had a relative in Tibenham. I saw her from time to time when I visited the village. She told me Eliza died," said Mary.

"Is her relative still alive?"

"Beth? Yes. But she's frail now and in the workhouse, poor thing. Why?"

"I just wondered. I find the whole thing fascinating."

"Don't go poking your nose into other people's business," said Mary sharply. "It's one thing me telling you a story, and quite another you bothering people about it."

"I won't," said Violet. "Really. But I would like to know one more thing. Just out of interest, you understand. Do you think Eliza Sage poisoned your family?"

Mary fixed Violet with a steely glare. "I told you I wouldn't speculate, and I won't. It's old news. I wouldn't have said a word in other circumstances, but it's been a long time since I've thought about family, and the words spilt out. But that's it now. I won't speak of it again, and I'm tired. Let's finish this tree."

CHAPTER TEN

Something's Afoot

Harry Redgrift was lying on his belly on an old tarpaulin in the grounds of the hall when Lawrence caught up with him.

"Excuse me," said Lawrence as he approached the prone man.

"What?" snapped Redgrift, heaving himself to his knees.

"Are you Harry Redgrift?"

"Who's asking?"

"Lawrence Harpham, private investigator."

"Well, you can sling your hook. I've nothing to say to you."

Lawrence did not beat about the bush trying to convince the recalcitrant man. Instead, he employed the tactic that had worked so well with Alf Grice and dropped a coin on the hard ground by Redgrift's feet.

"What's that for?"

"Your time," said Lawrence, hoping it was worth it. Still, the Goddard brothers hadn't so much as blinked when he mentioned his fees, and he could consider this and Grice's small bribe as an investment for the future.

Redgrift's hand closed over the coin, and groaning in pain, he got to his feet. Lawrence reached for a handshake while Redgrift wiped grubby fingers on a tatty apron tied around his middle before returning the gesture. His hand was iron cold and caked with soil. Lawrence, always averse to mess, resisted the temptation to clean his palms on his handkerchief and instead shoved them deep in his pocket, fiddling with a piece of paper inside.

"What do you want, then?" asked Harry Redgrift.

"Information," said Lawrence, then relayed the gist of his mission curtly and without fuss. He had already noted that Redgrift was not a man of words and was fidgeting like a bored child, keen to return to the odd task he had been undertaking when Lawrence interrupted him.

"That's as maybe," said Redgrift. "But I've nothing to tell you."

"You know your stepson," said Lawrence.

"Aye. And he knows more than I do. The boy is in Ipswich. Ask him."

"I know where he is. And without boring you with details, it's easier to speak to people not directly involved in the trial. Everything they've said is already well documented."

"I'm not telling tales on our lad."

"I'm not asking you to. Just give me your version of events – what you've seen and heard around the village."

Redgrift opened his palm and looked at the coin, evidently in two minds whether to return it and tell Lawrence to leave him alone. But greed got the better of him."

"You can have ten minutes of my time. And that's your lot."

Lawrence rubbed his hands together, cursing his lack of gloves. He had stopped disguising his scarred hand a long time ago, but it ached more than ever on cold days like these. "Can we go indoors?"

"Oh yes. Let's pop in through the front door like Lord and Mr Muck and watch me get my marching orders. I'm a market gardener and here to advise, not one of the servants." Harry Redgrift raised his eyes heavenwards in undisguised ridicule.

"Don't you have a shed or a barn we can go to?"

Redgrift scowled. "There's a bench in the boot room. No one will bother us there."

Lawrence trailed behind as the bad-tempered gardener huffed and puffed his way towards the rear of the house. Despite the cold, the back door was wide open. They entered, went a short way down the corridor, then Redgrift pushed open a stable-style door with an iron hasp and theatrically waved Lawrence through. "Sit there," he said abruptly, pointing to a long wooden bench.

Lawrence obliged, and Redgrift sat heavily beside him. "Wait a moment," he said before reaching into his pocket and withdrawing a pipe and a battered tin. He rapped the pipe on the bench, filled it and struck a match. Seconds later, the acrid smell of burning tobacco filled the air. Lawrence moved a few inches to the left and would have moved even further had it been possible. Redgrave spread his legs, leaned back, and puffed a contented plume of smoke into the room.

"What can I tell you about young Bill?"

"I hear he caught William Gardiner in a compromising position with Rose Harsent."

"That's one way of putting it," spluttered Redgrift, grinning for the first time.

"Was there any doubt about what he thought he saw?"

"Not a scintilla," said Redgrift, slowly separating the syllables as he spoke.

"He couldn't have been mistaken?"

"Nope."

"How can you be so sure?"

"Because when he saw Gardiner sneaking into the doctor's chapel, he came home and fetched Fonso."

"Alfonso Skinner?"

"Yes. My other lodger. The boys are employed at the drill works."

"So, they followed Gardiner?"

"No. He was already there. They made their way south of the chapel and hid behind a hurdle fence just outside the window."

"Could they hear anything?"

Redgrift nodded. "Talking and laughing, then a noise that sounded like rustling. You know what I mean?"

Lawrence feigned ignorance. "No."

"As if they were lying together."

"And then what?"

"The woman cried out."

"She screamed?"

"No. I didn't say that. It was more like groaning. Then the rustling began again, and the voices started talking about reading the Bible."

"So, on the evidence of a few incoherent sounds, sight unseen, they assumed that William Gardiner and Rose Harsent were indulging in intercourse?"

"It's more than that," said Redgrift, chewing the stem of his pipe. "Our Bill heard the girl say that she had been reading about what they had been doing that night."

"Reading what?"

"The thirty-eighth chapter of Genesis."

"I'm sorry. I'm not familiar with the Bible."

Redgrift raised an eyebrow and looked down his nose in disgust. "I suggest you read it then. Pay particular attention to Onan spilling his seed on the ground."

"Ah." Lawrence looked at the floor, hoping that he wouldn't embarrass himself by blushing now that he understood the inference. "Is Bill certain?"

"Oh, yes."

"It couldn't have been another chapter?"

"Bill said thirty-eight, and Alfonso agreed. It's two against one, despite what those self-interested preachers said, including your friends the Goddards."

"They didn't believe Bill."

"Because it suited them not to. But I do. And you want to know something else?"

"Anything."

"My brother, George, is Captain Levett-Scrivenor's gamekeeper. And old James Morris, who works alongside him from time to time, found a set of footprints running from Alma Cottage to Providence House, the day after the murders."

Lawrence looked at him blankly, and Redgrift tutted. "William Gardiner lived at Alma Cottage, and Rose died at Providence House."

"I see," said Lawrence slowly, his brain trying to catch up with Redgrift's words. "You think Gardiner murdered Rose and left footprints?"

"It's obvious, isn't it? It's a pity the jury couldn't see sense at the first trial, or they wouldn't have dragged Bill and Fonso away again. Best they get it right this time."

"Bill's a young man, I believe?" said Lawrence.

"Yes.".

"And young men are prone to exaggeration from time to time."

"I told you. I believe Bill."

"Hear me out. Is there any reason that Bill might have embellished events at the doctor's chapel? Did he know Gardiner?"

"Of course. It's a small town."

"In any other capacity."

"Gardiner was foreman up at the drill works if that's what you're getting at."

"And your stepson?"

"He's a wheelwright."

"At the works?"

Redgrift nodded.

"Who does he work for?"

85

"Gardiner," mumbled Redgrift.

"William Gardiner?"

"Yes. But that doesn't have any bearing on Bill Wright's word," said Redgrift.

"Did Gardiner treat him well at work?"

"He was a hard taskmaster."

"I see."

"No, you don't. You're trying to make a liar out of Bill. Well, you won't succeed any more than they did in court. Now, you've had your money's worth. It's time for you to go."

Lawrence racked his brains. He hadn't finished with Redgrift, but he was losing him. The man was chewing his pipe aggressively beneath his white moustache and his hands, formerly red with cold, were now clenched and white with anger.

"Tell me about the Creeper?" asked Lawrence, trying to diffuse Harry Redgrift's temper.

His ruse succeeded. Redgrift's eyes grew wide as his forehead furrowed. "How do you know about that?" he asked.

#

"The Goddards mentioned it," said Lawrence.

Redgrift snorted. "As if they would believe a word. Anyway, things like that don't happen to the likes of them."

"The Goddard brothers don't seem any different to you."

"Yes, but they're Methodists, aren't they? Godly and better than the rest of us. Especially Pious Willy."

"By that, I assume you mean Gardiner?"

"Who else?"

"Have you always disliked him?"

"I never gave him much thought one way or the other. Our paths didn't cross. He preferred the church while Bill and I take our pleasure in the public house."

Redgrift turned towards Lawrence, winked, and blew a fug of smoke directly in his face. It was all Lawrence could do to keep his breakfast down.

"You never spoke?"

"Aye. From time to time. I would greet Gardiner once in a while when passing his cottage. That wife of his is pleasant enough. She always had a kind word to say, especially when my wife took ill. But we're not alike, and I wouldn't pass the time of day with him even if we were the only two men living in Peasenhall."

"Because he's a Methodist?"

"Partly. And because he looks down on everyone else. But you're right, of course. That's typical of the Methodists around here and in Sibton. They think that anyone who doesn't worship in their congregation isn't worthy. That's why they didn't believe Bill."

"But what's that got to do with the Creeper?"

"Only that I'm surprised they've spoken of it."

"Well, they have, and I would like to know more."

"I thought you were investigating Rose?"

"I am. But I keep hearing about this man. It is a man, isn't it?"

"Unless it's the devil himself."

Lawrence glanced at Redgrift to see if he was smiling, but if he was, he concealed it well beneath his moustache. Instead, his eyes darkened, and one leg jiggled quickly up and down.

"Why do you call him the Creeper?"

"Because that's what he does," said Redgrift. "He slinks around Peasenhall in the dead of night, following folk who ought to be in their beds."

"Including Bill?"

"Yes."

"But not Alfonso?"

"Meaning?"

"It was just a question," said Lawrence, noting Harry Redgrift's defensive stance. "I meant nothing by it. Tell me, how did Bill describe the Creeper?"

"He heard him twice," said Redgrift. "The first time, Bill was returning from the alehouse, merry but not in his cups. Fonso was bad with the stomach flu, and Bill walked alone. It was late at night, close to midnight, I think. They were drinking past hours, a few of them, you know, favourites of the publican. Anyway, it wasn't far to come, and Bill was making his way down the street, as usual, when he heard a sound. You know, as if someone had kicked a stone behind him. So, he stopped and looked around. He couldn't see anyone and thought he must have imagined it. Then not five yards farther on, the same thing happened again. This time, Bill slowed down but carried on walking until he reached a lit window. He passed it, then quick as a flash, he turned around, taking advantage of the light. This time he saw something – a man in a shabby overcoat who ran away as soon as Bill turned. And you know what Bill said?"

"No."

"He said that the man was wearing a scarf around his face."

"What's wrong with that?"

"In the middle of June."

"It still gets cold at night."

"Whatever. Anyway, about a month later, Bill encountered him again. And once more, Bill was alone. This time, he didn't hear the Creeper until it was too late."

"What do you mean?"

"I mean, the brute put his hand on Bill's shoulder, and if it wasn't for John Mill's dog, anything could have happened."

"Where was this?"

"At the back of The Street. It was late at night, and Bill was playing a trick on John Mills. He'd given him grief at the drill works earlier that day, and Bill thought it would be amusing to fill his boots with horse muck. One of the lads had put him up to it while they were drinking."

"He does a lot of that," said Lawrence, regretting his words the moment they slipped out. But instead of taking his usual defensive stance, Harry Redgrift continued.

"Yes, always one for tricks was our Bill. And John Mills had mentioned his new boots that day. John should have known better than to brag in front of Bill when he had upset him. But he did, and that was that. Bill, fired up by his friends, said he would take care of it on the way home. So, he went around the back of Mills' house in the dark and was about to open the side gate when he felt this hand on his shoulder, and he swears something sharp touched his back. But the dog sensed danger and burst from his kennel, barking fit to wake the neighbourhood. The Creeper fled, and Bill couldn't get home quickly enough in case old man Mills saw him and reported him to the gaffer. And that was the last time he saw the Creeper."

"Right," said Lawrence, swallowing his disappointment. Redgrift's story sounded far-fetched and unlikely. If that was the quality of evidence Wright was currently feeding to the jury, then the Goddards were right, and William Gardiner would soon come home.

"Don't pull that face," said Redgrift intuitively. "Bill can embellish all day long, but he doesn't lie. There's always a germ of truth in everything he says."

"Don't you think it's curious that he's only seen this man twice?"

"He doesn't go out alone anymore."

"At all?"

"No. And don't you go telling anyone that Bill Wright fears his own shadow. He won't even go to the privy without the light on. That's how much he believes this. And he's not the only one."

"Yes. I've heard about Ellen Blowers."

"Who told you?"

"Never mind who. But it's on good authority. Something is going on in Peasenhall. I just hope it's something simple like a vagrant or simpleton."

"That's what I said," agreed Redgrift. "Though Bill disagrees with me, he didn't see enough to be sure. Yet I can't help thinking this has something to do with Rose."

"An interesting thought, but I heard the sightings occurred after Rose Harsent died?"

"They did. But it doesn't mean they weren't happening before. Just that nobody knew."

"Has anyone else seen this man?"

"Fred Davies," said Redgrift, "but he's in court."

"Damn," said Lawrence.

"Are you talking to anyone else?"

"Kate Pepper and James Crisp."

"Then you're in luck. Crisp lives next door to Fred Davies. His father has taken him to court, but I bet Caroline is at home. Ask her. Fred's a proper mother's boy for all his dirty talk. If he's told anyone about the Creeper, it will be her."

CHAPTER ELEVEN

Gibraltar – The Aftermath

March 1902

HMS *Devastation* left Gibraltar in February 1902, but I was not aboard. They left without me, having decided that I was not fit to sail. It was nonsense, of course. I was as well as I ever would be, but an embarrassment to the Royal Navy and a reminder of their dereliction of duty. It would have been better for them if I'd died. Not only better for them but a mercy for me. But I did not. Despite the horror of my injuries, I survived.

My shipmates left me bloodied and broken on the bow of the fishing boat they had borrowed in Gibraltar. I was barely alive, and even Sludge must have known he had gone too far this time and fled with the others to establish an alibi. I never found out how much the boat owner knew in advance, but he wasn't alone when he returned to his vessel, and his companion insisted on getting me medical help. But for his intervention, the owner might have tossed me into the sea. It would have saved him a lot of trouble when the navy came calling to find out what had happened that terrible night.

I was unconscious for days as the doctors tended to my wounds in the civil hospital ward where military medics worked alongside Spanish doctors. As I gradually came to, I vacillated between understanding what was happening around me and being lost in a sea of words I didn't understand. But the disorientation was nothing to the constant grinding pain of my existence, the enduring agony in every cell of my body. I couldn't move, couldn't so much as flutter an eyelash without needle-like pains stabbing across my flesh. In the early days, I heard myself making guttural animal sounds that seemed to come from another body as if I was looking down at somebody else. But eventually, I stopped keening, somehow understanding at a subliminal level that it was making the pain worse. I retreated inside myself, kept silent, thought of England. Even the barbaric punishments meted out by my father were nothing to this. But I bypassed those memories and thought instead of Cyril, Georgie and I tossing a ball or fishing by the brook. Mornings at school learning our letters, singing psalms, even the daily grind of the Lord's prayer before we went home. Old pedestrian memories grew into the happiest of times as I embellished them to tune out the agony of my existence.

After a week, the drugs they gave to dull the pain finally felt like they were working. After a month, I could conduct a conversation and comprehend the reply. The doctors dressed my wounds, the odour of my damaged flesh diminished, and I finally left the comfort of my memories to confront the truth of my injuries, both graphic and horrifying. I remember the day that Dr Franco Santos sat beside me with Victoria Flemming, a young Scottish nurse. She held my hand as the doctor spoke, biting her lip as she contemplated what would follow. Dr Santos gently asked how I had come by my injuries, having seen nothing like it in his many years of medical work. I didn't want to relive that night, to own the horror of the memories I had largely shut away. But Santos said that he could offer no further help until he understood what had happened. So, I told him. And when I finished, he strode from the room and straight to the army medical officer tending to wounded soldiers on the second floor. Between them, they contacted the navy demanding an immediate investigation which began the next day. But I didn't know this until afterwards and lay shivering under a sheet, tears streaming down my face, the salt spiking fresh pain into my wounds while Victoria stroked my brow. She stayed there until I finally fell asleep and returned when I woke screaming in the small hours, reliving the ordeal of being repeatedly dragged beneath the jagged hull of a boat.

Shellfish caused the worst of my injuries. The doctors hadn't realised when they started treating me, but all became clear once I explained the keelhauling. Barnacles cluster beneath the waterline, their razor-like edges ripping through anything coming in close contact. And they had pulled me across them on multiple occasions. Every time Sludge and his crew hauled the rope around the boat, the barnacles sliced through my skin, their sharp edges lacerating my body, exacerbating open wounds. And when they'd left me for dead, with my salt-covered skin exposed to the elements, the cuts became infected. By the time I reached the hospital, the raging pain was all-consuming. They expected me to die. And that was not the worst, it turned out.

Santos came again the next day, bringing Victoria with him. They stood on either side of my bed and hauled me into a sitting position. Santos explained that naval investigators would visit later that day. That nobody had the right to torture a serving naval seaman. I was to tell them everything I knew, to name names, and hold nothing back. But the investigators would need to see the extent of my wounds, which meant that at long last, so would I. Victoria took my hand, then reached into her apron for a mirror. Santos passed me a nip of rum, and then they made me look. A stranger stared back. A man I didn't recognise, a fiery half-made thing from the rivers of hell, blackened and demonic. Blood rushed to my head.

I felt hot, cold, and hot again. I couldn't speak, couldn't think. They took the mirror away and tried again a few hours later – this time, I was better prepared. My face, as I remembered it, was lost forever, my nose slashed away by the barnacle shells. My eyes had survived, but not my right eyelid and my lips were a pulpy mess, with my skin slashed and scarred. I stared at the hole in my face where my nose used to be and felt the bile rise inside. I was hideous and did not belong in public view. I asked them to take the mirror away, and to this day, I have never looked at another.

CHAPTER TWELVE

Recalling the Past

Lawrence was undressing for the night and was about to slip into the single bed at the Angel Inn when he had an inexplicable urge to see Violet. He grabbed a book to distract himself and started reading on top of the covers, but the words slipped through his mind, elusive and meaningless. And the more Lawrence thought about it, the more he wondered at the point of staying here at all. He'd only secured the room for one night, and Peasenhall was a little over an hour away from Bury if the roads were clear. If he went home now, he could sleep in a familiar bed, and catch up with Violet first thing in the morning. Assuming nothing untoward came about, he could return to Peasenhall in the afternoon to continue his investigation.

Lawrence glanced at his watch, wondering if he could muster the energy to dress and drive in the dark. But although they lived in separate homes, he had spent little time apart from Violet and Daisy since their return from Swaffham. He'd only been absent from town a few times, mostly during investigations and, notably, once while visiting Isabel Smith in London. Lawrence's news about Daisy had delighted Isabel, who promised to see them in Bury as soon as her responsibilities allowed her to leave London. So far, they hadn't. Her vocation protecting children in the capital was never-ending. There was always something to do and someone to save. But as much as Lawrence admired Isabel, his heart was with Violet. She had visited him almost daily during the long weeks he lay in hospital, sometimes with Daisy, occasionally alone. Violet brought comfort when he thought he would never come to terms with Francis Farrow's behaviour. Lawrence took it personally, unable to comprehend how a man he had grown up with, his best man and boyhood friend, could have betrayed him so comprehensively. Francis had set fire to Lawrence's house, intending to murder his friend. But by a terrible intervention of fate, he had succeeded in killing Catherine and Lily instead. And if that hadn't been enough to send Lawrence into a spiralling depression, Francis had then claimed Catherine as his lover and Lily as his daughter.

Though Francis held Violet as his prisoner and she still suffered nightmares, she could, at least, detach herself emotionally. In coming to terms with what happened, Violet had analysed Francis Farrow's behaviour and concluded that he was far from well himself. Lawrence found her attitude puzzling, and when she consoled him about the lost friendship, Violet had insisted that Farrow's earlier fraternal feelings for Lawrence were genuine and only changed because of his later fixation with Catherine. She had said that Francis had rambled enthusiastically about strange esoteric matters while holding her in Swaffham, and Violet felt sure that he was under the influence of other people. When Lawrence questioned her further, Violet said his ideas were similar to Freemasonry. But then she changed her mind. In hindsight, some words Farrow used during their time in Swaffham were sinister and otherworldly, sounding like the ravings of a madman. Violet said that Francis spoke of friends she didn't know and that Lawrence had never mentioned. All of which, Violet had concluded, meant that something had gone wrong inside Francis Farrow's head. A frantic, angry persona had replaced his once amiable nature, previously so calm and unruffled. Perhaps the long-term effects of Catherine's death had warped his sense of right and wrong. Or worse, one of his so-called new friends had led him astray. In short, she said, Lawrence shouldn't dwell on the lost friendship but take comfort in knowing that the problem was with Francis Farrow's mind. He probably needed medical counsel, if not a spell in an asylum. Lawrence wished he could sympathise with Francis, as Violet did. He had tried and sometimes pretended to understand in front of her, but he didn't mean it, and his mediocre efforts didn't fool Violet one bit. Lawrence hated Francis, and if he ever met him again, blood would spill from one of them.

But while Lawrence disagreed with Violet, he appreciated her efforts to help. When she moved back to Bury and purchased a cottage, he thought it would only be a matter of time until they married. He was unprepared for Violet's resistance and didn't understand it, supposing it to be a reaction to his dalliance with Loveday, but that had been a long time ago, and she ought to be over it by now. Lawrence had tried his best to demonstrate his admiration for Violet, though he found it next to impossible to talk about love. He could think about the word and hear it inside his head, but the words wouldn't come when he opened his lips to speak. And though his love for Violet was true and ever-present, Lawrence wondered whether she realised the extent of it. Now that Violet had shown an interest in suffrage and women's rights, she was more independent than ever. Lawrence was navigating his way through complex emotional matters that he didn't understand and couldn't resolve. But one thing was sure. If he spent too much time away from Violet, they never would be.

His mind made up, Lawrence dressed and threw his few possessions in his bag. Straightening his bed, he crept downstairs, unlatched the door, and left, relieved that he had left his room fee on arrival. He dropped his bag into his seat, and cranked the car, then slid into the vehicle, feeling the cold leather through his greatcoat. Violet might tease him about his vehicle's colour, but it was reliable and started first time every time. He pressed his foot on the pedal and began the journey to Bury.

CHAPTER THIRTEEN

Back to Bury

Friday, January 23, 1903

Lawrence arrived back in Bury a little before midnight and fell exhausted into bed. He blinked his eyes blearily as a weak light filtered through his bedroom curtains the following day. A glance at the familiar surroundings of the room invigorated him, and, full of energy, he jumped out of bed, dressed, breakfasted, and left for the office, greeting the new day with an unexpected spring in his step. The morning was young, and Lawrence assumed the office would be empty, but a shape caught his eye as he walked towards the window. He cleared the frosted pane with his sleeve and peered inside to see Violet, her head bowed, writing in her daybook. She wrote with her right hand and clasped her forehead with her left, her elbow ground into the desk in complete concentration. His heart leapt as he watched her profile, no longer seeing her plain, almost manly features, tousled hair, or deep laughter lines. Instead, he felt a swell of admiration, a surge of passion for this clever, uncomplicated woman he had loved without knowing it for so many years. He opened the door, and the bell jangled as he went inside.

Violet looked up, clutching her chest. "Oh, what are you doing here?" she asked.

Lawrence's smile froze on his face. He wanted to tell her that he'd missed her and had come back early just to glimpse her face, but the words wouldn't leave his mouth. "I thought I'd be more useful in the office today," he replied.

"I don't see how."

"To consolidate a few thoughts, plan ahead – you know what I mean."

"I don't, but never mind. Would you like a cup of tea now you're here?"

"Yes. It's chilly in here. You haven't set the fire. You must be freezing."

"I barely noticed. My mind is otherwise occupied."

"It's not Daisy, is it? Where is she?"

"With Pat Lampard. I took her there for breakfast so Pat can walk her to school with her two."

"That's a shame. Perhaps I'll collect her."

"No need. I should be back in time."

Lawrence knelt by the fire, lit a spill, and ignited the crumpled newspaper, adding a few pieces of coal as it sparked into life. "Back from where?" he asked.

"The workhouse."

"Surely things aren't that bad?"

"It's not funny," said Violet sternly. "I've got to see someone about a servant girl. She's the main suspect in my case."

"How are you getting on?"

"I'll tell you over tea."

Violet left the room, and Lawrence followed her to the kitchen, watching as she filled the kettle and placed it on the hob. Violet reached for two cups, and a teapot, then leaned against the cupboard facing Lawrence. For one wild moment, he almost kissed her, but fear of rejection stopped him. Violet sighed and spoke. "I think you were right. I spoke to Gracie's grandmother, and she's told me a lot, but I can't see a way of solving the murders so long after they happened."

Lawrence resisted the temptation to agree. "If it's possible, you'll do it," he said. "But tell me about the maid."

"I know little about her. Only that she was bad-tempered, recalcitrant and nobody liked her."

"Why didn't they send her packing?"

"Mrs Pearson had a soft spot for the young woman, despite everything. But Mary hated her and said she was a troublemaker. She's left me with visions of a pixie-like character, causing mayhem about the home."

"Lawrence laughed. A maleficent maid," he said. "You make her sound almost supernatural."

"I know," said Violet as the kettle whistled." That's the problem. I can't get a proper perspective on her, which is why I'm going to see Mrs Briggs."

"How are you getting there?" asked Lawrence. Violet handed him a mug of tea, and he followed her back to the office.

"Bus, I suppose. It's not very far."

"I'll take you."

"Really? What about your case?"

"It can wait. Tomorrow is the last day of William Gardiner's trial. I thought long and hard about the Harsent case while driving back last night, and I've changed my mind. I'm going to Ipswich tomorrow to see how the trial goes. The Goddards think they'll acquit Gardiner, though it doesn't make any difference to me."

"Then why are you going?"

"Because I've met none of the main characters in this case. I'm making progress with others, and it feels like the right way to go about it, but I should at least glimpse Gardiner. And I would like to understand Bill Wright's character better. I'll go to Ipswich, then straight back to Peasenhall. And that leaves today free to help you."

Lawrence waited for Violet to speak, but she wasn't listening. Something outside had caught her attention, and she stared transfixed at the other side of the street.

"I say?" said Lawrence.

Violet stood and smiled, then advanced to the window and waved outside. She returned to her desk, still smiling.

"Who's that?" asked Lawrence, as a smart-looking man dressed in a frock overcoat acknowledged Violet's gesture and waved a silver-topped walking stick towards the window.

"Alexander Jameson."

"Never heard of him."

"You wouldn't. He only arrived last Thursday. Alexander is Libby Marshall's brother."

Lawrence stared blankly, still none the wiser.

"Honestly, Lawrence. You never listen to a word I say. Libby is on the suffrage committee."

"I'm surprised her husband allows it."

Violet raised an eyebrow. "It's just as well I know you don't mean that. Anyway, Alexander is visiting for the next few months. I'm going to tea with him next week."

"Don't you mean them?"

"No. I mean him. He's invited me out."

Lawrence was unprepared for the stab of jealousy accompanying her words. "He looks a little young."

"I beg your pardon?"

"I mean, he looks younger than us."

"He is. Five years, to be precise. What's that got to do with it?"

"Only that, well, is it wise?"

"We're friends," said Violet, coldly. "At least for now."

Lawrence sat quietly for a moment, analysing her words. Violet didn't take tea, supper, or any other meal with men as a rule. Not unless it was with Michael or himself. A shiver of doubt made the hairs on his arms stand on end. He didn't like change, especially not behavioural.

"So, are you coming to the workhouse or not?" asked Violet.

Lawrence nodded, pleased he had returned to Bury, and determined to keep a closer eye on things.

CHAPTER FOURTEEN

Depwade Workhouse

The road to Pulham Market stretched into the distance, long, straight, and lonely. The occasional cottage was dotted here and there, but otherwise, it was a grim walk for those who faced the prospect of voluntary admission to the workhouse. Lawrence shuddered at the thought of it. Lawrence had always understood the privilege of his position for all his faults, both as a young man largely free from financial worry and more recently as the recipient of his Uncle Max's legacy. The tidy sum he inherited should comfortably keep him for the rest of his life, though he didn't spend money to excess. Even in the intervening years, when Lawrence had struggled to cope with a detective business that regularly failed to pay the bills, he always knew his relatives could help. Even Francis, who loathed Lawrence and ruined his life, as it transpired, wouldn't have hesitated to advance funds had Lawrence asked. Lawrence never took his good fortune for granted, least of all, when he learned of Violet's less than salubrious upbringing. She was acutely aware of the value of money, constantly worrying about how to make ends meet, with her eye on the next case and never advancing credit. Violet always insisted that fees were paid in full, preferably in advance, but never late. And it was not that she was greedy, just fearful of the prospect of being solvent one day and penniless the next. As the sprawling red brick workhouse loomed into sight, Lawrence wished he had paid more heed to her concerns in the earlier days of their partnership, when he took a laissez-faire attitude to their finances.

They approached the front of the building, drove past a small chapel and towards the front, where Lawrence parked the car. Today was his first visit to a workhouse outside of London, and although the setting was more pleasant, albeit isolated, he didn't expect the inside to be any different. But with a lifelong interest in architecture, Lawrence couldn't help but admire the workhouse configuration. The short drive into the grounds had revealed the building's central hub with wings radiating from the centre. The chapel, porter's lodge and other external structures had given the whole thing an octagonal appearance. Lawrence appreciated the planning and design involved, though the absence of anyone in the grounds gave it a sinister feel, and he couldn't suppress a shudder.

Violet glared at him. She had been quiet for most of the journey, only discussing Daisy's progress at school. He had tried everything to draw her out, but she seemed detached, and he could tell that something was playing on her mind.

"Don't go inside wearing that expression," she snapped.

Lawrence raised an eyebrow." What do you mean?"

"Like it's beneath you. Most of the inmates have no choice in being here."

"I know. I understand."

"Then, you might try rearranging your features to match your thoughts." Violet was harsh, cruel even. It wasn't like her, and

Lawrence barely recognised the hard-faced woman beside him, so different from earlier in the day.

"I'm sorry," he stuttered, not knowing what else to say. Violet ignored him and strode ahead, then opened the double doors. Lawrence followed, somewhat surprised that they could walk into the building without being challenged. The doors opened into an entrance hall, and they saw, to their immediate right, a glassless window to a small office with a counter running across the front. A middle-aged man dressed in a grey serge uniform stood behind the wooden worktop and looked up as they approached.

"I'm here to see Beth Briggs," said Violet curtly. "I should be on your list. I telephoned ahead."

The man sighed and glanced at his journal. Then turned to his left and flipped open a long box of cards. He withdrew one, glanced at it, and then spoke. "B wing, infirm, women," he mechanically chanted as if he had lost all humanity.

Violet aped his tone. "Directions, to the ward, point," she said, staccato. The man adjusted his head, took a pencil, and jabbed it in the air towards an accommodation wing radiating off to the right of the office.

"Thank you," said Lawrence as Violet marched away.

Lawrence struggled to keep up with her as Violet traversed the corridor, ignoring the side rooms and stomping towards the end of the passage as if she knew the layout. Lawrence paused, and the penny dropped. This angry woman wasn't the Violet he knew and loved. Something was badly wrong, and her behaviour could mean only one thing. Lawrence quickened his pace and caught up with her just as she arrived at an office near the far end. He grabbed Violet's hand, and she snatched it back. He retook it, pulled her towards him and stared into her face.

"You've been here before, haven't you?"

Violet's eyes welled. "I don't want to talk about it," she said as a tear leaked down her face.

"You must," said Lawrence, guiding her to a bench outside the room. "You can't go in there looking like that."

Violet stared at the ground and sniffed. Lawrence released her hand and reached for a handkerchief as a female orderly passed by. "You alright?" she asked disinterestedly, seeming relieved when Lawrence nodded.

"Talk to me, Violet," he said.

Violet sniffed again, her head still down. "I've told you about my father, haven't I?"

"Yes. Didn't Harold Smith rescue you from poverty?"

"He did. I'd be nothing without him. When Father was alive, he sold enough paintings to make ends meet, but he left us destitute when he died. I rarely speak about that time in my life, but if I do, I tell people that Harold Smith saved us from the workhouse. It isn't quite true. Victor and I spent several weeks here when we were children while our newly widowed mother searched for work to support us."

"Who is Victor?"

"My brother."

"I didn't know you had a brother."

"I don't. We came to the workhouse together, but I left it alone. Victor died a few days after we got here, but they kept us on separate wings. I was in women, able-bodied, and Victor stayed in the male equivalent. After Victor's accident, they transferred him to men, infirm, but they didn't tell me. I didn't know he was hurt, and I didn't know he had died. I found out the same time as Mother did – when she came to collect me. So, there it is. Now you know."

"I'm so sorry," said Lawrence, stroking her hand. Violet flinched but didn't pull away. "How did he die?"

"They put him to work in the garden, and he put a fork through his foot. Three days later, he developed lockjaw and died soon after. Complications from the toxins. His heart was too weak to cope."

"Why didn't they tell you?"

"Because of the stupid disjointed system, they run. The divisiveness of running separate wards for sick and able-bodied is bad enough, but when you factor in gender, you have four different accommodation wings with poor information sharing. The men who treated him probably didn't know he had a sister and that she was here."

"It looks fairly well organised to me," said Lawrence, thinking of the alphabetised box of cards in the reception office.

"It might be now, but I was here thirty years ago. I can assure you that it didn't look or smell like this back then."

"You seem to know the ward."

"Not really. But the accommodation wards are all the same. There's an office through there," Violet said, pointing ahead. "And before you ask, I don't remember it. They told me when I telephoned."

"Are you well enough to continue?" asked Lawrence.

Violet dabbed the last of the tears from her eyes. "Perfectly, thank you. I'm sorry you had to see that."

"I'm not. I wish you'd told me sooner."

"Some things are best left in the past, Lawrence. Shall we go?"

"If, you're sure."

Violet didn't answer but walked towards the door, this time, less certainly. She was about to enter when a woman dressed in a nurse's uniform approached her.

"Can I help you?" she asked, starchily.

"I'm looking for Beth Briggs."

"What's he doing here?" She flashed a glare at Lawrence as if he was a convict on the run.

"He's accompanying me."

"This is a women's ward, and he is a man."

"And also, a psychiatrist," said Lawrence, quickly. "Alistair Blatworthy at your service."

"Do you have a card?"

Lawrence patted his jacket and made to retrieve one, then tutted. "I normally do, but I seem to have come out without them."

"Where do you practice?"

"The Bury and Suffolk general," he said.

"Oh. You must know Dr Allen."

"Only by sight," said Lawrence, crossing his fingers and hoping he wouldn't have to describe him.

"In that case, go back the way you came," said the nurse, "and take the third door on your right. "Mrs Briggs is in ward six."

They followed her instructions and retreated down the corridor, but the closer they came, the slower Violet walked.

"Bear up, old girl," said Lawrence, touching her elbow. Violet moved away but smiled at him as they reached the door. She swallowed, then pushed it open.

Ward six was pleasant and homely. Rows of beds lay on either side of the room, and light flooded in from expansive sash windows. Tented flowery privacy curtains hung above the beds, and a long table and chairs occupied the centre of the room. Two uniformed nurses in long white aprons flitted busily around tending to their charges, all of whom were elderly.

"I don't remember it being like this," said Violet.

"Times have changed," Lawrence replied. "We're more civilised now. The inmates can't help being ill, and they run the workhouses more compassionately. Take a seat, Violet. I'll find your lady."

Violet opened her mouth to refuse, but a wave of tiredness overcame her. She had known the visit would be an ordeal, but the worst had already happened. She'd unburdened herself to Lawrence, and now she was in the ward, her gloomy mood had lifted. Violet took a seat and leaned against the small, knitted blanket covering the wooden struts of the chair, watching as Lawrence approached a nurse. He announced himself as Dr Blatworthy, and the nurse smiled as she spoke. Violet felt a pang of envy at the young woman's figure. Violet's midriff had never quite recovered from carrying Daisy and her days of wearing fashionable clothing were long past.

Lawrence, on the other hand, was as slim as he had ever been. Too thin, she thought. Never able to tolerate so much as a stray hair on his clothing, Lawrence was always dapper and well dressed – and handsome. Age had sprinkled white flecks in his hair, but it was still there, and his high cheekbones and clean-shaven face rendered him easily one of the most attractive men in Bury. Violet wished she wasn't a slave to her pride, but she was what she was, and as much as Violet cared for Lawrence, she couldn't accept his marriage proposal. Perhaps he meant it, but she could never be sure. And how long would it be before another Loveday tempted him? What would that do to her? Her pride would never recover. Lawrence had broken her heart too many times to risk further damage, and Violet had resigned herself to spinsterhood, despite the sniffy remarks from her former friends in the Primrose League. The suffrage girls were different. They admired independence and respected woman who coped alone. She had recently confided in Libby, who dismissed the idea of Lawrence's proposal with disgust. "You don't need him, dear," she had said. "A man like that will never settle down." And Violet hadn't needed telling. Deep down, she knew it, but that didn't mean she enjoyed seeing another woman in thrall to him. And the nurse was not only smiling at Lawrence, but she had just touched his arm with a familiarity that shocked Violet. She wondered what young girls were coming to if they thought touching was an acceptable reaction when someone asked for directions. Violet was still scowling when Lawrence returned and pointed to a bed at the front of the room.

"Sheila says she's over here," he said.

"Sheila," Violet exclaimed, then bit her tongue when Lawrence cocked his head. "Never mind," she said. "I hope Mrs Briggs doesn't mind you being here."

"I'll keep up the psychiatrist story," said Lawrence. "It seems to be working rather well."

Violet approached the bed and announced herself to Mrs Briggs. The old woman wore a lace cap over a shock of white hair, and spindly arms protruded from a nightgown that engulfed her frail body. What they could see of her parchment-like skin was speckled with raised blue-green veins, and a yellow pallor clung to her face. She looked close to death, and Lawrence wondered whether she would be of any use to them. But her voice, when she spoke, was clear and strong.

"Are you Violet?" she asked.

Violet nodded.

"They said you were coming. I don't know you, but it doesn't matter. I don't see anyone now, so you can be a vagrant, for all I care."

"I'm not, though."

"What did you say? Speak up, girl."

"I'm not a vagrant," said Violet, a few decibels higher.

"What do you want to talk about? And who is he?"

"I'd like to talk about Eliza Sage, and he's a psychiatrist."

"Are you one too?"

"No. I'm an inheritance seeker."

"What's that?"

"Never mind," said Violet. She hated lying at the best of times, but Beth Briggs' deafness meant that she was spouting untruths in an ear-splitting voice for all the ward to hear. And Nurse Sheila seemed to be taking a particular interest, casting glances towards Lawrence, and smiling when he met her eyes.

"Do you remember Eliza Sage?" asked Violet quickly.

The old woman chuckled. "Eliza Sage. Well, that's a name I never thought I'd hear again."

"Did you know her well?"

"Of course, I did. Eliza was my cousin's girl."

"Oh, good. I hoped you could help."

"How did you know?"

"Know what?"

"That I'd be able to help with Eliza?"

The old woman's eyes flicked across Violet's face. She might be frail, and a few steps from death, but her mind was alert and curious.

"Oh, I see. Mary Leverett gave me your name."

"Well, well. Is Mary still alive? And her husband?"

"Both alive as of yesterday."

Beth's face fell. "Pity. I'd like to have outlived them. It seems unlikely now."

"I thought you were friends."

"Acquaintances. She's alright for an Everett."

"Didn't you get on with the family?"

"Yes, until they started making free and loose with Eliza's good name."

Violet paused, trying to phrase her question tactfully. "I hear that Eliza didn't get on with her mistress."

"She wouldn't. Eliza was a free spirit," said Beth. She stared into the distance as if trying to recall her face. "Yes. Young Eliza was born to be a servant, but she wasn't made that way. She didn't like taking orders and couldn't stand being told what to do, especially by someone with Mary Pearson's standards. You know the kind, impossible to satisfy because nobody can do it as well as they can. And if that's how she felt, she should have kept the house herself instead of always finding fault with Eliza."

"I heard she had a soft spot for the girl."

"Well, if she did, I never witnessed it."

"Was Eliza quarrelsome?" asked Lawrence, with none of Violet's diplomacy. He was getting hungry and hoped to get back to Bury by lunchtime. It was all very well pandering to the old lady, but too much beating about the bush would get them nowhere.

"Some might see it that way."

"Did they argue?"

"Sometimes. The lad James said they'd fallen out about some weeding the week before she died. He stood there in court and said that Eliza had threatened to stive her old eyes."

Lawrence looked blankly.

"Suffocate her, make her lights go out, you know what I mean."

"That sounds very much like a threat."

"I'm sure it was. Eliza didn't mince her words." The old woman chuckled to herself.

"Then I can see why she was the primary suspect," said Violet, dropping all pretence at tact.

"That's because you didn't know her. She was all talk," said Beth Briggs. "Eliza was like a farm cat, always spitting and snarling, and when she'd got it out of her system, she'd settle down and purr. She wasn't sneaky or underhand. If Eliza had killed Mary Pearson, she'd have stabbed her in the face with a knife."

"I see what you mean," said Lawrence. "Do you think that the method used to commit the murder rules Eliza out?"

"Yes," said Beth, nodding her head. She raised a fragile hand to her face and wiped a crumb from the side of her mouth. "That's exactly it. On her day, Eliza could have cheerfully killed the woman. But not that way."

"Well, if she didn't, then who did?"

"The lad James. He didn't like his mistress either, and he hated Eliza. You should have seen him at the inquest tying himself in knots trying to find ways to do her down. And then there's John Everett. He fell out with his mother, and she drank from the poisoned kettle and died too."

"But could he reasonably have predicted that his mother would go to Mary Pearson's that day?" asked Violet.

"Perhaps not. But they were sisters and spent a lot of time together, so it was possible."

"Were you there that day?" asked Lawrence.

"No. But I went to the inquest."

"Good. Violet knows all about this case, but I don't. What can you tell me about it?"

"I thought you were a doctor. Why should you care?"

"Violet's my friend. I'm trying to help her."

The old woman stared straight into his eyes." That's a load of old squit. Don't take me for a fool. I don't care who you are, and I'm glad of the company, but talk straight bor', or you can go."

Lawrence leaned back and smiled at the Norfolk slang.

"We're both private investigators," he said. "I won't tell you who we're working for, but it's in connection with the Tibenham poisonings, as I'm sure you've realised."

"That's better," said the woman smugly, her beady eyes taking in every moment of Violet's discomfort. "It's a rum 'un, and that's for sure, but if you want to waste your lives on an old, unsolved murder, that's your lookout."

"Will you tell me all about it?"

"Gladly," said Beth Briggs. "Fetch me a glass of water, first," she said, nodding towards Violet.

\#

"You think you like Violet more than she likes you," said Beth Briggs matter-of-factly as Violet reluctantly walked to Nurse Sheila to ask for a drink.

"I beg your pardon?" asked Lawrence.

"Violet. You like her a lot. Why don't you marry her?"

"How is that any of your business?" asked Lawrence. "And more to the point, how can you tell?"

"Because that young nurse has been making eyes at you, but you haven't noticed because all you can see is Violet. Well," she continued, looking at Lawrence through rheumy eyes, "Violet doesn't like it."

"Doesn't like what?"

"The nurse's interest in you. Keep up, young man."

"I don't know what you're driving at, and I don't feel very comfortable having this conversation with a stranger."

"Life's too short to worry about your feelings," said Beth Briggs. "But listen and listen good. If she's jealous, then you've still got a chance."

"Are you a witch?" asked Lawrence.

The old woman cackled. "No. But I know people. I'm in my eighties, and I've seen it all. Take my advice, young man. Wait it out and let her come to you."

"What if she doesn't?"

"Who doesn't what?" asked Violet, placing a glass of water by Beth's bed.

"Miss Briggs doesn't think Eliza is guilty," Lawrence replied glibly.

"I know," said Violet. "How far have you got?"

"I was telling Mr Harpham that Mary Pearson died first and Elizabeth Everett later that day. The poison was in the kettle, and there's no doubt about it. So please don't imagine that it got into their bodies by any other means. I won't dwell on what happened that day because I wasn't there. But I'll tell you as much as I can remember of the inquest. And if you have any questions, then ask me. I don't suppose we'll meet again. I'm sure you can see that I'm not long for this world."

"Thank you," said Lawrence, uncharacteristically patting the old lady on the hand. Violet watched with wary indulgence. The two seemed to share a bond to which she was not privy. Lawrence rarely displayed such open compassion, and although Violet was pleased to see it, she couldn't help wondering if it was an act for her benefit. "Do go on," she said.

"Well, let's start with Eliza. She gave a good account of herself to the coroner and came out all guns blazing. People had been talking about her and spreading rumours that she'd poisoned Mary Pearson. Eliza was particularly unhappy with Joseph Pearson's brother."

"Mary's husband?"

"Yes. John Pearson and his wife visited his brother's home not long after Mary died. They took it upon themselves to ask Eliza to empty the kettle in front of them in case there was a toad in the bottom. Riled her greatly, it did. Then they went next door and borrowed some tea as they wouldn't risk drinking anything that had been in the house."

"Why were they looking for a toad?"

"I don't know," said Beth." They were a backwards-looking lot, heads full of straw and a bit daft. Perhaps they suspected witchcraft or that the girl was slovenly. Who can say, but it fair upset Eliza."

"I can imagine," said Lawrence. "She was a sparky little thing to raise objections in front of the inquest."

Beth smiled. "She was," she said proudly. "Anyway, the lad James came to the stand and spouted a load of nonsense. He said that Eliza hadn't taken breakfast that day."

"So, she didn't drink from the kettle?"

"No. And that could have gone against Eliza, but she wasn't the only one. Mr Pearson didn't either. What's sauce for the goose is sauce for the gander."

Lawrence nodded. "A fair point," he said. "Now, tell me what you know about the contents of the kettle?"

Beth Briggs closed her eyes and furrowed her forehead in concentration. "There were no fancy taps back then," she said. "They took their water from a pit by the side of the road. Not a stagnant puddle, you know. More like a running stream. Eliza fetched the water in a pail and used it to fill the kettle which she placed in the copper hole."

"Was it the day they fell ill?"

"Young man. These poisonings happened over forty years ago. I simply can't remember. It might have been any time. I really can't say."

"Sorry. I'm sure someone will have recorded the date somewhere."

"It was in all the papers. Read one of them instead of bothering me."

Violet sighed and shook her head. "The newspapers won't be any substitute for your memories," she said. "Much better to hear your thoughts and feelings than read cold, emotionless facts."

"Oh, right," said Beth. "Anyway, the coroner asked Eliza how the poison got in the kettle. She said she didn't know, and he asked her if there had been any poisonous material in the house. Well, shortly before her death Mary Pearson had shown the girl some mouse holes in a closet. She mixed up arsenic in a bowl and put it in the holes. But the kettle didn't come into contact with the poison."

"So, the arsenic belonged to Mrs Pearson?"

116

"More than likely," said Beth. "Anyway, the constables took away everything that looked suspicious, and they found arsenic not only in the kettle but also in a bowl and a stone bottle. The stuff in the bowl was probably the remains of the mouse poison. And clearly, Mary hadn't been too careful about disposing of it, not to mention the ready availability of poison around the house for anyone to lay their hands on. And it made the family very cautious."

"Which is no doubt why John Pearson wouldn't drink anything in the house."

"Quite. I wouldn't have either under those circumstances. Nor spared the feelings of those who might be offended at a refusal of their hospitality. It wasn't like Mary to leave muddles. She liked a tidy home."

"Can you remember anything else about the inquest?"

"Oh, my memory comes and goes in waves. Wait a moment." Beth reached for the water and took a tiny sip which dripped down her chin."

"Let me help," said Violet, replacing the glass. She gently lifted Beth into a better position before returning it to her hand. Beth took another sip.

"I remember Hannah Everett finding the poison."

"The mouse poison in the bowl?"

"No, the actual bottle itself. Hannah was Elizabeth Everett's niece. She lived in Norwich, I think. Anyway, Hannah came down for Elizabeth's funeral. Well, she would have anyway, truth be told, as she visited every week. But the day after the funeral, Joseph Pearson invited her to his home. Hannah opened the bureau to check her aunt's possessions and came across a bottle of poison."

"How did she know it was poison?"

"The bottle contained a white powder with a label on it."

Lawrence raised an eyebrow.

"Arsenic," said Beth, preempting his question.

"Pretty conclusive then."

"Most definitely. Now, you must understand that everyone in the house was under suspicion, and they were all very anxious, paranoid, even. Well, Mrs Reeve didn't help matters."

"Mrs Reeve?"

"A friend of the family – a relative too, I think. Well, she stuck her beak in and told Eliza that if anyone found anything that looked like poison, they should get rid of it straight away so that nobody else came to any harm. A sensible enough idea if circumstances were different, but not so clever with an investigation going on. She more or less told the girl to dispose of the evidence."

"It might have saved several lives."

"Only if you think Eliza did it," said Beth Briggs, looking down her nose. "As you know, I do not."

"So, did they dispose of the poison?"

"They did. Or rather, Hannah did, by burning the powder in the fire, but she knew the bottle wouldn't ignite so she asked Eliza to bury it outside."

"Did Eliza do as she was asked?"

"That's what the constable asked Hannah, and she said she assumed Eliza had buried it but hadn't seen her do it. But the truth will always come out in the end, and in this case, it was from worry. Eliza knew it wouldn't do her any good to tell, but she fretted about burying the bottle, and in the end, it got too much. Eliza told the lad that it would be Hannah Everett's fault if she went to prison because she'd asked her to bury the bottle, and neither of them had said a word about it."

"How did the authorities find out?"

"The lad talked to the housekeeper, and before long, it was out in the open. Someone told Constable Bloomfield, who came to the house and asked for the bottle. Hannah was still there and showed him where it was, so he took it away and tested it. And that was that."

"Who do you think did it, if not Eliza?"

"I don't know. The boy was too young, in my opinion. Elizabeth Everett had fallen out with two of her sons. It could have been one of them, but it's unlikely."

"So, you don't know."

"No. But if you knew Eliza, you would understand why I don't think she did it."

"Could it have been one of the family? One of the Everetts?" asked Violet.

"Of course."

"Oh, dear."

"Would that be so bad?" asked Beth without missing a beat.

Violet hesitated. Only for a second, but it was enough to confirm Beth's suspicions.

"So, it would matter," she said triumphantly. "What's this all about then? I'm dying to know."

Lawrence smiled. "You should have been a detective," he said, turning to Violet. "Can I tell her?" he asked.

Violet flashed an exasperated glare, but she was in an impossible position to decline and nodded her consent.

"I won't give you names," said Lawrence, with a twinkle in his eye. "And I can't remember them anyway, but a couple of lovebirds want to marry, and the male party would prefer to know the female party won't poison him next time they argue."

"I see," said Beth. "Not much of a gentleman, is he? It really shouldn't matter if he loves the young lady."

"In an ideal world," said Violet. "But if Eliza were the culprit, it would help enormously."

"Then tell them Eliza killed the women. She's dead now and can't complain."

"I wouldn't dream of lying to them," protested Violet.

"Then try harder," Beth responded curtly. "Tell them what they want to hear. But if you want my opinion, your girl should run a mile."

"Her intended is only being cautious."

"Pah. The man's a fool. The urge to murder doesn't pass through families. And most of the time, it's a spur of the moment thing. I take it there's no parental objection to this marriage?"

"There won't be if I can prove her family aren't murderers," said Violet.

"It's a funny old world," said Beth. "You've seen Mary Leverett, and she, of all people, knows what it's like to fight family for love. They didn't want her to marry George, you know."

"Why not?"

"They didn't think he was good enough."

"But she married him anyway?"

"Yes, and they came around in the end. But Mary didn't speak to her family for a while. As a matter of interest, who did she blame for the murders?"

"She wouldn't be drawn on it," said Violet. "I tried, and she's unwell, so I didn't want to push her too hard."

Beth cocked her head and stared at Violet. "Is she as ill as I am?"

"It's hard to say."

"I would love to outlive her."

"That's the second time you've said that." Lawrence's careless glance at his timepiece did not escape Beth.

"Feel free to leave if I'm keeping you," she said.

"Sorry. You're not. But why do you want to outlive Mary?"

"Oh, it's just an old lady's fancy. One likes to think one would be the last. Now, Violet," she said, turning away from Lawrence. "A word of advice."

Lawrence's head jerked up in horror, and he hoped she wasn't about to launch into relationship advice in front of him. But it was not her intention.

"I think you should go back and see Mary. You employed subterfuge to see me, and I'm quite sure you did the same to her."

Violet lowered her gaze, unable to meet Beth Briggs' eyes.

"I thought so. Return to Bunwell and do it soon. Tell Mary the truth. You may get to know something important that way. Mary will sympathise more than you expect. The younger generation always thinks their problems are new, but we've seen it all before. Ask for her help. Will you do that for me?"

Violet nodded. She wasn't sure what sort of reception she would get from Mary Leverett, but under Beth's commanding glance, she wasn't about to argue.

"Good. Off you go now, my dears. We won't meet again, but you've been very entertaining."

Nurse Sheila stared disappointedly as Lawrence and Violet left the ward. They walked to the motor car in silence, feeling an inexplicable sadness for the woman they had just left.

"What now?" asked Violet.

"Home. And a big hug for Daisy before I go back to Peasenhall."

CHAPTER FIFTEEN

Ipswich Shire Hall

Saturday, January 24, 1903

Lawrence set off from Bury St Edmunds intending to return to Peasenhall, but having pondered the case overnight, he abruptly turned the Wolseley around after five minutes driving and set off for Ipswich instead. He was still content to interview those not directly involved in the trials, but the more he heard about William Gardiner, the less he understood him. Today could be his last chance to meet the man in person and form an idea of his character.

An hour later, Lawrence pulled up outside Ipswich Shire Hall in St Helen's Street and tidily parked the automobile only a few yards away from the main door. It was just as well. The barristers were already inside, and if he wanted to assess William Gardiner, there was no time to lose. Lawrence strode purposefully through the door and towards the courtroom, where a burly looking uniformed man carrying a journal challenged him immediately. The man flipped the cover open to reveal a typewritten page.

"Name?" he asked.

Lawrence employed his well-honed ability to read upside down, quickly searching for one of only a few unticked entries. "Sydney Diamond," he said.

The man grunted and placed a pencilled tick near a name at the bottom of the page. "You'll be with the other reporters," he said. "Go quietly. You're lucky they're running late."

Lawrence apologised and slunk silently into the courtroom, sitting on the first empty seat. Apart from a low buzz of whispered voices, the room was largely silent in anticipation of the jury's arrival. Lawrence fidgeted as he glanced around the room, looking for William Gardiner. But if he was there, it wasn't obvious.

"Excuse me." The man sitting beside him stood and slid past Lawrence before making his way towards the door leaving a rolled-up newspaper on the chair. Lawrence seized the opportunity and quickly scanned the front page. Mr Wild, William Gardiner's barrister, had put up a robust defence of his client during yesterday's hearing, but Sir Henry Fielding Dickens was doing his level best for the prosecution. The verdict was by no means certain, and today's evidence would be crucial. Lawrence was still reading when the man returned.

"Sorry," he said, handing over the newspaper.

"I don't mind," said the man. "Fascinating, isn't it? And a celebrity prosecutor, to boot."

"Oh, he's not, is he?"

The man nodded. "Yes. Charles Dickens' son. This trial is more plausible than any of his father's books."

"I'm rather partial to them," said Lawrence.

The man raised a weak smile and opened his paper. Lawrence gazed around the room again. He'd missed them the first time, but now he could see the Goddard brothers sitting side by side across the court. He raised his hand, and Samuel Goddard nodded in recognition. Another fifteen minutes dragged by, and just as Lawrence was on the verge of leaving, the judge entered and announced himself. The room buzzed into life, and the court orderly quietened the spectators with a bang of the gavel before announcing William Gardiner's wife's arrival. Lawrence watched as a female orderly guided Mrs Gardiner to the box. When she got there, she clutched the sides uncertainly, swaying from side to side as if close to collapse.

"Would the witness like a chair?"

The judge gazed at the pale and shaking woman standing before him, his face creased in concern.

Georgiana Gardiner nodded, too distraught to speak, and a uniformed man carried a chair into the box, steadying her as she sat. The judge waited for a moment, then gestured to the defence barrister to begin his questions.

Ernest Wild, a plain-faced, confident-sounding man, addressed her with compassion. "I'd like you to tell me about the night of the murder. Do you think you can do that?"

Her lip trembled, and her hands visibly shook. Lawrence watched as a bearded man standing in the dock leaned towards her, clutching his hands across his face. Lawrence couldn't see the man's mouth through his bushy black beard but felt his despair and sensed that tears were not far away. The man must be William Gardiner, thought Lawrence, wondering why he hadn't seen him enter the courtroom. The orderly beside Gardiner placed a hand on his shoulder and gently pushed him back to a seated position. He obliged but looked longingly towards his long-suffering wife. Lawrence removed his notebook from his pocket and scribbled a note: *Gardiner undoubtedly loves his wife.*

Mrs Gardiner coughed, then began to speak. "The weather was stormy the night Rose died," she said. "Not just a little, but

124

thunderclaps and lightning, as if the world were about to end. My neighbour, Mrs Dickinson, had recently been widowed, and I promised I'd sit with her if the weather worsened. Well, it did, so I went over, and William joined us after a short time. We left about half past one and were in bed for two o'clock."

"How do you know?"

"I'm sorry?"

"How do you know what the time was?"

"Oh, I see." Mrs Gardiner played with a strand of hair as she remembered. "The clock chimed – that's how I know. We were just getting into bed when the clock struck two."

"And you had a disturbed night?"

"I did. My son, Bertie, cried out not long after I went to bed, so I got up and tended to him. But the storm kept me awake and made me feel so ill that I got up again around three for a little medicinal brandy. I barely slept a wink that night and heard every chime of the clock. Then, the twins woke up at five, and I brought them back to bed with me. We finally got up at eight o'clock."

"And did your husband leave the bed at any time?"

"Not once. William was with me all night, and he slept through the storm."

"What were your feelings regarding the rumours about your husband's conduct at the doctor's chapel?"

"I didn't believe a word of it."

"You forgave him?"

"There was nothing to forgive. Rose was a family friend. She visited often. There was no impropriety between her and my husband."

"Now, you are no doubt aware that they found a medicine bottle bearing your name at the scene of the murder?"

"Yes."

"How did it come to be there?"

"As I've said, Rose was a friend. I gave her some camphorated oil in an old medicine bottle."

"Did she take it?"

"Yes. I gave it to her."
"Are you quite sure?"
"I'm quite sure."
"What sort of girl was Rose Harsent?"
Mrs Gardiner sat quietly with her hands in her lap as she considered the question. "Rose was a most respectable girl," she said.
"Yet she was six months pregnant when she died."
Lawrence waited for Mrs Gardiner to speak, but she remained silent and looked at her feet.
"Did you ever see Miss Harsent with a man?"
"I don't recall."
"I mean, in an improper manner?"
"No."
"Never?"
"Well, I heard it said that Rose and Fred Davies were on friendly terms, but whether that went any further, I couldn't say."
"But she still came to your house?"
"Often."
"And she never went with any other young man?"
"Only Bob Kerridge. Rose was engaged to be married to him but broke it off."
"Now, to PC Nunn's visits to your home."
Georgiana Gardiner's face crumpled. It was a question too far, and her hands visibly trembled again. Lawrence sat forward in his seat, straining to see as Ernest Wild whipped a bottle of smelling salts from his pocket and held them under the shaken woman's nose.
Wild gently guided her through his questions, and after an hour, the court rose for lunch. Mrs Gardiner stood shakily before clutching the back of the chair. An orderly rushed forward, but it was too late, and she slumped to the floor. Mr Wild produced his smelling salts again, but when Mrs Gardiner resumed consciousness, she let out a guttural moan of despair before launching into full-blown hysterics. Lawrence could still hear her

cries as she followed the warden into the bowels of the court. William Gardiner sat with his head in his hands, and when he finally raised his head, Lawrence saw the tracks of recently shed tears running down his cheeks. He left the court feeling saddened at the raw display of emotion and walked towards a pie shop, where he purchased a pasty and took it to a nearby bench.

Lawrence sat there alone, the echo of Mrs Gardiner's cries lasting longer in his head than the reality of the courtroom. They disturbed him in a way he didn't understand, reminding him of the dark days after Catherine's death – Catherine, who may have been a disloyal, faithless wife, not that he would ever know the truth with Francis long gone. But the Gardiners' relationship was anything but. If ever Lawrence had seen a genuine display of mutual love and affection, this was it. Gardiner, sitting thin and dark-eyed in the docks, pain etched across his features at the situation with which his beloved wife was now dealing. And Mrs Gardiner, distraught at the prospect that her husband might face the rest of his life in prison, or worse – his ultimate fate only a few hours away. No wonder Lawrence felt their discomfort across the courtroom. And finally, he appreciated the Goddard brothers concern. Gardiner was in the dock because others assumed he was the father of Rose Harsent's child. Not because of any physical evidence, but because of rumour, speculation, and Bill Wright's allegations. Even if they were true, and Gardiner had dallied with the young maid, it didn't make him a murderer. Lawrence stood and paid a penny for a newspaper at a nearby booth, then finished his pasty while reading another account of yesterday's trial. This newspaper focused on the sequence of events on the night of Rose's murder, publishing the note found in Rose's room in full. It was the first time Lawrence had read it, and he scrutinised every word.

D R

I will try to see you tonight at midnight at your place. If you put a light in your window at 10 o'clock for about ten minutes, then you can take it out again. Don't have a light in your room at midnight as I will come around the back.

Lawrence frowned. Rose doubtless kept an assignation with a man, but was it remotely plausible that William Gardiner would have risked meeting her so close to his cottage? Such a foolhardy risk, considering the rumours had never gone away, and they would suspect him no matter what. No, it made little sense. If Gardiner and Rose were as familiar as reputed, William would have known of her pregnancy well before that night and could have taken a more considered approach to her disposal. Rose's killer wasn't Gardiner; of that, he was increasingly confident. Lawrence rolled the newspaper, tucked it under his arm and headed towards his vehicle. He had seen enough, and the verdict would go one way or the other whether he was in Ipswich or not. Better to spend his time in Peasenhall. If he put his foot down, he could get there by mid-afternoon, a good few hours before word of the verdict would reach the villagers. Lawrence opened the door, lay a blanket over his lap, and commenced his journey.

CHAPTER SIXTEEN

Progress in Peasenhall

As an opportunistic private detective, Lawrence was used to treading a thin line when it came to morals. Even so, the audacity of his next decision brought unfamiliar pangs of conscience as he planned his afternoon's work. Lawrence intended to access Rose Harsent's room in Providence House, if possible. He had to gain entry within the next few hours and certainly before tomorrow morning when the owners, Mr and Mrs Crisp, would likely return from Ipswich. It was a gamble, of course. The house might not be empty, or worse still, occupied by another maid who was unlikely to admit Lawrence without her mistress's permission. But remembering his conversations with Alf Grice and George Whiting, Lawrence decided to throw himself on the mercy of James Crisp, brother of the owner, who lived on the other side of

Providence House. Ideally, Lawrence would access Rose's room after dark, which left a few hours to fill. Hours he could use finding out more about Fred Davis, with whom Rose may or may not have had a dalliance. The plan was sound in principle, but whether luck went his way was a different matter. Still, better to have an objective in mind than flounder.

Lawrence pulled up outside Providence House, an attractive three-storey home with steep, red-tiled gables. The building was divided into three, with the middle part facing the front of the road and the two end homes side on. Lawrence looked up, immediately noticing an attic window overlooking The Street. If Rose had placed a candle in the window at night, it would be easily visible directly below, but how much farther down could someone reasonably see it? No doubt the authorities had considered this point in the most minute detail, but that was no excuse for failing to check it himself.

Lawrence was still sitting in his car pondering the matter when the occupant of the middle cottage opened the door and shook a colourful tablecloth onto the small frontage surrounded by a bowed fence. When satisfied that she'd disposed of all the crumbs, the woman folded it into four, glaring at Lawrence as she tucked it under her arm.

"Are you lost?" she asked.

"No. Might I ask your name?"

"Why?" Her tone was defensive, but she didn't turn away.

Lawrence searched his repertoire of excuses and opted for the truth. "I'm investigating Rose Harsent's death," he said.

The woman stared incredulously. "You're a bit late for that."

"Not really," said Lawrence, launching into the explanation he'd used on Harry Redgrift. The woman still wore a puzzled frown.

"I spoke to Alf Grice yesterday, and he said I should speak to Frederick."

"Oh. You're the man with the deep pockets?"

Lawrence took the hint and handed over the smallest denomination coin he could find.

"That's not what I meant," the woman snapped, handing it back to him.

"I'm sorry," said Lawrence. "I didn't mean to offend you. Do you know Frederick Davis?"

"I should do. I birthed him."

"Ah. Then are you prepared to speak to me? I would really like the benefit of your opinion, and I'll do whatever it takes."

"Asking nicely is good enough for me," she said, pushing her front door open and gesturing for Lawrence to go inside.

"Much appreciated," he said gratefully.

"Sit in the parlour," said the woman. "The fire's lit, and it's warm."

Lawrence removed his coat and settled into a winged chair before placing the coat across his lap.

"The name's Caroline," said the woman. "Caroline Davis – pleased to make your acquaintance."

She was oddly formal, thought Lawrence as he surveyed the room, trying to work out her social status. Not that it always mattered, but sometimes knowing whether a family faced hardship was a helpful thing.

"Ask what you will," she said, leaning forward as she took the chair opposite.

"What did you think of Rose?" he asked.

"Now, there's a question," said Caroline. "And not an easy one to answer."

"Why?"

"Because I liked Rose at first when I thought she was stepping out with my boy. But she gave him the run around good and proper, the little minx. And she's ruined his good name, as you very well know."

"I've read the newspapers," said Lawrence, "but I don't necessarily believe them."

Caroline Davis nodded. "Good for you," she said.

"Why did he write out the obscene verses for her? And why, for that matter, did he give her a leaflet about contraception?"

Lawrence dispensed with tact, rightly assuming that they were past that point.

"Isn't it obvious?"

"Because he liked her?"

"It was more than that. Fred wanted to walk out with her, but she didn't like him that way."

"Yet he carried on hoping?"

"Any man would if he was encouraged to."

"So Rose Harsent wasn't above using a man for her own ends?"

"Quite," said Caroline Davis, "though it's stretching a point to call Fred a man. He's only twenty, a few years younger than Rose was, and considerably less mature. My son is a silly boy when he gets a few ales inside him, but he's neither a killer nor a pervert."

"Thank you for being so frank," said Lawrence. "I gathered as much from Alf Grice."

"He's loyal, that one," said Caroline, pursing her lips. "Though I'm not sure about the company he keeps."

"Who do you mean?"

"Harry Smith and George Whiting. Harry is only a teenager and has the sense of a child. Fred said Harry gave him the leaflet that he passed on to Rose. And as for Whiting, why does a man his age spend so much time with the young 'uns? That's what they should ask in court, not waste their time defaming Fred's good name."

"I see," said Lawrence, making a mental note to revisit Whiting tomorrow. The men probably drank together in the public house where age was no boundary, but it was worth asking the question. "Now, what do you think of William Gardiner?"

Caroline visibly shuddered. "I don't like him," she said. "He's a hypocrite. Always preaching to others, without following his own teachings."

"How do you know?"

"I don't," she said. "It's just a feeling. I try not to listen to gossip. God knows, my Fred would be guilty as sin if I believed every word that went around this village, but there's something sinister about Gardiner. Perhaps it's his beard."

"You don't like it?"

"I prefer to see someone's lips move when they talk to me. Anyway, it's Gardiner's wife I feel sorry for."

"Why?"

"She's a trusting little thing, always friendly with Rose despite the scandal."

"Isn't that a good quality?"

"Trust? I suppose so if it's not misplaced."

"Do you have a concrete reason for believing Gardiner's guilty?"

"No, and I don't pretend to. But I trust my intuition. I was the only one who believed Ellen Blowers at first."

"Ah, yes. The Creeper. How do you know she's not making it up?"

"He terrified poor Ellen," said Caroline. "Just because she's loose-tongued doesn't mean she's without feelings. I know fear when I see it."

"Have you come across this man?"

"If it is a man," said Caroline. "But no, I haven't, although Fred thinks someone has been following him."

"Are you implying a woman?"

"Of course not," said Caroline, rolling her eyes.

"Then a monster, a devil?"

"It sounds ridiculous when you say it like that, but people see Black Shuck all the time."

"I don't," said Lawrence, dismissing the idea of the East Anglian ghost dog out of hand. Caroline Davis was a disappointment. She had seemed so rational earlier in the conversation, but if she didn't think the Creeper was a man or a woman, she must have considered something supernatural.

"Could the Creeper have murdered Rose?"

"Obviously, if he'd been around when she died. But he's only appeared recently."

"Have the police investigated?"

"They think it's village superstition," said Caroline, shaking her head. "Even Eli Nunn, who ought to know better."

"The village constable?"

"Yes. He's known Ellen long enough to take her seriously. If it wasn't for Bill Wright and his tall tales, they might look into it."

"Did the Crisps replace Rose with another domestic?"

"Of course."

"Ah." Lawrence grimaced as he felt his plan slipping away.

"She's quite a nice girl, the new maid. But she won't move into the attic room after what happened. Lucy comes in daily from her father's house."

"Is anyone at Providence House now?"

"Not that I know of. Deacon Crisp and his wife are in court, and they've given the girl a few days off while they're away. Why? You're not going in there, are you?"

"Of course not," said Lawrence, knowing that was precisely what he intended to do if James Crisp wouldn't grant access. But he didn't need Caroline Davis's watchful eyes, and the lie was necessary.

"Well, thank you for your help," said Lawrence. "I appreciate your time."

"You're welcome. It breaks up the day," she said, rising from her chair. Caroline Davis walked to the door and watched Lawrence leave. He considered getting something to eat but decided instead to call on James Crisp without delay. As he walked next door, he could still see Caroline gazing at him through her window, eyes distant and no doubt waiting for the return of her much-maligned son.

#

Lawrence knocked on the door of Church House, which opened to reveal the rotund form of an elderly woman and not the man he was hoping to see. He doffed his hat and asked if the man of the house was at home. The woman said nothing but retreated and called out for her husband, who emerged, hunched over a walking stick some moments later.

"Sorry to disturb you," said Lawrence, disappointment washing over him at the sight of the man's frail frame. Lawrence had intended to be pushy, demanding even. Whatever it took to secure access to Providence House. He needn't have worried. Beneath the skeletal form of James Crisp lived an ebullient, helpful man who greeted his visitor with unexpected courtesy.

"Hello," said Crisp. "Do I know you?"

"No, I don't think so."

"You look familiar, doesn't he, Hannah. He reminds me of that chap – you know the one." Crisp clicked his fingers as he searched his memory. "Oh, dear. It's gone. Never mind. How can I help?"

Lawrence offered his card and succinctly explained his mission while James nodded. "A detective," he said. "Well, well. Come through and take the first right. I can't hang around on the doorstep. The old legs aren't what they used to be."

Lawrence followed him into a workroom with a table, chairs, and a bench containing leather and lasts. He took a seat and tucked his new shoes out of sight. It did not go unnoticed.

"I'm a retired shoemaker," said James Crisp. "But I like to keep my hand in. And Hannah keeps a tidy parlour, so this room is mine and set out as I choose. Would you like a glass of water?"

Lawrence resisted the urge to ask for something stronger and accepted it gratefully. He took a sip, but an embarrassing gurgle emerged from his stomach."

"How rude of me," said James. "I'll only be a moment," he limped to the door, leaning heavily on his stick, and shouted down the hallway in a robust voice. By the time he returned to the table and sat down, a woman of middling years, bearing a tray of bread and cheese, had opened the door.

"Help yourself," said James, gesturing to a loaf of brown bread.

"That's extremely kind," said Lawrence, slicing two pieces and handing one back to the old man. They buttered their bread in silence, then Lawrence hacked off a couple of triangles of cheese and passed one over.

"You don't even know who I am," said Lawrence through a mouthful of bread.

"Godly men extend their hospitality to strangers," said Crisp. "Especially those taken in by their next-door neighbours."

"Ah," said Lawrence. "Did you see me coming out of Mrs Davis's house?"

"No. I saw you parking your car and going in. And I said to Hannah, he'll be coming to see us next."

"That was percipient."

"Not to mention nosy. Now, how can I help?"

Lawrence faltered before he spoke. Having sought the benefit of Dr Lay's knowledge earlier in the week, he already knew that James Crisp had seen Rose's body. The sight of a murdered young girl would be traumatic for anyone, but more so for a man of advancing years. "Rose Harsent," he said, wondering how to finish the sentence.

Crisp sighed. "I see," he said.

"But only if it won't distress you."

"I've had eight months to get used to it. What do you want to know?"

"Nothing relating to the body," said Lawrence. "I've already spoken to Dr Lay and he was very obliging. But I would like to hear your first impressions and anything as you can tell me about Rose."

"I didn't really know her," said James Crisp. "She was my brother's housemaid, and we were on nodding terms only. I heard the rumours, of course. But in accordance with my faith, I ignored them, and so did my brother. Judge not, lest you be judged."

"Quite," said Lawrence, nodding sagely.

"The first I knew of it," said Crisp, "was when William Harsent hammered on my door. My daughter answered and came to fetch me. I went to the house, saw the girl, then fetched Dr Lay while Harsent stayed with his daughter. The poor man was deeply shocked. He'd covered her body with a rug but kept peeling it back and stroking her arm as if he couldn't believe she was dead. I told him to fetch my brother, who was still sleeping upstairs, to give him something productive to do. And when my brother came down, he said a prayer for Rose."

"It was rather a commotion to sleep through."

"William is deaf," said James. "That's why his wife has given evidence instead."

"And you've had no further involvement than that?"

"No."

"Do you know William Gardiner?"

"We're acquainted, but he's a Methodist," said Crisp dismissively.

"You move in different circles?"

"We do."

James Crisp glanced at his watch. "Can I help with anything else?" he asked.

"There is one thing."

"Name it."

"Do you have a key to your brother's house?"

"Naturally."

"I would like to see Rose Harsent's room."

"Isn't it a bit late for that? And why are you still in Peasenhall at this time of night? Surely you don't want to be driving your vehicle home in the dark?"

Lawrence glanced outside. Dusk had fallen while they were talking, and leaving now would mean a cold, poorly lit journey back to Bury.

He sighed. "I lost track of time," he said.

"Well. Let's kill two birds with one stone," Crisp replied. "How do you fancy a bed for the night? My brother is out of town, and he will not mind."

"But you don't know me."

"Share your food with the hungry and provide the poor wanderer with shelter," said James.

"Well, if you're sure."

"If William were here, he would agree. Now, I'm exhausted. Call Gertrude for me, will you?"

Lawrence walked to the door and gingerly shouted the girl's name. She responded at once and came to her father while Lawrence waited at the door.

"Give this chap the key to your uncle's house," he said. "He is staying the night."

Gertrude left, returning moments later with a chunky iron key, tagged with a piece of rough string.

"I'll return it first thing," said Lawrence.

"Please do. I'm expecting William back tomorrow."

Lawrence took the key, unable to believe his good fortune. The plan had gone swimmingly, and not only would he get inside Providence House, but he'd be doing it alone. He left Church House in good spirits and was about to go next door when he thought better of it. His parked car was still outside Caroline Davis's house, a bright lemon beacon of his intent. He started the engine and moved it a short distance away, parking it outside the Angel Inn where he had stayed earlier in the week. It would attract less attention there, and nobody would know where he was really staying.

Lawrence whistled as he walked down The Causeway, feeling on top of his investigation for the first time. He didn't know whether he could help Gardiner's sullied reputation, but at least he was dealing with the matter methodically. Violet would be proud. He felt a pang as he thought of her. Daisy would be home from school, and they would be taking supper about now. It felt like he hadn't seen his daughter in days, and he missed her warm little hand in his, her unconditional love for a father who hadn't been there in her early years. Daisy had accepted his role in her life gladly and without question. She was an affectionate, talkative little thing, personable and self-contained, just like Violet. If only they could live together as a family. If only Violet hadn't lost faith in him. But Lawrence had grown more self-aware and accepted that the situation was of his own making. He had behaved badly, not with malice or intent, but he'd hurt Violet all the same. And he didn't blame her for wanting to live an independent life.

Lawrence passed a row of cottages as he proceeded towards Providence House. A curtain twitched in an upstairs room, but he didn't see it. Nor did Lawrence notice the pair of eyes staring from a mess of bandages. Instead, he sauntered towards his destination with a spring in his step.

#

Lawrence turned the key, and the door creaked open into a dark hallway. He fumbled for a light, leaving the door ajar while he opened his tin and struck a match, immediately seeing an oil light on a table to his side. He lit the lamp and three candles, then commenced his investigation of the property. The parlour, to the left, bore all the furnishings of a man with a respectable trade and comfortable life. The dining room opposite was slightly smaller and set for a meal. Neither room was worth spending time on, and Lawrence took the stairs two at a time, keen to see Rose's part of the house. It didn't take long for him to realise that there must be another staircase. No matter how hard he looked, Rose's room remained tantalisingly out of sight. Lawrence had noticed the master bedroom window overlooking Church Street earlier and knew it was directly below Rose's room. But knowing where the attic was and getting there were two different matters. Having opened all the upstairs doors, Lawrence returned to the staircase and towards the right of the house, noticing the kitchen door for the first time. William Harsent had found Rose there, dead and burned on the floor, and to Lawrence's disgust, a well-scrubbed brown stain was still visible on the brick floor near the staircase that Lawrence had been seeking.

He walked towards it while examining the small kitchen, almost too small for an otherwise fine house. A large scullery at the end occupied space which might have increased the overall size of the kitchen but instead drew attention to its lowly dimensions. Lawrence spared a thought for William Harsent, who would have stumbled straight into his daughter's body immediately upon entering the kitchen.

Lawrence slowly climbed the stairs, arriving at the end of the house directly opposite Rose's room. He traversed the corridor and opened the door to Rose's bedroom with trepidation. The room was clean but dusty, appearing as if it might have remained empty since Rose Harsent's death. A single bed lay under the window with a dresser against the sidewall. But there was nothing inside. Rose's possessions were gone, her life erased as if she had never existed at all. Lawrence leaned against the window and looked down The Street. The view from Rose's attic room window was limited, not only by distance but by the bough of a large tree on the right-hand side of the road. He doubted that William Gardiner could see her from Alma Cottage, but there was only one way to be sure.

Lawrence glanced at his watch. It was only half past five, and if he was going to make the most of the opportunity, he should follow Rose Harsent's movements and timing as far as he could. But that left a few hours to kill. He returned to the kitchen, boiled a pan, and made himself a cup of tea before taking a seat in the parlour where he found a novel by HG Wells among the religious paraphernalia. He settled down to read, drawing a blanket over his lap instead of lighting the fire. Candles flickered around the room as the wind increased outside, forcing itself through chinks in the window. Lawrence heard a rumble and then another. A storm was brewing outside, just as it had on the night of Rose's death. He lowered his book and listened. More rumbling, a flash of lightning, then the rain came down in a torrent, hammering against the window. Lawrence sighed. He needed to go out later, and at this rate, he would end up soaked to the skin. Lawrence continued to read, checking his watch every few minutes until it was five minutes to ten. Then he rose and took a candle upstairs before setting it down in Rose Harsent's attic room window. He peered outside, but it was too dark to see anything. Besides, Rose's ten o'clock signal was meant for someone else to see and not as a means of illumination for her. Lawrence returned to the kitchen and rummaged through a rack before finding a waterproof cape, which he slung over his shoulders. It was a little large, but it would do the trick and protect him from the worst of the rain. He opened the door, grabbed an oil lamp which he had lit earlier, and stepped outside.

The Street was dark and silent, apart from the relentlessly driving rain which had left Peasenhall deserted. Everyone was inside, huddling by their fires or preparing for bed. The rain was icy cold and puddling across the earthen paths. It was no place to be, but Lawrence had no choice if he wanted to see the extent of the light. He picked his way up The Street, avoiding the worst of the puddles until he found Alma Cottage, fortunately clearly signed and not far from Providence House. The Gardiners were in Ipswich, but someone must have been caring for their children elsewhere as the cottage was silent, dark, and unoccupied. Lawrence leaned against the door, looking out as if he was peering from a window. Then he did it again a few feet farther down in case one window gave an enhanced view that the other did not. Neither way worked. Although Rose's window was faintly illuminated, the light could have come from anywhere within the room. Whether the candle sat on the window ledge as the letter requested was impossible to tell from a distance. Lawrence returned down The Street, walking towards Providence House. He was almost underneath Rose's window before he was confident of seeing the candle's location on the ledge, a fact that went in William Gardiner's favour. Satisfied, Lawrence headed towards Providence House but chose not to return through the front entrance, deciding instead to inspect the grounds. He walked across the usually quiet brook and into the gardens of Providence House. Rain lashed against the tall trees surrounding the property, and Lawrence stood for a moment, imagining how it must have felt that night.

Lawrence was cold, and although dressed in a waterproof cape, he was uncomfortable, and his trousers sodden. Whoever had kept the assignation with Rose might have faced similar problems that fateful night when the storm hit. Lawrence shivered and decided not to prolong the discomfort, but as he moved towards a small gate at the rear of the property, he heard a rustle behind him. He stopped, turned slowly around, and raised the lamp, seeing nothing save for a gently swaying tree. The rear gate was still ajar just as he'd found it, and he headed towards the tumbledown conservatory in curiously poor repair. The small, glassed room, evidently used as a rudimentary boot room, encompassed the even smaller kitchen. Lawrence peered inside, his breath misting against a cracked glass pane as he spied a pair of goloshes and an upside-down bucket in the corner of the room. His fingers closed over the keys in his pocket, and he withdrew them, intending to try the smaller brass key in the conservatory door, but as he did so, he heard the crunch of gravel and spun around. He was not alone. Someone was in the grounds and close to him.

Lawrence's heart raced as he stared silently into the darkness, trying to make out the shape of the intruder. Then he slowly raised his lamp and held it towards the trees where a figure crouched in the darkness, a homburg hat jammed over his head and his face covered by a scarf. Lawrence took a step forward, and the man stood, then backed away, intending to flee. But Lawrence was in no mood to let him go. Dropping the lamp, he darted forward towards the trees. The man bolted, and Lawrence followed, running through the garden and towards a small lane. His quarry sprinted, but Lawrence was quicker and, panting hard, he followed him into the back of St Michael's church and through the graveyard. The sky was cloudy, and the moon cast little light, but every so often, Lawrence could see the flash of rain on the man's coat and hear the crunch of twigs as he ran.

Lawrence was gaining ground and almost upon him when the man dropped to his haunches behind a high gravestone. Lawrence slowed and approached him, confident that he had trapped the stranger. With only feet between them, Lawrence advanced from the side, seeing the glint of the man's frightened eyes above the scarf. His quarry blinked, but something was wrong. Lawrence saw one eyelid move through the moonlight and the still falling rain, but the other was missing. The man stared at him, panting ragged breaths into the air, then reaching to his side, he grabbed a rock and hurled it at Lawrence. It slammed against his shoulder, throwing him off balance, and the split second it took to recover was enough for the man to run full pelt towards Church Street. Lawrence cursed loudly. The distance was too great, and the man had escaped for now. But Lawrence had learned much from the night's events. He no longer doubted the recent village rumours and was confident that he had just encountered the Creeper.

CHAPTER SEVENTEEN

The Secret Drawer

"Where's Lawrence today?" asked Michael, grabbing the poker and jabbing it into the waning fire. He stared disappointedly at the lack of flames and placed another log in the grate.

"Peasenhall, I think," said Violet.

"Is he making any progress?"

"It's hard to tell. We were too busy with my case yesterday. Oh, dear. I've made a mistake. Can I have another piece of paper?"

"Of course. It will be easier if you use a pencil this time. I'll fetch one."

Michael left the room, and Violet crumpled the spoiled paper and tossed it into the fire before propping up her notebook against a vase of flowers in the centre of the table.

"There," said Michael, placing several large sheets of paper and a blotter in front of Violet.

"Oh, that's better." Violet took a ruler, drew a horizontal line across the page and several vertical lines beneath.

"Were they helpful?" asked Michael.

"The archdeacon's records?"

Michael nodded.

"Somewhat, I suppose, and they will improve the accuracy of this family tree. But the newspaper archives were better still. We're quite friendly with one of the press compositors, and he's given me a couple of clippings about the Tibenham poisonings. They make for interesting reading. Mrs Leverett was adamant that the maid was an unruly, unpleasant character, and the article supports her story."

"That will help your client," said Michael.

"Only if I can prove it," Violet sighed. "And that's looking unlikely."

"What does Lawrence think?"

"He agrees with Beth Briggs, who says that I ought to see Mrs Leverett again and tell her the truth. But I doubt my client would like it."

"What will you do?"

"I've already written to Mrs Leverett, but I ought to see Gracie and explain myself. Otherwise, she might hear something from one of her relatives, and that would be unprofessional. I'll catch a train to Norwich tomorrow."

"I could drive if you like?"

"Really? It would be a great help."

"Well, you'll need someone to mind Daisy, won't you?"

"You're so good to us, Michael."

Michael pulled back a chair and took a seat next to Violet. "That looks better," he said, pointing to Violet's diagram, which was now resembling a competently drawn family tree.

"Wait until you see my next effort. I'm going to create a timeline showing who was where and when. I'm not like Lawrence.

He writes everything down in that tiny little notebook and sees the bigger picture in his head. But the older I get, the more I need to visualise facts."

"I'll help," said Michael. "Show me what to do." But as he picked up a pencil, the door opened to reveal Aurora carrying a tea tray, which she placed at the far end of the table.

"Thank you," said Michael. "Won't you join us?"

Aurora shook her head and smiled nervously. "Here's some post for you," she said before leaving the room.

Michael poured two cups of tea and offered one to Violet. "Biscuit?"

"No, thank you. Aurora's still not very talkative, is she?"

"Yes, but did you see her smile?"

"If you could call it that."

"Come now, Violet. She's making a tremendous effort. Aurora is a lovely girl when you get to know her."

"How can you say that? You've been acquainted for less than a week. And she moved into Netherwood barely two days ago."

"Yes. But we've done an awful lot together since then, and she's been like a breath of fresh air. I didn't realise how lonely it was living alone."

"You're not falling in love, are you?" Violet barked the words abruptly, employing none of her usual empathy.

Michael blushed. "Violet, I'm not ready to discuss my feelings. I'm not even sure myself."

"Oh, Michael. You know nothing about her."

"Except that she's a gentle soul, a kind woman and excellent company."

"Did you write to her previous employer?"

"No, and I'm not going to. Let's not quarrel, Violet. I'm happy for the first time in a long while and willing to invest my trust in Aurora."

"Then I'm happy for you," said Violet, squeezing his hand and trying to bury the feeling of disquiet that had enveloped her. She would speak to Lawrence at the first opportunity. Michael was clearly reluctant to check Aurora's background, but Violet would. She was too fond of Michael to let him risk his heart to a stranger.

Michael reached for the letter Aurora had tucked beneath the sugar bowl on the tea tray.

"Ah. I think it's from Albert," he said, ripping the envelope open. "Yes, it is. Oh, that's good news. He's been contemplating the missing keys."

"Does he know where they are?"

"No. Not the originals. But Albert thinks Francis kept a spare set in his safety deposit box."

"At the bank?"

"Yes. And according to Albert, the box key should be in the desk in the study."

"Is it?"

"I don't know. Shall we find out?"

Michael left the room with Violet trailing behind. He opened the door and stood back while Violet entered first.

"I can't believe the difference in here," she said, admiring the polished wood panelling which shone with a warm glow. The last time she'd seen it, the room was heavy with dust and cobwebs.

"Aurora has worked like a Trojan," said Michael. "It's hard to get her to slow down. She's up with the lark, and if I didn't make her stop, she wouldn't. She's beginning to love this place as much as I do."

"Good for her," said Violet, trying to keep her features impassive but taking Michael's words as more evidence of the young girl's dubious intentions.

"Right. I've been through this desk a few times, and I don't recall seeing any keys," said Michael, tugging out the drawers one after the other. The desk contained little of interest apart from a few items of stationery and one or two documents. Violet watched as Michael pulled out the bottom drawer, removed a couple of household journals, and replaced them again.

"No. Albert was wrong. They're not here," he said disappointedly.

147

"Let me try," said Violet.

"There's nothing to see."

Violet ignored him and opened the top left-hand drawer. She placed her hand inside and cocked her head in concentration. Seconds later, Michael heard a click, and a star-shaped piece of marquetry in the centre of the desk stood proud of its surroundings. Violet pulled it open to reveal a tiny inset drawer, inside which were two keys and a silver cardholder.

"How did you guess?" asked Michael.

"I didn't. Francis showed me a few years ago when he first bought the desk. He was very proud of it."

"Look, Violet. There's a tag on this key."

Michael held the brass key aloft, and Violet examined it.

"Yes. I think you're right. Now, just the small matter of opening the safety deposit box."

"That won't be a problem," grinned Michael. "I've known the bank manager for years."

CHAPTER EIGHTEEN

Back to Blighty

April 1902

I returned to Blighty on a British cargo vessel, landing at Plymouth on the first day of April 1902 – April Fool's day. The Royal Navy paid my passage home and couldn't get me away from Gibraltar quickly enough. I never knew whether the investigation into my injuries bore any consequences, and nobody ever said. But they discharged me with a small and wholly inadequate pension with just enough travel allowance to get me back to Suffolk.

I spent the return voyage alone in a single officer's cabin, well away from the other men. A crew member brought food to my cabin and another, with rudimentary medical training, changed my bandages every other day. Apart from that, they left me well alone, and I spent the time reading and improving my writing skills. The days went slowly, but at least they were bearable, unlike the nights when I fought like a tiger to stay awake for fear of the nightmares returning. I lost, of course. Nobody can stay awake indefinitely. And inevitably, the dream horrors came, each one worse than the last.

I took a train from Plymouth to London and from there to Suffolk, arriving a few days into April. I had avoided travelling during the day, having heard several cruel comments about my appearance. It wasn't so bad in London, where the population was dense and differences less obvious. But the closer I got to Suffolk, the more I noticed the horrified reactions of my fellow travellers. I disembarked the train at Saxmundham station, leaving the platform to seek transport for the rest of the journey. But as I rounded the corner, I almost stepped into the path of a well-dressed young lady who shrieked and fainted clean away at the sight of me. Her gentleman friend caught her and eased her gently to the ground, but as I stopped and offered to help, briefly forgetting my situation, he swore at me and told me to leave at once, shouting that my face wasn't fit for public view. And that moment encapsulated the direction that the rest of my life would take. I was a pariah, deformed, ugly and unloved, and destined to be alone. So, I trudged across the fields to Peasenhall and arrived late in the evening under cover of darkness at the place where I hoped my father still lived.

It had been over a decade since I'd last seen him. I hadn't written in that time, and neither had he. Nor was I in touch with any of my siblings. They could all be dead for all I knew. I did not expect a warm welcome, and the best I could hope for was an offer of shelter for a night or two. After that, I didn't know what I would do with limited funds and a face so repulsive that no decent person would take me in.

I approached the cottage where my father dwelled and peered inside through a chink in the threadbare curtains. Two women were sitting in the parlour, one clutching a swaddled baby, the other brushing her hair on a stool by the fire. It took a few moments to recognise them, given the poorly lit room and the passage of time, but as my eyes grew accustomed to the lighting, I realised to my relief that I was looking at my sisters, Phoebe, and Louisa. I couldn't risk knocking on the front door for fear that one of them might scream, so I crept around the back, unlatched the rear door, and went inside.

It took a long time to calm my sisters down and convince them of my identity. I will never forget their reaction to my appearance and their revulsion at the sight of me. But they did not eject me from the house that night and agreed that I could stay in the attic room providing that nobody found out. I did not ask them why I must remain hidden, for that would force them to acknowledge their shame. But I knew. And I did as they asked and paid board money from my pension despite the scant living conditions. After all, they might be poor, but my sisters were entitled to their pride.

A few days turned into weeks, then months, and they didn't move me on. At first, I kept to my sisters' rules. I did not need to go out and spent my days watching the world go by from my tiny attic room window facing onto The Street. The window was fortuitously angled, allowing me to see a long way, almost as far as the road junction. I soon learned the rituals and routines of my fellow villagers until I felt as if I knew them, and from time to time, Phoebe and Louisa shared snippets of gossip, rich fare for a lonely man. My sisters kept me fed and watered, told me about my father's death and my brother Mark's descent into lunacy. Phoebe charred for a living, Louisa stayed at home, and occasionally male visitors appeared at the house, but I remained in my garret and did not ask questions. And because I handed over my pension and caused no trouble, my sisters did not object when I left the house after a few weeks for a late-night walk. It was the first moment of joy I had experienced in a long time. The late April day had been balmy, and although I left the house a little before midnight, the temperature was still bearable without a coat. I exited through the rear gate and kept well away from any lit areas, then I went to the church and walked among the gravestones. I sat on the remains of a tomb, crumbled and defaced, watching the bats swoop overhead. And my heart lightened a little, and life seemed more bearable as I perambulated the churchyard until dawn. And that became my habit. Late-night walks, scratching the heads of friendly cats as I slunk through the darkness, nocturnal ramblings through fields – I even ventured to nearby villages under cover of darkness if the weather allowed. But I was careful never to be seen and always to return home before dawn.

I soon learned the scope of information I could glean after dark and often visited houses in the dead of night, entering gardens from the rear and pressing my face against the windowpanes to see inside. Although most villagers were strangers, I saw some familiar faces from the past. Several were acquaintances, but one was once a dear friend. I found myself sorely tempted to test the friendship and reveal myself, but I could not risk the wrath of my sisters and possible ejection from my home, so I stayed hidden.

I took an interest in the local gossip. Stories from my sisters gained greater importance, bringing an irresistible urge to find out more about the parties involved. I came to know the vagaries of the townsfolk. Ellen Blowers and Henry Rouse were malicious gossips, Henry Ludbrook, an inveterate womaniser, and a couple of young lads were well-known troublemakers with a penchant for spying. Peasenhall was buzzing with rumour and had been for over a year, according to Phoebe. A tall, black-bearded man called William Gardiner was making a fool of himself with a young girl, so they said. I could see Gardiner's home from my attic room window and often watched as he went to work or chapel. I quickly learned his daily routines, together with those of his long-suffering wife, and I decided to find out more about the man and his accusers. I did not ask questions for fear of upsetting Phoebe but instead waited for morsels of gossip as and when she chose to share them. To her credit, my sister was not a tittle-tattle so much as a bearer of news, so I had to be patient or attempt to uncover more myself. And that's why I began following people, the first of whom was a young man called Billy Wright.

I hadn't originally set out with that purpose in mind, but on walking around the village one night, alone, so I had thought, I heard chatter behind me. I concealed myself behind a bush and peered out to see two drunken young men weaving their way home from an unusually late night at the inn. Loud and carefree, they were talking in the most disrespectful terms about William Gardiner. I seized on their words, listening in as the older man recounted the same story I had already heard regarding an intimate meeting in the doctor's chapel. Their words faded as they walked away, and I followed beside them, creeping along the other side of the hedge only feet away, so I didn't miss a word. And in their drunken state, they didn't see me and continued to talk as if conducting a private conversation. Wright spoke angrily about the Methodist ministers' refusal to believe his story. My sister Phoebe had speculated that he might have been making it up, but Wright's words left me with no doubt that he believed what he said, which surprised me somewhat. My observations of Gardiner gave the impression of a hard-working, God-fearing man, and I was minded to give him the benefit of the doubt. But Wright's impassioned condemnation immediately changed my mind, and I began to question William Gardiner's integrity. As the days went on, I roamed the village, looking for clues. Then one night, quite unexpectedly, I encountered Rose Harsent.

CHAPTER NINETEEN

Amelia Pepper

Sunday, January 25, 1903

Lawrence woke fully dressed in Rose Harsent's former bed, wondering for a moment whether he'd dreamed up the stranger from the previous night. He had fallen asleep on top of the covers with his coat slung across him for warmth. It was wholly inadequate in an unheated house, but Lawrence was on high alert after encountering the Creeper. He had no intention of shedding any of his clothes, especially having arrived without nightwear. He yawned, stretched, and walked towards the window overlooking The Street. The weather was clement for January, and a low sun shone encouragingly in pale blue skies. Lawrence straightened the bed and proceeded downstairs before locking the door and leaving.

He had already decided to vacate the house before Deacon and Mrs Crisp arrived back home in case they were not as benevolent as their brother. Lawrence walked to Church House, tapped on the door, and gave the key to Gertrude Crisp, then walked back towards his car. In the distance, he saw a familiar face and recognised it as George Whiting.

"Glad to see you're still wearing them," said Whiting affably, nodding towards Lawrence's new shoes.

"Yes. They're very comfortable," said Lawrence. "I'll recommend your services next time I come across anyone in need of a shoemaker."

"Mind you do," said George. "How are you getting on? They've cleared pious Willie's name again, and we need another candidate."

"Sorry?"

"Haven't you heard? The jury acquitted William Gardiner yesterday – eleven to one in his favour."

"How do you know?"

"From a reporter in the village first thing this morning. He was hanging around Alma Cottage with the others, clustered around like a pack of vultures waiting for their prey. Gardiner would be off his chump to turn up now. They'll be there for the rest of the day."

"Well, I'm not entirely surprised."

"About Gardiner or the reporters?"

"Either, I suppose. It was only to be expected, given the amount of circumstantial evidence. I was unimpressed with what I saw in court yesterday."

"Do you think he's innocent?"

Lawrence nodded. "Yes. I do. At the very least, there isn't enough evidence for a justifiable conviction."

"I don't know. Gardiner is a slimy one, Harpham. If you met him, you'd know."

"I saw him yesterday, and I'm sure that he loves his wife very much and is in agony at the trouble he has brought to her door."

Whiting snorted. "He's got you fooled then."

"I take it you think otherwise. Are you suggesting he killed Miss Harsent?"

"I don't know about that, but those little trysts weren't as innocent as he pretends."

Lawrence took his hands from his greatcoat pocket and rubbed them firmly.

"It's colder than it looks," said Whiting, watching him grimace.

"Hmmm," said Lawrence, distractedly, thoughts of the night before still uppermost in his mind. "Can I ask you something?"

"Be my guest."

"Have you seen the Creeper?"

"Have I seen Old Shuck?"

"I'm serious. Have you encountered anyone who fits the description of the Creeper?"

Whiting sighed. "I haven't, but I've heard things. You know, dogs barking in the night for no good reason, things going missing or turning up in different places."

"But you haven't seen anyone?"

"No."

"Have any strangers arrived in the village recently?"

"Since when?"

"Since Miss Harsent's death."

"Not that I know about unless you count old Molly Rogers who left the workhouse last month."

"No. This stranger was a man."

"Was?"

"Yes. I saw him last night. There was something wrong with his face."

Whiting cocked his head. "Are you sure? I don't know anyone of that description. Did you have a drink too many?"

"Perhaps," said Lawrence, not wanting to dwell on the subject if the man couldn't help. "Who's that?" he asked, pointing to a woman who was entering the neighbouring property to Alma Cottage.

"That's Mrs Pepper," said Whiting. "Amelia Pepper. I'm surprised you didn't see her in court."

"I wasn't there for long," said Lawrence. "Is she worth talking to?"

George Whiting nodded. "I would say so, for all the good it will do. Now here's where we part ways," Whiting continued. He raised a hand in mock salute and strode down the road.

Lawrence waited for a moment, trying to decide whether it was worth risking the attention of the half dozen reporters milling around Alma Cottage to talk to Amelia Pepper. But he might not return to Peasenhall for a while, and this was his last chance to collect more information before he sat down to analyse it. So far, the case was unresolvable, and he had visions of having to return some of the advance fees to the Goddard brothers. Violet would be unamused. So, against his better judgement, he approached the Pepper house, ignoring questions from reporters as he strode up the path. Lawrence knocked firmly on the door and waited a few seconds before the woman he had seen earlier answered. She stood uncertainly in the doorway.

"Yes?" she asked suspiciously.

A newspaper photographer moved his tripod closer and began lining up a shot. "Can I come in?" asked Lawrence, nodding towards the hack. "I'd rather not explain on the doorstep."

The woman raised her eyes and opened the door slightly wider, shutting it with a deliberate bang once Lawrence was safely inside.

"I've seen enough of them to last a lifetime," she said. "God smite me down if I'm wrong, but I will never willingly set foot in a court of law again with all that carry on."

"I was in Ipswich yesterday," said Lawrence.

"At the trial?"

He nodded.

"Then you know what they're like. Worse than a plague of rats. Get away!" she shrieked suddenly, flinging the curtains shut as a whiskered face peered into her living room. "No peace, no privacy. I can't bear it. No wonder the Gardiners are slowly going mad."

"It's rather intrusive," said Lawrence. "Bear with me a moment." He approached the window and opened it. "What paper are you representing?"

"*The Bury Post*. How does it concern you?" said the man rudely.

"Good answer," said Lawrence. "I am a personal friend of the owner, and if you don't leave this lady alone, I will make sure he knows all about it."

"Alright. Keep your hair on," said the man, reaching for his camera. He nodded towards his colleague. "Come on, Ned. Nothing to see here."

"Well, thank you," said Amelia Pepper, beaming widely. "How fortunate that you're so well connected."

Lawrence smiled. There was no need to reveal that the only friendships he enjoyed at *The Bury Post* were with the sub-editor and the chief compositor. Lawrence wouldn't know the owner if he fell over him, but it didn't matter. Not only had he seen the reporter off, but he had made himself the hero of Amelia Pepper's day.

"Can I offer you a cup of tea?" she asked. Lawrence nodded. He was hungry, and a mug of tea would bridge the gap until his next meal. He sat down in a comfortable chair in the parlour while Amelia fetched a tray.

"Help yourself," she said when she returned, placing the well-stocked tray on the side table. "I'd pour the tea, but I don't know how you take it, or which cake you would like."

Lawrence glanced gratefully at a plate next to the teapot containing, if he wasn't mistaken, chunks of gingerbread and honey cake. He cut a slice of each and settled back down.

"I'd like to ask some questions," he said, then quickly added," but I'm not a reporter."

"It didn't cross my mind," said Mrs Pepper. "You're far too well-mannered."

Lawrence smiled. "I am a private detective, though. I am trying to find Rose Harsent's murderer."

"They've acquitted Mr Gardiner," Amelia replied defensively.

"I know. And I'd still be looking for somebody else even if they hadn't."

"You believe him?" Her eyes widened in surprise.

"Of course. Do you?"

"Yes. Oh, yes. I have always known William Gardiner was innocent. We both did, that is to say, Mrs Gardiner and me. It couldn't have been William, and I have told them that repeatedly. What's happened to that family is wicked. Simply wrong and with no basis in fact."

"We are like-minded in that regard," said Lawrence.

"Thank goodness someone is on his side. Poor William is still under lock and key," said Amelia. "And there's talk of a third trial."

"It won't happen," said Lawrence.

"How do you know?"

"I was in the Suffolk constabulary before I started consulting privately. A third trial would waste everyone's time and money and is highly unlikely to result in a guilty verdict. They'll let him go. Mark my words."

Amelia Pepper beamed. "You're like a breath of fresh air," she said. "Now, what do you want to know. I'll tell you anything."

"Just remind me what you heard that night," said Lawrence.

"The night of the murder?"

"Yes."

"Well, I was in court to back up Mrs Gardiner's account," she said. "But it didn't go very well. I got my words confused, and I wasn't much help in the end."

"Slow down," said Lawrence, acknowledging Mrs Pepper's discomfort as she recalled the events of that night. She was the type of person who rushed to get her words out, not deliberately to confuse, but because she wanted so badly to help. And as commendable as her attitude was, Lawrence guessed she would be a frustrating witness, sacrificing detail for speed.

"I'm sorry," she said, flushing.

"Please don't be. What were you doing that night?"

"We all stayed up," she said. "Such a shocking storm, it was. I've never heard the like before in my lifetime. The claps of thunder were enough to rouse the dead. Well, we were all frightened, especially Mrs Dickinson. So, we were up later than usual, and I heard when the Gardiners went to bed. The walls are paper-thin, you see. Not so much as a squeak on the stair passes me by when I'm awake. Especially if I have insomnia and I was tossing and turning until four that morning."

"Then what did you hear?"

"I heard Mrs Gardiner come down the stairs and deal with her child. He was crying."

"How do you know it was Mrs Gardiner?"

"Because her tread was light on the stairs."

"Are you certain?"

"Not really," she said miserably. "That's where it went wrong in court. They pulled out my witness statement, and it was slightly different to what I remembered afterwards."

"In what way?"

"I said that Mrs Gardiner told me she had gone to the child, but in court, I remembered hearing a light tread. They believe I said it just to agree with Mrs Gardiner, but I remember thinking at the time that the footsteps weren't heavy. I just didn't say it."

"But in terms of evidence, you didn't hear Mr Gardiner leave the property."

"No, I did not," she said firmly. "It's no good them trying to make out that William murdered Rose Harsent when his wife went to check on the baby. I would have heard it. He didn't get out of bed. I didn't hear him, and Mrs Gardiner didn't hear him either because he didn't do it. He couldn't have."

"And we already know that Rose Harsent was killed that night," said Lawrence.

"Exactly. Somebody else got Rose, and I am so pleased that William is safe from a wrongful conviction. Perhaps they can come home now."

"That's what I'm hoping for," said Lawrence. "Well, that's all I need," he continued. "I'll leave you in peace."

Amelia Pepper stood and offered her hand. "Thank you for helping my friends," she said. Lawrence smiled. "I'll do my utmost to clear Gardiner's name."

CHAPTER TWENTY

Gracie's Fiancé

Monday, January 26, 1903

Violet checked and re-checked her watch before reaching into her bag for the note she had written after the day before's telephone call with Gracie Francis. "I'm sure she said one o'clock," Violet repeated.

"Perhaps she's been delayed," said Michael.

"She must have been. But I can't wait for much longer. School finishes in an hour, and I must get home for Daisy."

"Well, we know where the young lady works. Let's go inside."

Violet nodded. She would rather have met Gracie in the tea shop as planned, but they'd been waiting outside for fifteen minutes already. And unless the typing manageress was an unreasonable martinet, there was no reason why they couldn't collect Gracie instead. It was just a pity that the meeting wasn't sooner, which would have suited Violet better. But Gracie's young man had suddenly made other arrangements, necessitating a Monday trip.

The offices of Brown and Co were only a few doors down from the tea shop, and Violet and Michael entered, making their way upstairs as directed by a large sign. They arrived in a reception area, but the desk was empty. Violet opened a nearby door and peered inside to see a busy room containing half a dozen desks, each with a typewriter on top. Typists were sitting behind some desks while others were left vacant. A young man looked up, saw Violet, and hastened towards them before beckoning them back into the reception room.

"How can I help?" he asked warmly.

"I'm looking for Gracie Francis," said Violet.

"Ah," said the man. "Are you Miss Smith?"

"Yes. How do you know?"

"I'm Edward Fisher," he said, extending his hand. "Gracie's colleague and friend. She asked me to come and find you to say she will be a few moments late. Unfortunately, Miss Anderson collared me first, and I couldn't get away. I'm so sorry."

"Oh, dear. Will Gracie be much longer?"

"No. It's just that Phillip, her fiancé, has turned up. She wasn't expecting him and, well, you know how it is."

"Can I help?" A tall, thin, middle-aged woman opened the door and cast a steely gaze towards Michael and Violet.

Edward responded. "Nothing to worry about, Miss Anderson," he said cheerfully. "Miss Smith is here to see Miss Francis, but I'll take care of them. I'll break for lunch now if you don't mind."

Miss Anderson removed her glasses. "As you wish. And where is Miss Francis?"

"She's taking an early lunch, if you remember."

"No, I don't."

"Well, she'll be back soon. We're leaving now." Edward flashed an anxious smile at Violet, and she took the hint and followed him through the door.

"Sorry about that," he said when they reached the bottom of the stairs. "Phillip has turned up unexpectedly a few times now, and Miss Anderson is taking an interest. She's not as fearsome as she looks, but it's her job to maintain discipline, and I didn't want to draw too much attention to Gracie's absence. May I escort you to the tea shop? Gracie will be along shortly. I promise she won't take long."

They followed Edward inside. "Is it easier if I order tea and sandwiches all round?" he asked.

Violet nodded. She wasn't particularly hungry and didn't care whether she ate, as long as Gracie wasn't too late.

Edward placed the order and returned to the table. "I've requested high tea for four, but we might have to share if Phillip turns up."

"Is that likely?" Violet glanced at Michael, and he acknowledged her frustration with a thin smile.

"It's not ideal," said Edward. "But anything is possible with Phillip. He doesn't need to work, you see. He's not a selfish man, but he doesn't understand the demands of an employer. Poor Gracie wants to keep her job for as long as possible, although she will have to give it up in the end."

"Why?"

"Because Phillip insists. She's making a good marriage, but it comes at a price."

"Do you approve of the marriage?" The question slipped out before Violet considered the consequences and it created a moment of tension as the young man fell quiet. He picked at the corner of the menu, eyes downcast, as he pondered his reply.

"No, I don't, as it happens," he said, raising his head and staring directly into Violet's eyes.

"Why?"

"Because she deserves better. Gracie will want for nothing materially when they marry. But his parents have high expectations, and Phillip obeys their every word. I suppose he has no choice to be sure of his inheritance. But they must have reservations about the marriage already to put this latest barrier in the way. They've created a virtually insolvable situation. Have you made any progress?"

"Not much," Violet admitted truthfully, acknowledging his candour. "As you say, it isn't easy after all this time, but I'm not giving up yet. I've still got another iron in the fire if Gracie agrees."

"She'll agree to anything," said Edward.

"She must be deeply in love with Phillip."

"What woman wouldn't be? He drives a splendid automobile, lives in a mansion and has money to burn."

Violet watched the young man as he spoke without malice and detected a sadness in his demeanour.

"Have you known Gracie long?"

"Three years," said Edward. "Harry, Gracie and I have been as close as the three musketeers since we met. We all joined Browns during the same week."

"And what about Harry. Does he like Phillip?"

"Harry is short for Harriet, and no, she doesn't like or approve of him. Harry thinks Gracie would be better off with someone else. Someone who loves her unconditionally."

Michael, who had been listening quietly in the background, leaned forward. "Someone like you?" he asked.

Edward blushed furiously and cast an anxious glance towards the door. "Is it that obvious?"

Michael nodded.

"Then thank God she hasn't noticed."

Violet opened her mouth to reply, but as she did, the door opened, and a young couple walked through.

"Gracie, Phillip," said Edward, jumping to his feet and hastening towards them. He returned to the table and made their introductions before pulling out a chair for Gracie.

Edward turned to Phillip. "Would you like my seat? I've got to go in a minute."

"But you haven't eaten yet," said Violet.

"Not to worry."

"Don't inconvenience yourself on my account," said Phillip. "I'm not staying. Just doing my duty and escorting my fiancée to her appointment."

He smiled and nodded affably in Michael's and Violet's direction before turning to Gracie.

"Now, don't forget, dinner will be at six thirty on Tuesday night and wear something smart." Then he turned and strode towards the door as Gracie watched him retreat.

"Oh dear," she said. "Dinner with Phillip's parents is always an ordeal, but at least they've invited me. Perhaps they are coming around at last. Please accept my apologies for running late. I hope Edward has kept you company."

"Admirably," said Michael.

A waitress arrived bearing a stand of assorted sandwiches and a pot of tea. Silence momentarily reigned as they filled their plates and started eating. Then Gracie looked up and spoke.

"Have you uncovered anything yet? Do tell me you've found proof that the maid did it?"

Violet shook her head and finished her mouthful. "No, I haven't. I've made some progress, but it's difficult after all this time."

Gracie frowned. "That's disappointing news. Phillip says we can start planning for the wedding as soon as you've settled this matter."

"What if I can't?"

"Don't say that. My future happiness depends upon it." Gracie's lip trembled, and her eyes filled with tears. Edward flashed a wide smile. "Don't think like that," he said. "There's always a way."

Gracie smiled gratefully. "Is there anything else you can do? I can pay more if it helps. I have a little money put away for a rainy day."

Violet spontaneously reached forwards and took Gracie's hand. "Keep your money," she said. "That's not the problem. I've spoken to your grandmother, and she's told me about the poisonings. But she thinks I'm an inheritance finder and has little reason to help."

"Oh, dear. What can I do?"

"I've spoken to a friend of hers, Beth Briggs. She told me that your great grandparents disapproved of your grandmother's husband."

"I didn't know that. But how does it help me?"

"Well, your grandmother married him despite parental opposition and may have some sympathy with your situation."

Gracie raised a weak smile. "I daresay. But what's the good of it if she's already told you everything?"

"I can't be sure that she has. She refused to speculate on the murderer, despite her obvious dislike for Eliza Sage. Mrs Briggs is a very astute lady, for all her years. She thinks we should be honest with Mrs Leverett and appeal to her better nature."

"You've got nothing to lose," said Edward. "Surely it's worth a try?"

"I don't want to upset my mother," said Gracie. "She's been so poorly this year, and if Granny reacts badly, she's bound to make a fuss."

"Then what's the alternative?"

Gracie sighed. "There isn't one. Not if I'm to marry in April."

"And grandmothers love a wedding," smiled Michael.

"Oh, it won't be a big wedding," said Gracie. "The Wild family always hold their weddings in their private chapel. Close family only."

"That's a shame," said Violet. "But can I go ahead and consult your grandmother?"

Gracie nodded. "Yes. But let me know what she says. I can't afford any more worry."

#

"What did you make of that?" asked Michael, as he reversed away from the tea shop, feeling the heater box with his gloved hand. It was tepid, and the hot brick he'd thoughtfully inserted earlier in anticipation of the frosty day had long since cooled. He drew his collar higher and rearranged his scarf.

"Be careful," said Violet, as he veered towards the middle of the road and an oncoming car.

"Sorry," said Michael. "I seem to feel the cold so much more these days."

"And you're the youngest of us. It doesn't bode well for Lawrence and me. Anyway, what do I make of what?"

"Your client and her young man."

"They're not very well suited," said Violet. "She's a lovely girl and could do so much better."

"It's a good marriage," said Michael. "Too good in some ways."

"Only when judged in the context of material wealth. I don't think Phillip will make her happy."

"She might be one of those girls who is perfectly content as a wife and mother."

"I don't know," said Violet. "I couldn't do it."

"That's a pity. I know someone who will marry you tomorrow if you'd only agree."

Violet shot him a withering look. "Out of pity."

"Out of love. How long do you intend to continue making him pay?"

"Michael!" Violet's sudden exclamation shocked them both. She stared at him, her mouth open in horror at his harsh words. He had never spoken to her like that before, or anyone else as far as she knew.

"Is that really what you think of me?"

"No, it isn't. I'm sorry. I shouldn't have said it. I only want the best for you. But Aurora has brought such happiness into my life that naturally, I want the same for you and Lawrence."

"Lawrence thinks he loves me because we share a child. But he doesn't, and he wouldn't look twice in my direction if Daisy hadn't been born. And I'm perfectly at peace knowing this. I understand him better than you do."

"You sound more than a little defensive."

"It's sensible to protect yourself, Michael."

"Why are relationships so complicated?" he asked.

"You're the minister. You tell me."

"God's love is unconditional. And so, it appears, is mine. Perhaps Aurora will break my heart, but I don't know any other way. I'm afraid the same applies to the young man, Edward."

"Yes. He has got it rather badly, poor thing. I wonder how he will cope. Gracie won't move in the same circles after her marriage."

"He should tell her how he feels."

"Not a good idea," said Violet, shaking her head. "I disapprove of marrying for money. But if Gracie loves Phillip, and I think it's obvious that she does, then why should Edward risk his pride and her feelings in unburdening himself. It will only make them both feel uncomfortable and could ruin a friendship forever."

"But does she love Phillip?" asked Michael. "Or is she flattered that someone in her position has secured such a good match?"

"Oh, Michael. Really. A good match doesn't depend on power or status. Consider our situations. You, Lawrence, and Phillip Wild are much the same. What's the common factor?"

"We are men," said Michael.

"I know, but it's not the only similarity. My background does not compare with yours, but I wouldn't have the same earning potential even if it did. And neither does Aurora. What would your father say if he was still alive? What would Francis think, for that matter?"

"They would strongly disapprove."

"Exactly. They would worry about Aurora's prospects."

"Yes. But you don't approve either, yet you say it doesn't matter."

"Only because you don't know anything about her. Aurora's occupation is less of an issue than the implausible story she has told you."

"We're talking about Gracie Francis, not Aurora. And I didn't detect any great love between her and Phillip, but her easy affection towards Edward was undeniable."

"Perhaps you're right," Violet conceded. "But it's too late to matter, and it would only cause problems. I need to concentrate on the job that Gracie's given me."

"What will you do?"

"See Mary Leverett and hopefully conclude this case before the end of the week."

CHAPTER TWENTY-ONE

Bunwell Revisited

Tuesday, January 27, 1903

"Here we go again," said Lawrence as they climbed out of his vehicle and walked towards Mary Leverett's cottage in Bunwell.

"I don't know what you mean by we. Michael brought me last time."

"I mean, the two of us investigating cases as we've done so often in the past?"

"More apart than together," said Violet pensively.

"Do you mind?"

"Not anymore. I found working alone harder at the start, but I got used to it when you were in Bury hospital. You do when there's no alternative. Still, I'm glad you're here now. Mrs Leverett is sure to be cross with me. I hope that Beth Briggs was right, and this visit is worth the upset."

"She's a very astute woman," said Lawrence. "And we've nothing to lose. How did Michael get on with Mrs Leverett?"

"He didn't meet her," said Violet. "You know what Michael's like – more than happy to sit in the background playing with Daisy. He's a kind man."

"Isn't he, "said Lawrence. "And how is he getting on at Netherwood?" They were nearing the cottage now, Violet having asked Lawrence to park near the church so she could stretch her legs for the first time that day.

"I'm worried about him," said Violet.

"Really. Why?"

"He's only fallen in love with the maid."

"Michael in love? I didn't know he had it in him."

"It surprised me too. I thought Michael would end up a confirmed bachelor, like, well, you know who."

Lawrence frowned. "Let's not talk about Francis," he said, swiftly changing the subject. "Don't you approve?"

"Of Aurora?"

"Who else?"

Violet sighed. "I don't dislike her, but she's an enigma. There's something about her that worries me, and her background is unusual."

"Oh yes. This religious organisation she mentioned to Michael. Do we know any more about it?"

"No. But we ought to find out. And if we can't get any details, then at the very least, we should take up references from Aurora's last position."

"Hasn't Michael already done it?"

"No. And he's not going to," said Violet.

"Michael is in far too deep. I agree with you, Violet. Write to her last employer and see what you can uncover."

"I've already written, and I posted the letter this morning. I was going to wait until we had spoken, but I knew you'd see it my way."

"I do. Anyway. We're here. Nervous?"

Violet nodded. She had thrust her hands deep into her camel overcoat to stop herself from picking at her cuticles, a lifelong reaction to anxiety. "I wish we hadn't lied," she said.

"You, not we."

"Don't start, Lawrence," Violet snapped defensively.

"I didn't mean it like that," Lawrence replied, looking downcast. "I mean, let's use it to our advantage. Mary Leverett might be angry with you, but she can't take it out on me. We've never met."

"She doesn't like men," said Violet. "She may not let you through the door."

"But she married one."

"Even so."

Lawrence stopped, grabbed Violet's hand, and pulled her close. He tipped her face towards him as he towered above her. "Stop worrying," he smiled.

Violet's legs almost buckled at the tender gesture. She watched him without speaking for a moment, torn between anger at his familiarity, yet unexpectedly overwhelmed with a surge of affection that made her heart flutter. "We'd better get on with it," she muttered.

Lawrence stood respectfully behind as she swallowed, then banged on the door.

"Come in," commanded a querulous voice.

Violet smiled nervously, opened the door, and went inside while Lawrence trailed behind.

"Oh, it's you," said Mary Leverett as Violet entered the parlour. "And who is your man friend? You said nothing about bringing him. And he's not the same one who came last time."

"No," said Violet. "This is my business partner, Lawrence Harpham."

"Another inheritance seeker. How many do you need, for goodness' sake?"

"He's not an inheritance seeker. He's a private detective. We both are."

Mary Leverett's eyes narrowed. "I should have known better. I thought your tale sounded like a cock and bull story. How dare you enter my house under false pretences?"

"I shouldn't have," said Violet. "It was a bad idea, but we didn't want to upset you."

"Well, you have. And if I were in better health, I would take the broom to you. Get out of my house."

"Please. I need to speak to you," said Violet.

"I don't want to listen. Go away."

"Excuse me," said Lawrence.

"No. I don't know you. Leave my house now, or I'll call the police."

"Be my guest," said Lawrence.

"I haven't got a telephone."

"Wouldn't it be easier to sacrifice five minutes of your life and listen to Miss Smith?"

Mary Leverett scowled. "Miss Smith, the liar. I won't believe a word she utters." Her lips disappeared in a thin line, and her jowls trembled with anger as she spoke.

"I am so very sorry," said Violet. "But Gracie and I thought it would be better this way."

"Gracie?" Mrs Leverett's demeanour changed from angry to interested in seconds.

"Yes. Gracie Francis."

"My granddaughter?"

Violet nodded.

"What about her?"

"She's getting married," said Violet.

"So I've heard. What of it?"

"There's a problem."

"There often is. Marriages are tricky things to arrange."

"This one is more difficult than most. Her fiancé's parents object to the marriage."

Mary Leverett snorted. "I hope the young people have the means and good sense to proceed regardless."

"They don't," said Violet.

"Poor, is he? In that case, he's not good enough for my Gracie, and she'd better walk away."

"The opposite," said Lawrence, wading in. It was Violet's case, and she knew more about it than he did, but it didn't do to sit silently for too long and seem like an irrelevance. "The young man is very well off. It is, if you don't mind me saying, an unequal match."

"Nobody tells me anything," complained Mary Leverett. "Though I haven't seen my daughter in a long while. She's ill, you know. Well, well. Some things change, and others stay the same."

"I'm sorry?" Violet stared quizzically into the old woman's eyes.

"My father objected to my marriage," said Mary. "But it didn't make any difference. I was going to wed my husband one way or the other. Where there's love, there's hope. So, Gracie's folks aren't good enough for this young man's family?"

"It's not that," said Violet. "It's the murders."

"I see." Mary Leverett sat back in her chair, removed a handkerchief from her sleeve and dabbed at her rheumy eyes. "No wonder you resorted to subterfuge. Exactly what have they asked you to do?"

"Gracie employed us," said Violet. "Her young man, Phillip, became sick after eating something, and his parents caused a fuss. I think they are using the murders as a reason to stop the wedding, but Phillip says he is happy to marry as long as Gracie can prove that the murderer wasn't a member of her family."

"And how is she supposed to do that after all this time?" asked Mary.

"That's why we're involved. We've had some past success in solving historical crimes," said Violet. "Nothing as old as this, unfortunately, but, nevertheless, it's possible under the right circumstances."

"Then how are you getting on?"

Violet hesitated. "We're not. But I saw Beth Briggs, and she thought you might be able to help if you knew the reason why."

"Hmm. So, you went poking around in my business, after all. Well, I will have to give it some thought. It rather depends."

"On what?"

"Whether I like the young man."

"But your granddaughter's happiness is at stake."

"Precisely."

"I don't know what you mean."

"Let me ask you a question," said the old lady, picking threads from the blanket draped across her lap.

"Please do."

"Would you want to marry a man who thought you had a predisposition to murder?"

"No," said Violet quickly. "I would want him to love me enough that my background didn't matter."

"You mean unconditionally?"

Violet nodded.

"Well, think again. There are good reasons not to rush into wedlock. My granddaughter's betrothed might be a cautious young fellow," said Mary Leverett. "Or is perhaps humouring his relatives. He may be looking for a route to marriage that keeps everyone happy."

Violet considered her words. "You may be right," she conceded.

Lawrence flashed an encouraging smile. "Then there could be a happy ending," he said.

"Not necessarily," said Mrs Leverett. "I must judge this situation carefully."

"Can you help?" asked Violet.

"Perhaps. But you must do something for me in return."

"Anything."

"I want to meet them."

"Both of them?"

Mary nodded. "It's the only way."

"I'm not sure they will agree," said Violet. "Gracie will want to see you, of course. But her young man, well – he's awfully busy."

"He will find the time," said Mary. "And if he doesn't, I will know as much as I need to."

"Then I'll telephone Gracie as soon as I return to Bury," said Violet.

"Do that," said the old lady. "And don't waste any more time."

#

"That went well," said Lawrence, smiling at Violet as they approached Bury St Edmunds at a sedate pace. He had tried to engage her in conversation a few times since leaving Mary Leverett, but Violet had been withdrawn, only offering one-word answers and clearly deep in thought. And, after their long acquaintance, Lawrence knew why. Violet was more than capable of lying, but though convincing, she didn't like doing it. Violet was tactful and appropriately forthright, generally seeing little need for dishonesty when a dose of truth usually produced the right outcome. But this time, she'd let herself get carried away and had given a poor account of herself. It was a shame. Had Mary Leverett known Violet's true personality, she would have liked and trusted her. Yet today, Mary had come within a whisker of ejecting them from the property. It was just as well that she was frail, with no one at home to help her.

Violet sighed. "It wasn't a complete disaster."

"You've achieved your objective."

"I'm not so sure. Who's to say that Mary won't embarrass Gracie in front of her young man."

"She seemed very fond of her granddaughter. You've done as much as possible, Violet."

"But will it end well?"

Lawrence glanced towards her. Violet was facing ahead, her mouth set into a thin line and her eyes lacking their usual sparkle.

"If you mean will she suddenly produce a piece of evidence that will solve a decades-old crime, then probably not. But she has the wisdom and the background to guide Miss Francis in the right direction. The trouble with the young is that they underestimate the value of their elders. She should have approached Mrs Leverett directly in the first place."

"If everyone turned to friends and relatives, we'd be out of a job," said Violet.

"I know. But in this case, it's the right thing to do. Cheer up, old girl."

Violet returned a weak smile. "Drop me at the office, please," she said, as Lawrence indicated towards Angel Hill. Lawrence changed direction and was about to pull up outside The Butter Market when Michael marched briskly towards him.

"Hello, old man," said Lawrence cheerfully, then his face fell as he noticed Michael's worried demeanour. "What's wrong? You look as if you've seen a ghost."

Michael leaned against the side of the car and caught his breath. "I've just seen the oddest thing," he said.

"What is it? And where?"

"Back at Netherwood."

"Tell me."

"I think it's better if I show you," he said grimly.

CHAPTER TWENTY-TWO

One Secret Too Many

Lawrence strode through the hallway of the property he knew so well, wondering how many times he had passed through the front door during his lifetime. He had known Francis and Michael since his schooldays when Netherwood belonged to Sir Archibald Farrow, and the place was almost as familiar as his father's home in Great Finborough. Yet from the moment he entered, trailing behind Michael with Violet even farther behind, something felt chillingly wrong.

"Slow down," said Lawrence, as he turned around to give Violet a fighting chance to catch up. Michael had not explained himself in the car, simply sat there brooding while Lawrence drove. And he had left the vehicle before it stopped, dashing to the house as if his life depended on it. Yet Michael had chosen to walk to The Butter

Market, forgoing the Arnold Benz for reasons best known to himself. And Lawrence wondered if he had been so flustered that it simply hadn't occurred to him to drive.

They finally caught up with Michael just outside his brother's old study.

"Where is she?" asked Michael, glancing up and down the corridor.

"Who?"

"Aurora. I left without telling her what I'd found. I didn't want to unsettle the poor girl, but she'll be wondering where I am. She must be in her room."

Michael turned as if he was about to go looking, but Lawrence grabbed his arm.

"Concentrate," he said. "Why are we here?"

Michael took a key from his pocket and inserted it into the study lock, frowning as it failed to rotate. He stood, perplexed for a few moments, then Lawrence reached across and turned the handle before pushing the door open.

"It was left unlocked," he said.

Michael shook his head. "Was it? I was preoccupied with other matters when I left. Never mind. Take a look at this." Michael walked towards a bookcase on the sidewall closest to the drawing room. He removed a book at the far end of the middle shelf, slid his hand inside, and pulled a lever. The bookcase swung silently towards them.

Lawrence turned to Violet. "Did you know about this?"

She shook her head. "No. Francis showed me the secret desk drawer, but that's all. What's inside? There can't be much room."

"There isn't," said Michael. "Not on this level, anyway."

He walked towards the bookshelf and pulled it away, revealing a small space just wide enough to contain a staircase.

"How did you know to find it?" asked Lawrence.

"I picked up a set of keys from the bank manager this morning," said Michael. "Francis had a safety deposit box, as you know, and Violet located the key a few days ago. There was little of interest left inside the box," he continued. "A few empty jewellery boxes and some paperwork, which leads me to suppose that Francis sold my father's stocks and my mother's diamonds before he left. But Albert was right. The spare household keys were still there, and I've been able to open all the empty rooms."

"But what luck to find a hidden room," said Violet.

"Not luck," said Michael. "Have you ever been in the attic, Lawrence?"

"Perhaps once or twice when I was younger."

"The same for me," said Michael. "But I remembered enough to know that it didn't feel right."

"What do you mean?"

"The attic room seemed smaller somehow. We didn't go upstairs very often, but Ann had an old doll's house there. Something that belonged to my mother and wasn't in good enough condition to keep in her bedroom. So occasionally, my parents let us play up there to keep Ann company. Anyway, I opened the basement room this morning, then went up to the attic for old times' sake. But it was too small."

"Things seem bigger when you're younger," said Violet.

"No. I mean, it was unrealistically disproportionate. I couldn't work it out. Then I started banging on the walls, and although they were mostly solid, certain hollow areas suggested something beyond them. It took a few hours before I comprehended what must have happened, but when I realised, I checked the downstairs rooms and the same applied to the study."

Lawrence glanced at his surroundings, then at Michael. "Apart from the open bookcase, it looks much the same as it ever did."

"Yes. But how often did you come in here when Father was alive?"

"Never," said Lawrence. "Do you think Francis created the room?"

Michael nodded. "I do. Anyway, I knew there wasn't enough space, but I couldn't work it out, so I took all the books off the shelves in desperation. And there, on the right-hand side, was a lever."

"Where do the stairs lead?" asked Lawrence.

"Follow me. I'll show you."

Michael approached the desk and ignited a gas lamp, which he held aloft as he entered the small space.

"Ladies first," said Lawrence, nodding to Violet.

The staircase was narrow, and Lawrence's shoulders brushed against the wood-panelled sides as he stepped up before arriving at a tiny dog-leg for a further climb. When he reached the top, Michael was waiting.

"Stay here," said Michael before opening the curtains and allowing natural light into the room.

Violet gasped as she looked down and found herself standing on the edge of a painted pentagram in the middle of the floor.

Lawrence placed a comforting hand on her shoulder. "Steady, now," he said as he gazed around the room.

Wall sconces containing old, half-burned candles dotted the walls, and at the far end, they saw a wooden stand, similar to a pulpit.

Michael approached the wooden object, then walked beyond. "Look at this," he said, sliding open another curtain to reveal a rack of robes.

"Freemasonry, perhaps?" asked Violet.

Lawrence removed a garment from the rail and examined the colourful embroidery. He turned it over and ran his fingers across a carefully sewn crescent moon. "No. This is something altogether different."

"What?"

"I'm not sure. What do you think, Michael?"

Michael said nothing but beckoned them towards a wooden chest beneath a bench in the sidewall. He tugged the chest free and opened the lid as Lawrence crouched beside him. "Don't worry. It's not full of crows," Michael said without raising a smile as he met Lawrence's eyes.

"Do you mind if I take a look?"

"Go ahead. I don't want to touch the filthy things."

Lawrence reached inside and removed a leather-bound book entitled Sacred Order of the Crescent Moon. He placed it on the bench, opened it, and flicked through the pages.

"What is it?" asked Violet.

Lawrence frowned. "I don't know. They've used cyphers." He turned a few more pages, "but not all the way through. Have a look, Violet. I'll see what else is in here."

He removed three additional books, a neck chain, and a viciously bladed knife, leaving several metal staffs in the trunk. And when he finished, he turned to Michael.

"I saw something similar when I broke into the Society for Psychical Research. But I don't think they were using it so much as studying it."

"Tell me it's not as bad as it looks," said Michael.

"I'm sorry. I can't. This paraphernalia explains a great deal about your brother's state of mind. We can't ignore the facts. Without doubt, Francis was dabbling in the occult."

#

Michael sat heavily on the bench with his head in his hands. "How can this be? Francis must have had his fill of esoteric matters in the Freemasons. They provided all the pomp and ceremony he could ever have craved, and they are a good and charitable organisation worthy of the attentions of a former superintendent. How could Francis stoop so low?"

"Do you know anything about the order?" asked Lawrence.

"No. Nothing. The church has an uneasy relationship with Freemasonry as it is, but secret societies are beyond the pale, presuming this is a secret society?"

"I'm not sure what it is," said Lawrence. "But the book clearly states that it runs on a hierarchy."

"Definitely," said Violet, who had been quietly skimming through the tome. "The leader's base advancement on degrees of initiation, and they're pleasingly enlightened. Women are equal to men."

"But what do they study?" asked Michael.

"The occult, metaphysics. Various aspects of the paranormal. There are references to astrology, alchemy and astral travel."

"Well, that's a relief," said Michael. "I was beginning to think it was something more sinister than a load of unscientific mumbo-jumbo. Francis comes from a God-fearing family, and he ought to know better. Our father would turn in his grave if he could see this. But as long as it's not harmful, it doesn't matter."

Lawrence was still holding the knife and inspected the blade beneath the lit gas lamp. "There's an inscription here," he said. "But my Latin isn't good enough to translate. Hold this for a moment," he continued, turning the knife, and handing it to Michael with the blade facing away. Michael recoiled.

"I can't," he said. "No matter how much recent events have challenged my faith, I will not touch that object."

"Understood," said Lawrence as he put the knife back in the chest. He picked up a second leather-bound book and peered inside, turned a few pages, and snapped it shut before quickly returning it to the chest.

"You don't want to know what's in that volume," he said, turning to Michael. "Perhaps the order started with innocent intentions, but I've just seen some very disturbing diagrams. God knows how deeply Francis was involved in this, but he's not a stupid man and must have known what he was doing."

"You mean it is dangerous, after all?"

"In a manner of speaking. I hope my views don't offend your faith, but I don't believe in evil, per se," said Lawrence. "I'm not suggesting that those who indulge in this cult-like behaviour will start raising demonic entities. But rituals and incantations of this nature can cause profound psychological disturbances, especially in the easily suggestible."

"But Francis was a leader of men, not a follower. My brother was rational and intelligent. I can't believe he would fall for this nonsense."

"Perhaps retirement didn't suit him," said Lawrence. "Or he couldn't live with himself after what he did to Catherine and..." Lawrence gulped, unable to utter the name of his dead daughter. Violet squeezed his hand.

"Something changed in him," said Michael. "And perhaps you're right. His altered behaviour may have dated from the fire. But what was he hoping to achieve?"

Lawrence stared around the room, trying to imagine a candlelit group of people dressed in embroidered robes inside a painted pentagram, one standing by a pulpit clasping a knife. He shuddered. "No good could come from such a thing," he muttered. "I'll find out more about this, Michael."

"How?"

"As much as it pains me, I'll have to contact the Society for Psychic Research."

"Lawrence, no." Violet stared at him, eyes round with worry.

"There's no choice."

"But it's not safe."

"I'll telephone," said Lawrence. "Myers and his brother are both dead. The danger has passed."

"Do whatever it takes," said Michael. "Francis may return one day, and we need to know how closely he relied on these people. But let's go now. I can't bear to spend another moment in this room."

They filed sombrely downstairs, through the study and into the passageway.

"Go into the drawing room," said Michael. "I'll ask Aurora to rustle up some tea unless you would prefer something stronger."

"Tea will be very welcome," said Violet.

Lawrence strode into the drawing room, opened an ebony cabinet, and helped himself to a glass of brandy. "Not for me," he said. "I'm afraid I need alcohol."

"Are you alright?" Violet touched his arm as she spoke.

"Not really. And you?"

"No. Francis has harmed everyone. But he's hurt you most of all."

"He took the two most precious things in my life and then tried again. But thank God, he failed the second time around."

Violet blushed and lowered her head.

"Violet, it's never too late..."

"She's gone." Michael slammed the door open and ran into the room.

"Aurora?"

"Yes. Aurora."

"Perhaps she's gone to pick up groceries."

"She's taken her clothes."

"What? Packed and left?"

"Only what she can carry. Come and see."

Lawrence gulped the brandy, then followed Michael upstairs and into the second guest room. Violet followed closely behind.

The bedroom was in chaos. The wardrobe stood open and empty, and drawers had been pulled out so quickly from the dresser that they had fallen to the floor. Lawrence pointed to an old trunk standing at the foot of the bed.

"Is that yours?" asked Lawrence.

"No. Aurora brought it with her," said Michael.

"Why would she leave in such a hurry?"

"I don't know. Aurora was happy here. I'm sure of it."

"I wonder if someone has taken her," mused Lawrence.

"I can't see how. I only left for half an hour. And anyway, why would they?"

"Didn't she have connections to a church?" asked Violet.

"I don't know. She wouldn't tell me. Aurora left her last employment suddenly and took great comfort in being here because I was a clergyman."

"So, you assumed she'd been involved with a religious organisation?"

"Well, yes."

Lawrence, who had been gazing out of the window, turned around. "From what you say, bolting isn't new to Aurora," he murmured softly. "She's done it before. She might be the type of girl who takes off when things get difficult."

"But they aren't difficult. Aurora has changed out of all recognition."

"Face it, Michael. You know nothing about her."

Michael sat on the bed, head bowed and staring at the chest as if Aurora might be inside. "I'm a fool," he said. "A weak and trusting fool."

"No," said Violet. "There must be another explanation. It makes no sense. Did she bring you breakfast this morning?"

"Yes. We ate together."

"What did you speak about?"

"I told her I was going to make a start on clearing the basement. I asked her to dig out a couple of buckets for me."

"And she agreed?"

"Of course. Aurora offered to help, but I said it would be better if she carried on cleaning the bedrooms."

"Was that the last you saw her?"

"No. She brought coffee and biscuits to the study. She must have wondered what I was doing with books all over the floor."

"Did she ask?"

"I wasn't paying attention, having just seen the mechanism on the side of the bookcase. I thanked Aurora for the tea and didn't even see her go."

"Did you tell her about the room?"

"No. And that was the last time I saw her."

"But you left the study door unlocked when you left Netherwood."

"By accident. Oh no. You don't think Aurora went inside?"

Violet nodded. "I'm afraid I do. I'm nosy by nature, and if I'd seen you tearing books out of a shelf, I'd be wondering why. And if you left the house, and I tried the study door and realised it was open, wild horses wouldn't stop me trying to find out what you were doing."

"Do you think she went upstairs?"

Violet nodded.

"Then ran off in fright at the sight of the secret room?"

"Not exactly. I suspect Aurora had better reasons to leave abruptly."

"What do you mean?" asked Lawrence.

"We've jumped to the conclusion that she left a religious order, but what if Aurora left a secret society?"

"I doubt it," said Lawrence. "That suggestion defies all credulity. You know I don't believe in coincidences."

"Why not? Francis's secret room is vast. He could have entertained many initiates in there. Who knows how many exist within the organisation and how many groups are scattered through the country?"

"Then why didn't she know it was here?"

"Because she's only recently moved to Suffolk. Before that, she lived in London."

"Did she?" asked Lawrence.

"Yes," said Michael. "At least, her previous employer's address was in the capital."

"Even so. The idea is rather thin," said Lawrence.

"I disagree," said Violet. "Aurora was perfectly happy this morning. While Michael was away from Netherwood, something happened that frightened her enough to leave voluntarily with all the possessions she could carry. It's the only explanation that makes any sense."

"Then we must find her at once," said Michael. "Oh, why didn't I tell her what I was doing? If I'd only said something, she would know that Francis built the room and that nobody's used it for years. She'll think I'm part of this order. This is terrible."

"Search the room," said Lawrence. "She may have forgotten something." He strode towards the bed and examined the pillows, then stripped the bedding and felt beneath the mattress. "Nothing," he said disappointedly. The three searched the room in vain. Then Violet spoke. "Has anyone opened the trunk?" she asked.

Lawrence and Michael exchanged glances. "I assumed it was empty," said Lawrence.

He knelt, loosened the clasp, and opened the lid. Inside was a wooden box containing costume jewellery and various papers and ephemera, including a birth certificate.

"The one thing I doubted turned out to be true," said Lawrence, handing the document to Michael. "Aurora is her real name. Aurora Sutherland, born in Ascot. It's not much help. We need something more recent."

He scrabbled in the trunk while Michael gripped the certificate as if holding it close provided protection.

"Here," said Lawrence, producing a small leather journal. "He flicked through it until he found an address in Bury. "Martha Brame, 14 Long Brackland. She must have lived somewhere before she came here. Does that sound right?"

Michael nodded, his eyes flashing with hope. "Yes. Yes. Aurora has mentioned Long Brackland. Do you think she's gone there?"

"I doubt it. If Violet's right, she will try to get far away. We must split up. Michael. You will best recognise her. Go to the train station via the coach stop and see if you can track her down. Violet and I will visit Martha Brame."

"I'll go at once," said Michael. They bolted from the house, Michael on foot, while Lawrence and Violet sped away in the Wolseley.

CHAPTER TWENTY-THREE

Wandering Rose

May 1902

Rose Harsent was a strange-looking girl. Not comely like some of the village maids, but there was something about her that defied convention, an allure that came from a vivacious personality, masking her plain looks. Rose was popular among the young men, not so much among the women. But I often saw William Gardiner's wife treating her like kin, and she was not alone in her kind and solicitous behaviour. For all those who frowned on Rose's rumoured misdemeanours, others rallied to her cause, taking the young woman beneath their wings like overprotective mother hens. Her behaviour divided the villagers, their opinions settling mainly across religious lines, for Rose was part of the Methodist church.

She was one of them. Some loved her, some loathed her, and some took advantage. I know this because I started following Rose early in May 1902.

I had tracked William Gardiner and found no fault in his behaviour, despite Billy Wright's claims. He was a family man, often lingering to chat with his dear wife as she saw him off on the doorstep. And she, in turn, seemed happy, despite the village gossip, except for one day when Ellen Blowers waylaid her as she was cleaning the windows. She must have delivered bad news, for as soon as Ellen left, Mrs Gardiner sat on the pavement with her head in her hands and remained there for some time. I watched her with deep concern until she was safely indoors. But other than that, the Gardiners seemed content with their lot, though William sported a bushy beard and could have concealed a great deal of emotion beneath it. I waited in vain for him to reveal himself as an adulterer, but he did not oblige. Occasionally, Gardiner passed the time of day with Rose, but only in the presence of others. And if he crossed her in the street, I might see him nod from my attic window, but he didn't spend enough time near Rose for conversation to develop. He rarely left the house after nightfall, which limited my ability to watch him, and in any case, I had decided that after the previous year's scandal, he would be highly cautious and not worth my time. Rose, however, was a young girl and more likely to act on impulse. She would be a better bet, and, as it turned out, she was not averse to leaving Providence House after dark.

I soon learned the patterns of Rose's movements. She would regularly shop on Wednesday afternoons, and I would watch her walking to the store with an empty basket, then see it groaning with provisions on her return. Rose liked to eat an apple on the way back and dallied until she finished, presumably to hide the evidence. She often went to chapel, not furtively as one would suppose, but with a smile, chatting to the villagers as she made her way along the road. Rose was still a topic of gossip, but she carried herself with dignity as if she had risen above it. No one ever ignored or avoided her, and William Gardiner clearly took the lion's share of the blame for the alleged indiscretion.

I saw Rose at her best in the day. There was much that I couldn't detect while hidden from sight, and I took her behaviour at face value. After all, she looked so innocent, so trusting and naive. But at night, she was a different animal. High shrubs surrounded the garden of Providence House, providing plenty of dark corners for a stranger to lurk in. Deacon Crisp had erected a semi-circular stone bench beneath an old oak tree, and I would sit there at night, safely cloaked from sight. Rose's room faced down the street, and I couldn't see it from the garden, but it didn't matter for she came and went through the kitchen, and I tracked her easily as soon as I heard the door unlatch. The Crisps rarely stayed up beyond ten o'clock, and Rose often went out once she knew her employers were asleep. She did not wander far at first but occasionally met with the son of the woman next door. His name was Fred Davis, and I thought him a simple-looking chap and beneath Rose's intellect. For reasons which later became clear, they did not want to be seen and would scurry across the road, one at a time, causing me much anxiety about whether I could get within listening distance quickly and without being seen. But as long as nobody else was around, I could cross the road and crouch beneath the hedge. It wasn't as comfortable as a seated position, and the scarred, twisted skin around my thighs felt tighter still when sitting on my haunches in the night-time cold. But it did the trick.

I learned the art of silence, kept still, shallow breathing my way to restfulness as I listened to them reveal their secrets. Fred, it turned out, was a fixer – a deliverer of useful items. He had procured a leaflet on contraception sometime previously at Rose's request. Fred evidently expected something in return, for he fawned by Rose's side like a spaniel, waiting ever patiently for a treat from his mistress – a treat that never came. Fred was her friend and confidant, but even I, inexperienced, broken and destined to be forever a bachelor, could see she had no romantic interest in the boy. Fred was a fixer, but Rose was a user. No doubt she was fond of the lad. They laughed together, told lewd jokes, shared village tittle-tattle, and she leaned in to kiss him once. Well, I presume it was only once. In reality, I couldn't usually see them. But on this particular occasion, the usually dense hedge had suffered from blight, causing a big enough hole for me to witness Rose plant a kiss on Fred's cheek beneath the full moon. Fred gasped aloud, but she laughed it off, openly teasing, keeping his interest aroused. A planned and deliberate ploy to entice the young man. Fred was not subtle, wearing his desires for all to see. A girl like Rose would never be interested in such an easy catch. But I knew something that the boy did not – several things, in fact.

The first of these came to light only a few days before I last saw them together. Rose had ventured into the garden after dark alone, tiptoeing from the house in her nightwear. She came straight towards me, and for one awful moment, I thought she had seen me. I moved from the bench and shrank into the bushes, turning my head away for fear that the moonlight would reveal my white bandages. I usually wore a scarf over my face, but I had suffered a chill, which had infected my nose hole. Neither Phoebe nor Louisa could bring themselves to clean it, and I could not consult a doctor. So, I made the best of it with saltwater and bandages, typically making myself more visible when I could least afford to. But Rose had not seen me after all, and I cautiously turned to find out what she was doing. Rose had forgotten to bring the laundry in, and I watched as she unpinned her clothes from the line, dropping pegs into her dressing gown pocket. She had nearly finished when her tie became loose, and the dressing gown fell open. Rose thought she was alone and felt no need to refasten it, giving me a glimpse of her full belly. Rose Harsent was with child. There was no doubt about it, and I was likely the only other person in the village who knew.

I kept the secret to myself, determined not to share it with my sisters, at least not until I had found out who had impregnated the girl. It wasn't Fred Davies but perhaps could have been William Gardiner. It almost didn't matter who it was. The village had long decided that Gardiner was predatory and had conducted an illicit affair. Gossip had become fact, and if a signed confession from another man purporting to be the father had turned up, it wouldn't have made any difference. Not that it was likely. Who else could be responsible for Rose's condition? I hadn't seen her with anybody else until then. But that changed at the end of May.

My time in the attic was boring, and I lived my life vicariously through the people I stalked. My forays had become more regular until they reached the stage where I routinely left home several times a night, desperate for news. Night after night, I walked the streets, the fields, the churchyard. But only occasionally did I find something worth waiting for. And on the last day of May, I saw the evidence of Rose's illicit affair with my own eyes. The truth of the matter was depressingly mundane. I was sitting in the garden, idly watching a candle travel through the upstairs rooms, no doubt held by one of the Crisps, when I heard a noise in the distance.

I slipped outside, through the gate and towards Hackney Road, where a figure waited in the shadows. No sooner had the candle gone out than the kitchen door opened and Rose appeared, hissing 'come in'. The man left the shadows and approached the door, and I saw his face in the candlelight. It was old man Ludbrook, a middle-aged lothario from the village, well known for his womanising. Rose Harsent was a crushing disappointment. The girl had no imagination or flair, falling for the age-old siren song of a man who says he will leave his wife but never does. The truth was so dull that I nearly left in disgust. But the thought of sitting all night in the attic, alone and with nothing to do, was unbearable. So, I waited until Ludbrook left again, some ninety minutes later. Rose came to see him off and waved him away with a smile on her face, seeming satisfied and happy. There being nothing else to see, I made for home, then chanced to look back at Rose's window as I crept past the church. A candle still burned in her room, illuminating her face pressed against the window as if she was waiting for something. I flattened my body against the wall and silently waited for Rose to return to her bed. But she did not move.

Rose was watching, lingering, but she had just waved goodbye to her lover, and they had parted on good terms. So, who was she waiting for? I couldn't go home, knowing that something was afoot, so I stayed where I was until she turned away, then I crept through the shadows until I reached the end of Providence House, when the heavens opened, and I sought shelter. Time passed quickly and I left as soon as I could. It was deathly quiet and as still as the grave when I first heard the soft sound of footsteps coming from The Street. When my eyes finally adjusted to the dark, I gasped aloud at the sight of the figure walking towards the kitchen door.

CHAPTER TWENTY-FOUR

Long Brackland

Lawrence and Violet pulled up outside the terraced cottage in Long Brackland. The car had barely stopped before Lawrence jumped out, solicitously opening the passenger door, and helping Violet to her feet.

"What do you expect to find in Aurora's lodgings?" asked Violet as she walked the short distance to the doorstep.

"Who knows? But I want to do something useful for Michael. The poor fellow is suffering terribly."

"I don't trust Aurora," said Violet.

"I'm not sure I do, but it's a matter of helping a friend."

"But is it right for Michael? Wouldn't it better to let her go?"

Lawrence was about to knock on the door but paused as Violet spoke. "It's up to Michael," he said quietly. "We can't decide for him."

Violet bit her lip. "I know. Really, I do. But Michael's been like a younger brother to me. I can't bear to see him ill-used."

"Give the girl a chance," said Lawrence. "We don't know her. There may be mitigating circumstances in the background."

"Very well. Let's see if someone's in."

Violet stepped forward and rapped on the door. They heard a shuffling sound, and the door opened to reveal a grey-haired woman wearing carpet slippers and a housecoat.

"Are you Martha Brame?"

The woman nodded.

Lawrence flipped open his wallet and produced a business card. She eyed it curiously, then dropped it in her pocket.

"What do you want with me?" she asked.

"Can we come in?"

"No. I'm cleaning. It's not convenient. What do you want?"

Lawrence sighed. The temperature had dropped, and snow was falling softly around them. "You'll let all the warmth out," he proffered.

"I don't care. You're not coming in, and if you don't tell me what you want, I'll shut the door on you."

"Do you know Aurora Sutherland?"

"Yes. But the girl doesn't live here anymore. Miss hoity-toity took herself off to a fancier establishment a short time ago."

"But she lived with you until then?"

Martha nodded and bent to pick up a small black object looking suspiciously like a mouse dropping, which she tossed outside.

"For how long?"

"About six months."

"What did she do?"

"A bit of sewing for the last few months and cleaning before that. Why?"

Lawrence ignored her question and fired back one of his own.

"Where did she come from?"

"London," said Martha. "At least that's what she said when she bothered speaking at all."

"Was she quiet?"

"Too quiet," said Martha. "Nobody wants a chatterbox for a lodger, but it wouldn't have done her any harm to pass the time of day with me occasionally. But no, not her. Too wrapped up in herself and scared of her own shadow, she was. Here, she's not in trouble, is she?"

Lawrence shook his head. "No. But we need to find her. Did she leave anything behind?"

"No. But then she wouldn't. She hardly brought anything with her. A change of clothes, a few trinkets and a few bits besides."

"Did anyone visit her?"

"No, never."

Violet pulled up her coat collar and shoved her hands deeper in her pockets. "Did Aurora mention any family?" she asked.

"She didn't have any," said Martha. "The girl was an orphan. Didn't you know?"

"Poor thing," said Violet. "No, we didn't. How sad."

"All alone in the world, she was," said Martha Brame, warming to her theme. "No friends or family. And that's why she surprised me when she upped sticks and moved into that big house. What's it called? You know, the one on Westgate Street.

"Netherwood," said Lawrence.

The woman raised an eyebrow. "Hmm. I won't ask how you know, but it's too grand for the likes of her. She said she'd got a housekeeping job, but I'm not sure about that. Why would a young girl go from sewing to keeping up with a big place like Netherwood? She'd no experience."

"You've said yourself that she was a cleaner," said Violet, jumping to Aurora's defence. "And perhaps she worked in a big house in London."

"She was a scullery maid," said Martha, standing pompously with her hands on hips. "And she only lived in London for a few weeks before coming here. She said she wanted a change of scenery, but it wasn't true. She was running away from something, mark my words."

"Was the house in Knightsbridge?"

"Probably. It was somewhere fancy. The girl said it looked over a little park."

"That sounds right," said Violet, turning to Lawrence. "My letter was addressed to Lowndes Gardens."

"That was it," said Martha. "I remember now. It's where Aurora saw the cats."

"Cats?"

"Yes. Half a dozen felines outside their front door one day. It gave her a right turn, so she said. The girl hated cats."

"So, she talked to you occasionally," said Lawrence.

"Not so as you'd notice," Martha replied, reaching into her apron pocket. She pulled out a lozenge and sucked noisily. "But I'd not long lost a cat before she came, and I was going to get another. Too many mice around here for my liking. And when I told her, she went pale and said she would have to leave."

"That's an extreme reaction."

Martha nodded. "It's a bloody cheek if you ask me. But I wouldn't lose the rent money for the sake of a cat, so I didn't bother."

"Do you know why she was so afraid of cats?"

"No. But it could have been anything. As I said, the girl was scared of her own shadow: cats, men, loud noises, the dark. I don't know how she got through the day. She was always peering out of the curtains at odd hours. Goodness knows why when she had no visitors. But that's what happens when you listen to superstition, so my mother used to say. She didn't have any truck with it."

"Superstition?"

"Yes. Aurora couldn't bear the sight of spilt salt or crossing people on the stairs. You know the type who would rather get hit by a cart than walk under a ladder. And she spent far too much time alone in the church if you ask my opinion. Not going to services like any normal person, but just sitting there, for hours at a time. Don't bring her back here if you find her. The more I think about it, the more strange she seems."

"But not in a bad way?"

"She never smiled," said Martha. "Not once. It's not normal. Now. Have you finished? I need to get on."

Lawrence nodded. "Thank you for your time," he said politely before doffing his hat. They had barely turned around before Martha slammed the door behind them. Violet shivered as she took her seat in the Wolseley.

"Here, take this," said Lawrence, passing over a tartan blanket, which Violet tucked around her knees. "What do you think about Aurora now?"

"I'm ashamed of myself," said Violet.

"Don't be," said Lawrence. "You've done nothing wrong."

"But I haven't been the least bit friendly," said Violet. "I thought she was taking advantage of Michael, but she's just a lonely girl. His kindness must have meant the world to her, and yet she's disappeared. It makes no sense."

Lawrence started the car and pulled away. "I think we must accept that Aurora is telling the truth regarding the little she has revealed about herself. The Brame woman wasn't exactly charming, but there's no advantage in her lying to us. We know Aurora came from London and spent a short time as a scullery maid in Knightsbridge. We don't know where she was before that, but she may have grown up in an orphanage."

"But how will we ever find her?"

"If Michael hasn't tracked her down, then we'll visit her previous employer," said Lawrence. "I've got to go to London, anyway. But let's return to Netherwood and hope for the best."

"Oh, dear," said Violet, as they drove towards Westgate Street, passing the entrance to The Butter Market. "Look over there."

Lawrence groaned as he saw Samuel and Abraham Goddard striding towards their office. "They probably want to know how I'm getting on," he said.

"Drop me here, and I'll walk to Netherwood," said Violet. "Off you go and face the music."

CHAPTER TWENTY-FIVE

Appeasing the Goddards

By the time Lawrence pulled up outside the offices of Harpham and Smith, the Goddard brothers were already outside and impatiently banging on the door.

"Where have you been?" demanded Abraham Goddard as Lawrence drew up, his face red with frustration. Lawrence ignored the question. Not even paying customers had the right to an account of how he spent his day.

"I'm here now," he said. "Come in."

Lawrence unlocked the door and was about to direct the Goddards to the chairs opposite his desk when he noticed a large white rabbit already in occupation.

"What the?" he exclaimed, finding himself lost for words.

Abraham Goddard was not. "There's a rabbit on your desk, Mr Harpham," he said coldly.

"So, I see."

"Is it customary for you to keep animals in your office?"

"Of course not. Did you see it during your last visit?"

"No," admitted Goddard. "But we are here on a serious matter, and this," he continued, nodding towards the rabbit, "does not fill me with confidence. Where did it come from, and what are you going to do about it?"

"I don't know," said Lawrence through gritted teeth, but I will take it outside at once. Now, please take a seat, and I'll be straight back."

Lawrence grabbed the animal, half expecting it to struggle. Instead, it nestled into his shoulder, clearly familiar with being handled. Samuel Goddard smiled sympathetically, but his brother raised an accusatory eyebrow as if finding random creatures around the place was only to be expected.

Lawrence strode into the kitchen and was about to fling open the back door when he noticed it was already ajar. He walked outside with the rabbit to find Cynthia emptying glass into the dustbin.

"Oh, don't bring Mopsy outside. She might escape," she scolded, dropping the dustpan, and snatching the rabbit from Lawrence's grasp. She hugged the animal into her chest and kissed its ears.

"What was it doing on my desk?" hissed Lawrence.

"I dropped a glass, and it shattered all over the floor. I didn't want Mopsy to cut her paws."

"I'll rephrase that. Why is your rabbit in my office?" Lawrence said slowly, emphasising every syllable.

"Because she's lonely," said Cynthia. "And I didn't think you would be in today."

"Why?"

"I don't know. You're in and out. There's no need to be cross. She won't do any harm."

Lawrence opened his mouth to reply, then remembered the Goddards still sitting in the other room. It wouldn't do to keep them waiting. "I'll deal with you later," he snapped.

"Mystery solved?" asked Samuel brightly as Lawrence walked back in and settled at his desk.

Lawrence grunted, trying to avoid further discussion, but Samuel persisted. "A fine, healthy animal," he said.

"It belongs to my cleaner," Lawrence replied.

"I don't care a fig for the rabbit," Abraham Goddard exploded. "And I'd be grateful if you could keep your mind fixed on our objective," he said, turning to Samuel.

"Sorry, brother."

"Let's begin again," said Lawrence, leaning forward and steepling his hands. "I suppose you want to know what progress I've made?"

"Naturally," said Abraham. "And to bring news. You will understand the urgency of the situation when I tell you what has happened."

"I've already heard about Gardiner. They've acquitted him, and he may face a third trial."

"Things have moved on," said Goddard. "Look at this." He thrust a copy of the London *Sun* towards Lawrence, with 'Special Edition' plastered across the top.

"They're expecting Gardiner to be released," said Lawrence. "Surely that's just speculation."

"Read on."

"Oh, released under a *nolle prosequi*. Well, well."

"Meaning that they won't proceed with any further prosecution," said Samuel Goddard, helpfully.

Even Lawrence's pitiful grasp of Latin was sufficient to understand, but he nodded his thanks, anyway. "Ah, I take your point. He will no doubt want to return home."

"Plans are afoot as we speak," said Abraham Goddard. "The Gardiner children will arrive home later today, and Mrs Goddard joins them tonight. If this story is true, and they seem to have an excellent source, then William Goddard should follow her within days, if not hours. But the village is still a seething mess of gossip, and that man deserves some peace of mind. As you probably know, Bottomley of the London *Sun* has set up a shilling fund for the Gardiners and their children, but it won't be enough to live on if the man cannot return to work. We must clear his name as soon as possible, so there's no objection to him resuming his employment at the drill works. What progress have you made?"

Lawrence rubbed his eyes. "Not enough," he said.

"Meaning what?"

"I don't think Gardiner committed the crime. One can never rely on an alibi given by a wife, but Amelia Pepper seems a reliable witness, despite her poor performance in court."

"I'm surprised you think so," said Samuel Goddard, sitting back in his chair and crossing his ankles. "I thought her wholly unconvincing."

"I visited Mrs Pepper yesterday, and she said as much herself. But giving evidence doesn't come naturally to everyone. Mrs Pepper relaxed in her own home and talked willingly and with confidence. I thought she recounted the night faithfully as she saw it."

"You are alone in that view," said Abraham Goddard. "And you cannot offer anything to convince the people of Peasenhall based on Amelia Pepper's word. If two acquittals haven't convinced them, only proof positive of the murderer will. Have you learned anything in that regard?"

"No, I need more time."

"There isn't any. You have twenty-four hours at the most. Or have we wasted our time in employing you?"

"It's not a straightforward case," said Lawrence. "And I have discovered something, but I don't know how it fits into the murder."

"What?"

"The man you call the Creeper is real."

"Is that the extent of your work?" snapped Abraham Goddard. "Is a stupid village superstition all we have for our money? You're a disgrace, Harpham. And I will make sure that your failure does not go unnoticed in this town. Come on, Samuel. We are leaving."

Abraham Goddard scraped his chair back and stood, glowering at Lawrence as Samuel sat quietly in his chair.

"I said we are leaving. Come now, Samuel."

"How do you know?" asked Samuel, ignoring his brother.

"I saw him," said Lawrence.

"Stuff and nonsense," spluttered Abraham, advancing towards the door.

"Wait," said Lawrence. "I am not a liar. I saw the Creeper, and I tell you, he is a real flesh and blood man."

"Where? When?"

"Earlier this week in the churchyard."

"What was he doing there?"

"Trying to hide. I chased him from Providence House."

Abraham Goddard blinked as he regarded Lawrence through suspicious eyes. "Are you sure?"

"Of course, I'm sure." Lawrence was getting irritable now and in no mood for Goddard's cynicism. "Sit down and listen."

Abraham Goddard returned to his chair and stroked his greying sideburns. "What did he look like?" he asked.

"I don't know. It was dark, and the Creeper had wrapped bandages over his head."

"As a disguise?"

"No. There was something wrong with the man's face."

"Then you are mistaken. Nobody in the village answers to that description."

"Perhaps he came from elsewhere?"

"I'm sorry, Mr Harpham. It's a little too convenient. And anyway, whether or not this man exists has no bearing on Rose Harsent's murder."

"That's just it. I think it does."

"No," said Samuel Goddard, who had been listening quietly. "I must agree with my brother. There were no reports of the Creeper until after Rose died. If he'd killed her, wouldn't we have heard something before?"

"I didn't say he committed the crime."

"What then?"

"Well, he's followed both Bill Wright and Fred Davies, who are witnesses in the case."

"Yes, but Ellen Blowers is not."

"No," said Lawrence slowly. "But I hear that she's a gossip."

"Irrelevant. Peasenhall is full of chatter. That's why we've paid for your services."

"Listen," said Lawrence, staring straight into Abraham Goddard's eyes. "If I'd realised the immediacy of the situation, I would have stayed in Peasenhall. Your religion relies on an unshakeable faith in God. You don't need proof to believe in him. When I investigate a case, I gather as much factual evidence as I can. But a point inevitably comes when logic isn't enough, and instinct takes over. And I am telling you that if you want to know the truth about Rose Harsent, we need to find the Creeper. At the very least, he is a distraction, but all my senses tell me he is key to solving this crime."

The Goddards exchanged glances, and Abraham gave an imperceptible nod. "Very well," said Samuel. "But there's no time to lose. You must come to Peasenhall now."

"Agreed," said Lawrence, taking his fountain pen from the stand. He strode towards Violet's desk and scribbled a note on her journal. "I'll be right behind you."

CHAPTER TWENTY-SIX

What Mary Knew

Wednesday, January 28, 1903

Violet sat at her desk and read Lawrence's note for the fourth time. She'd returned from Michael's yesterday, collecting Daisy from school, and had gone home without giving much thought to Lawrence. But now that she knew he was in Peasenhall, Violet felt a pang of guilt. Yesterday had been a busy day, and she'd had the pleasure of high tea with her little girl, followed by a relaxing evening reading a book. Yet Lawrence, it transpired, was back on the case and hard at it while a broken-hearted Michael languished alone in Netherwood. Of the three of them, she was definitely in the happiest position.

Violet stoked the fire and wandered towards Lawrence's desk. He had evidently left in a hurry as his chair, and the two opposite his desk were in the same state that the occupants had left them. Obsessively tidy, Lawrence would usually have tucked his chair under the desk and aligned the others with determined accuracy. His note said little, but having seen the Goddards the day before, Violet assumed they had recalled him to Peasenhall to finish the investigation. And from the little he had told her, Violet didn't like his chances of success. She liked, even less, the thought of Lawrence in a village with a predatory stalker and wondered, for a moment, whether she should join him. But the days were long gone when she could take off without a second thought. Daisy needed her, and although an unplanned and late-life surprise, Violet adored her daughter. And as independent and business-minded as she was, Violet wouldn't have changed the way things had worked out for the world. So, she dismissed the idea and accepted the limitation of her day.

As Violet rearranged the chairs, she noticed several round objects beneath Lawrence's desk and recoiled in disgust as she recognised them as droppings. Surely there couldn't be rats in the building, she thought, while simultaneously ruling out mice because of the size. Violet wandered into the kitchen and fetched a dustpan and brush before sweeping up the droppings and dumping the offending objects into the dustbin outside. Violet sighed as they dropped onto shards of glass, a sizeable chunk of which she suspected was from Lawrence's favourite whisky tumbler. Cynthia must have had another accident, and she was glad that Lawrence wasn't around to witness it. He'd changed considerably over the last few years and mellowed in ways Violet could never have imagined. But that did not include patience, and his tolerance for someone making repeated mistakes was negligible. It was only a matter of time until he lost his temper with Cynthia, resulting in the need to employ another cleaner. Good workers were scarce, and Violet did not relish the prospect. Still, that was a worry for another day.

Violet was back at her desk when the door went, and Michael appeared, rear first, shaking an umbrella onto the doorstep.

"Any news?" asked Violet?

Michael handed her the small pile of letters that the postman had just handed over. "I was hoping you had news for me," he said

Violet shook her head. "Sorry."

"What about Lawrence?"

"He's in Peasenhall."

Michael groaned. "What shall I do?" he asked, sitting heavily on Lawrence's chair.

Violet removed an envelope from the pile and examined the postmark. "This might help," she said, slitting it with a brass letter opener.

"What is it?"

"A letter from Aurora's previous employer. She must have written back by return."

"Why? But that must mean...?"

"Yes. I'm sorry. I was worried about you, and I wrote to her on Tuesday."

Michael swallowed his annoyance and approached Violet's desk. "What does it say?"

"That Mrs Sedgington employed Aurora, who was a good worker, but hurriedly handed in her notice without explanation, leaving some of her possessions behind. And on that basis, Mrs Sedgington cannot recommend her."

"Then I'll never find Aurora."

"You might. I'll write back and ask if Mrs Sedgington knows anything about Aurora's background."

"We should go there. Now."

"No, Michael. If we're going to do this, we'll do it properly."

"What do you mean?"

"Lawrence and I will take this on. We'll find Aurora. But Lawrence is on a case he cannot abandon, and I must take care of Daisy."

"That's not good enough. I can't wait."

"You must. We need Mrs Sedgington's cooperation. Be patient for a few more weeks, and we'll investigate Aurora's disappearance as we would do any other."

"But the trail will have gone cold."

"There is no trail. We don't know where Aurora has gone. But the best way to find her is to unravel her life. Backtrack and see if she has any family or friends, presently unknown, who she might have tried to find. I know it's hard, Michael. But we must do this well. Find something to do to keep your mind off it."

"You are right, Violet," said Michael, heading towards the door.

"Where are you going?"

"To find Lawrence in Peasenhall. I don't suppose I'll be much use to him, but anything is better than rattling around Netherwood without Aurora."

#

No sooner had Michael left the office than the doorbell jangled again. Violet looked up to see the unexpected sight of Gracie Francis and Edward Fisher entering the office.

"How lovely to see you both," she said. "Although I'm afraid I have made no further progress. Did you see your grandmother?"

"Yes," said Gracie, smiling at Violet. "This is for you." She handed Violet an envelope. "May we sit?"

"Of course," said Violet. "Excuse me for not offering. You surprised me. For me? Whatever is it?"

"Open it," said Gracie.

Violet did as she asked, and her eyes widened as she felt inside before retrieving several banknotes. "What's all this money for?"

"Your fee," said Gracie.

"But I haven't solved the murder."

"Not directly," said Gracie. "But your wise advice led me in the right direction."

"Anybody in?" came a voice from the rear.

Violet turned around to see Cynthia approaching via the kitchen door.

"How did you get in?" asked Violet.

"I took the second key."

"That belongs to Mr Harpham."

"He left it by the sink, and I prefer coming through the back door."

Under any other circumstance, Violet would have rebuked her, but now was not the time. "Can you bring us a pot of tea?" she asked.

"Of course."

Violet turned back to face the young couple.

"You look happy," she said to Gracie, peering closely at her face. The black circles under the young woman's eyes had disappeared, and she seemed relaxed and worry-free.

"I've got something to show you," she said. "My grandmother gave it to me the day that Phillip and I visited. When we first arrived, she said she couldn't help and knew nothing of any value. Grandmother feared I was wasting my time, but the longer we stayed, the more she came out of herself. And when we stood to leave, Grandmother asked Phillip if she could have a few moments alone with me and left the room for a while. When she returned, she handed me this letter. She insisted I open it alone and counselled me to use the information wisely. Well, my first instinct was to tell Phillip, of course. I kept meaning to on the way back, but fear stopped me every time I opened my mouth to talk. And loyalty to my grandmother took priority, I suppose. Anyway. I'm glad I didn't mention it."

Cynthia arrived with a tray of tea and set it on Violet's desk. Violet held her breath, waiting for the usual sloppy handling, but the tea, milk and sugar stayed firmly in their pots.

"Anything else?"

"No, you can go," said Violet, smiling at Cynthia as she walked towards the kitchen. Violet took a second look as the door closed. For one moment, she thought she saw something white and furry on the floor, then decided it must be her imagination.

"Here, take this," said Gracie, handing her another envelope with a small, folded note pinned to the outside.

"Do you want me to read it?" asked Violet.
Gracie nodded.
Violet unfolded the note and read the shaky hand.

Dear Gracie,

Excuse my poor writing. I have penned this in a hurry. I wanted you to know that I too, have faced adversity in my marriage plans and am the last person to stand in the way of yours. Before you arrived, I had decided to conceal the truth about the Tibenham poisonings, but now that I've met your young man, my conscience won't allow it. You must be in full possession of the facts to adequately determine your future. You will not like them, but life is full of difficult choices. Know that I do this with the best of intentions. I trust you will not reveal the contents of this letter to anyone in the family, although the person concerned is long dead,

Your loving grandmother.

"Is this what I think it is?" asked Violet, her heart thumping.
Gracie nodded. "Yes. It's a confession."

#

June 1872

My dearest niece,

I am an old lady now, in failing health. The best of my life has passed by with little time remaining here on earth. I have been a widow for thirty long years and lost many children along the way. I value those still living more than life itself, despite their faults, of which there are many. But in recent days, certain knowledge has come into my possession, causing much angst and regret. I have swayed between concealing this information or trusting it to another. I was minded to tell my eldest living daughter but soon

213

decided that it would bring too great a burden upon her. After a restless night of tossing and turning, I rose in the small hours to consider my options and concluded that I must keep it away from immediate family for not only is Susannah in low spirits of late, but she is prone to rapid judgement, and once she sets her mind against someone, she won't budge an inch. So, I thought back to the days before I lost my husband. What would William advise if he hadn't passed away?

Your uncle was not a man given to rash impulse. He would have considered the matter in his own quiet way. Although he had a trade, his mind was active, his intelligence profound. He liked to read, and he encouraged me to do likewise. And unlike other men, he would talk to me as an equal. I know how his mind worked and the methods he used to resolve problems. He would not have wanted to keep this a secret and would have turned to somebody he could trust. How I wish William had been alive when Mary and Elizabeth died, for he would have contributed much wisdom to the puzzle, but God called him some years before, and we faced the ordeal alone.

How selfish of me to describe it thus. Though Mary and Elizabeth were well-loved sisters-in-law, my grief cannot compare with yours, my dear Mary. You, the eldest child of Elizabeth, bore the brunt of her loss. I well remember how you gathered your younger siblings, comforting them as they tried to comprehend the death of their mother, helping your father with the day-to-day chores, while you sacrificed your feelings for the good of the family. And that is why I thought of you. For you alone can decide what to do with this information. You are far enough removed, both geographically and as a niece rather than a daughter. And despite your father's opinion of your husband George, I have always found him to be a good man, and I know he will support you, should you decide to tell him. Knowing how close you keep things, I suspect you will not.

Of all my children, Hannah was my greatest trial. I heaved a sigh of relief when she married, hoping that was the end of her immaturity. No parent can reasonably expect their children to be angels, but from the moment the police caught Hannah misbehaving when she was still a young woman, I feared she would bring trouble to my door. But she matured nicely after leaving for Norwich, working long hours, and coming home whenever she could. We grew close again, and I looked forward to her visits. Hannah wasn't just attentive to me, but to her uncles and aunts as well. And like the rest of us, she disliked Eliza Sage with a vengeance.

I never understood why Hannah was so passionately against Eliza. She was kindly, in other ways, impulsive, perhaps, hence her youthful brush with the law, but she wouldn't hurt a fly. Maybe it was because she was fond of her family, and none of us could bear Eliza. Wasn't it you, dear Mary, who called her the Maleficent Maid? Then again, it might be because Hannah is a quiet girl. She got into trouble trying to impress her friends, but ordinarily, she was slow to put herself forward, and others took advantage of her reticent nature.

Hannah has thrived since her marriage. Have you met her husband? He's a gruff old ex-army pensioner from Suffolk, and they are a good match. She seemed settled and content. At least I thought so until a few weeks ago when she came to see me in some distress. Hannah had taken herself for a walk and chanced to see a magpie along the way, and though usually as superstitious as I am, she thought nothing of it. But she made the mistake of returning on the same path. This time, there were several birds clustered around a fallen stump. Hannah counted seven and thought of the old song, One for sorrow, Two for mirth, Three for a funeral, Four for a birth, Five for heaven, Six for hell, Seven for the devil, his 'ain self. Thoughts of the rhyme consumed her. They would not leave her. It was, she said as if the devil was whispering in her ear. Naturally, she came to me and told me all about it, and I laughed it off. There are many versions of this song, I told her. Don't worry about Old Nick. Why should he bother with you? And she went silent, Mary. So eerily quiet that I feared she was unwell. Then she looked at me and asked if I would forgive her if she'd done something very wrong. I told her that, of course, I would. And that if she had something to say, she had better get on with it. For I knew then, as I do now, that time is not my friend.

Well, Mary. The tale she told me chilled me to the marrow. I can scarcely believe that it's true. And in my wilder moments, I hoped she had a nervous complaint that laid her low and caused her to misremember the past. But deep inside, I knew she had unburdened herself for a reason. She was in turmoil and has been for many a year because of a wicked and impulsive act. And because she is my child, I quite naturally forgave her, and I hope you will do likewise. For, Mary, in telling you this and transferring my burden to you, I must ask that you watch out for Hannah and keep her safe. I know it isn't easy, living in a different village. I don't expect you to live cheek by jowl trying to protect her, but when I am gone, write to her, visit occasionally, counsel her if she needs it. Her siblings, I fear, will not. They don't understand Hannah. You must wonder by now what Hannah did. Well, I will tell you.

You already know that Hannah found rat poison in my sister-in-law's possessions. At the time, it seemed logical for her to look. Mrs Reeve had said that if they found poison on the premises, it did not bode well for anyone. So, when Hannah received an invitation to her uncle's house, as she had done on so many previous occasions and went looking for the stuff, everyone sighed with relief when she found it. Nobody questioned why she went straight to the arsenic or why she asked Eliza Sage to dispose of the bottle later. After all, Hannah had been more or less instructed to by Mrs Reeve.

Hannah held her secret for years. And once she started telling me her story, she couldn't stop. Every little detail emerged, and as I looked at my daughter, the scales fell from my eyes, and I wondered why I had never guessed. But what mother would seek to know such a terrible truth? For Hannah had poisoned her aunt and uncle quite deliberately. And when I asked her why, she said,

216

at first, that she didn't know. Then the truth emerged. It was an act of revenge, pure and simple. The killings were typical of Hannah's rash behaviour. She had known her aunt kept rat poison on the premises and happened across the powder during a previous visit. She came to see me the day before her aunt died, but I didn't know then that she had also been to Mary's house. I doubt Mary or Joseph were aware either, for they weren't at home when Hannah saw Eliza Sage shaking a tablecloth outside. The two girls exchanged words about something that Hannah can no longer remember. Eliza, sharp-tongued as always, thought nothing of the argument, but Hannah took her cruel words to heart. And when Eliza went to the garden to feed the chickens, Hannah used the opportunity to slip inside the house. She could have stopped herself, thought better of it. But instead, she took the poison and shook a small amount over the bottom of the spare kettle, expecting to make her aunt and uncle poorly. Eliza was not the cleanest of servants and was sure to be blamed when they fell ill. Hannah returned to Norwich and did not discover the consequences of her actions for another two days. It shocked her to the core when she found out, but not enough to reveal her part in it.

I did not know this at the time, Mary, or even suspect it. Hannah was calm and unruffled at the inquest, her demeanour as innocent as the next persons. If it weren't for Constable Bloomfield, we would never have known that she asked Eliza Sage to bury the poison bottle, and he alone thought it odd that Hannah knew its precise location. My daughter escaped justice from the law, but not from the demons living inside her head. She has twice visited since she first told me only a short time ago, and death has dominated our conversations. Hannah regularly attends church to pray for forgiveness and fears she will go to hell on Judgement Day. I said she might find peace if she contacted Eliza Sage, but the girl married and went up north to who knows where. Besides, it wouldn't do to tell anyone outside the family. Even after all this time, the authorities could still charge Hannah, and I cannot risk it.

*So, Mary. I appeal to your kindness. Watch over Hannah, keep
her secret, and destroy this letter.*

Your loving aunt, Susannah

#

Violet lowered the letter. "I can't believe it," she said. "How utterly
extraordinary."

"Isn't it," said Gracie.

"You must be devastated. I'm so sorry."

"Whatever for?"

"Well, it's the news you dreaded. How has your fiancé taken it?
I see he isn't here. I hope that doesn't mean that your marriage
plans are over."

Gracie smiled and reached for Edward's hand. "Phillip doesn't
know about Hannah, and yes, we won't be marrying now."

Violet regarded her. Gracie was still smiling and far from the
upset woman she would have expected under the circumstances.
"Have you got something to tell me?" Violet asked, watching as
Edward entwined his fingers around Gracie's hand.

Edward grinned. "There will be a marriage," he said. "Gracie
has consented to be my wife."

"Congratulations," said Violet, jumping to her feet and shaking
his hand. "But you've well and truly got the better of me. How did
this happen?"

"You'd better start the story," said Edward, his eyes twinkling as
he regarded his intended.

"I said goodbye to Phillip and opened the letter as soon as I got
home," said Gracie. "And as you say, it devastated me and spelt the
end of my prospective marriage. For one brief moment, I truly
hated my grandmother for revealing her secret. She could so easily
have said nothing, and the wedding might have gone ahead."

"Doubtful," said Edward. "You had proved nothing to Phillip's
family's satisfaction."

"No, indeed," said Gracie. "Well, as you can imagine, I was beside myself. I didn't want to tell Phillip for obvious reasons, so I rushed to Edward, as I always do when I have a problem. He wasn't at home, and I walked back to an empty house feeling alone and bereft. I barely slept that night and couldn't wait to get into work to ask Edward what to do. I arrived early yesterday morning, and Edward was already in the office, thank goodness. I showed him the letter and asked for his advice, and he put his arms around me while I sobbed into his shoulder. He did nothing, said nothing, but let me cry until my tears had dried. There was still half an hour to go before anyone else was due, so Edward made me a cup of tea, and we sat on the stairs and talked. He told me he would employ someone to manufacture evidence against Eliza Sage and send it to Phillip if that's what I wanted. I told him that would be fraudulent, and he could get into trouble, and then, well – tell Miss Smith what you said."

Edward blushed and looked down. Then his eyes met Violet's. "I told Gracie that Phillip was a fool, and if he loved her as I do, her background wouldn't matter a jot. It was foolish, careless. I could have lost her friendship. The words left my mouth without thought of the consequences."

"But you didn't lose my friendship," said Gracie. "Instead, you gained a fiancée. Are you surprised, Miss Smith?"

"Not at all," smiled Violet. "I suspect you were the only one who didn't know Edward was in love with you. And it's rather wonderful that you feel the same."

"He didn't think he was good enough," said Gracie. "Not with Phillip's future inheritance in the background, and of course, we won't be able to get married straight away. We don't have enough money between us. We will never be rich or own a house in the country, but when I woke up this morning, the thought of not having to worry about Phillip's family anymore was a tremendous relief. And the joy of being loved by a man who doesn't judge me is best of all. I only regret that I didn't realise how Edward felt much sooner."

"What will you do about Phillip?" asked Violet.

"I'll see him today," said Gracie. "It won't be easy, but I owe him an explanation, and it's only right to tell him face to face. No doubt, his relief will be as great as mine."

"And your family?"

"I suspect my grandmother already knew what would happen. She gave me that letter for a reason and understood that in doing so, my prospects of convincing Phillip's family were over if I revealed what was inside. My grandmother is very wise. I could have destroyed the letter and pretended it didn't exist. But I'm not like that, Miss Smith. However uncomfortable, I value the truth. And as distressing as things were until Edward spoke up, it was worth it."

"And thank goodness for my impulsive declaration," laughed Edward. "If I'd given any thought to it, my pride and fear of rejection would have stopped me in my tracks. Our futures would look very different now." He beamed at Gracie as if she was the most precious thing in the world, and Violet's heart swelled with pleasure at the satisfactory ending to a complex case.

"I'm thrilled for you, but I can't justifiably take my fee," Violet said.

"You must," said Gracie. "None of this would have happened without you. It's money well spent."

"Goodbye," said Edward, offering his hand. "We won't hesitate to recommend your services."

Violet watched from the window as they walked down the street, Edward's arm protectively around Gracie. He was an impressive young man, naturally kind and considerate. But having seen him in Norwich, determinedly hiding his feelings for Gracie, it surprised her that he had lost his resolve to stay silent in the heat of the moment. She couldn't imagine impulse ever ruling her decisions. It wasn't Violet's way. But what Edward said about pride and rejection made her feel uneasy. Lawrence had rejected her for Loveday, and for the last three years, she had been firmly in control, determined to rise above her feelings for him. Her plan had been successful, and she was mostly content with life. But would she still be happy if Lawrence gave up hope and found somebody else? Not that he would if he truly loved her. He would persevere, no matter what. But over the years, Lawrence had become more logical and less reliant on his feelings.

Perhaps, one day, he would simply decide that it was not to be and move on with his life without her. After all, he could afford to do as he pleased. Violet tried to imagine another woman living at Lawrence's house in Angel Hill. An unintended vision of Loveday, dressed in her finest gown, barged into Violet's thoughts – Loveday playing the piano in the drawing room and sitting opposite Lawrence at the dinner table. But when Loveday appeared in the walled garden throwing a ball to Daisy, Violet found herself blinking tears away. She left the window and sat back at her desk before opening a journal to tally their accounts. It didn't distract her from the vision now rooted in her head.

CHAPTER TWENTY-SEVEN

A Shocking Gossip

Lawrence woke in a cold, damp room in a Peasenhall cottage, having finally found refuge late the previous night after an exhausting search for accommodation. He had approached the Angel Inn again, but now that the village was crawling with reporters pending the expected return of Mrs Gardiner, rooms were scarce. He had tried a second inn, and the same applied. No beds were available – not a single one. Lawrence had been heading for his car and about to face the prospect of a late, cold drive back to Bury when George Whiting had passed him on his way back from the public house. Lawrence had explained his problem, and Whiting had grinned. "I know just the thing for you," he had said before leading Lawrence to a ramshackle cottage on the edge of the village. He'd exchanged words with the elderly woman before requesting an unreasonably sizeable sum of money from Lawrence, most of which he trousered, before leaving him in the company of a half-deaf, half-blind woman. Lawrence attempted to engage her in conversation out of politeness, but it was futile. Nevertheless, she seemed unperturbed by her unexpected guest, showed him to his room and retreated to hers.

Lawrence slept surprisingly well. For a woman who had little income, she kept her spare room tidy, with plentiful blankets and a duck down bolster he'd sunk into before falling into a deep sleep. The lack of heating was a different matter. As soon as Lawrence peeled back the covers, chilly air crawled across his skin, and he dressed in indecent haste, forgoing his usual morning ablutions.

He descended the stairs and found, to his surprise, that his host, Mrs Fairweather, was not alone. She was sitting in the parlour with a man who turned out to be her husband and who had been absent the previous night. Unlike his wife, Samuel Fairweather was not hard of hearing and shook Lawrence's hand as if he was an old friend before offering him the room for another night if he required it. Mrs Fairweather suggested breakfast, but Lawrence declined. From the pitifully small loaf and the scraping of butter on a chipped saucer, he could see that they could ill afford to feed him. So, paying for his room in advance for a night that he may or may not need, he left the house with his stomach rumbling.

Lawrence walked towards the churchyard, remembering a convenient bench where he could sit and focus his thoughts. He had returned hotfoot to the village full of plans to find the Creeper. But truth to tell, Lawrence didn't know where to start. He knew first-hand that the Creeper was real, but if nobody had seen his face, then he would be impossible to find. Perhaps the Creeper was less deformed than he had first appeared and was simply wearing a clever disguise, which would make his mission harder still. Lawrence closed his eyes, trying to visualise the Creeper squatting behind the gravestone, and the memory returned with fearsome clarity. Those haunted eyes, the puckered skin, and the missing eyelid. No, the Creeper was wearing a mask to cover his face, not from an attempt at anonymity, but because he didn't want anyone to see the damage he had sustained. Lawrence wondered how the Creeper had kept his identity secret for so long. Somebody must have helped him – someone in the village who knew who he was and agreed to conceal him; family perhaps, or a loyal friend.

Lawrence removed his gloves and chewed a jagged nail on his scarred left hand. He stroked the raised bumps across his skin, remembering how he had hidden his hand from sight for many years after burning it in the fire that claimed his wife and child. Or, more accurately, Francis Farrow's lover and child. He hadn't used gloves out of vanity or shame but to hide the daily reminder of his loss. Surely, the Creeper was doing the same. Something had happened to him, and he couldn't bear the memories. But understanding his quarry did not make finding him any easier. Lawrence flexed his fingers forwards and back, stretching the scarred skin. His hand was almost fully functional again, weaker than the right, but with none of the earlier problems when he could barely use it. He had been lucky in that regard, and if he was going to solve this case, he needed another dose of luck.

"No, I don't." As the words left his lips, Lawrence realised he was speaking aloud and adopted an internal monologue instead. Good detective work has nothing to do with luck and everything to do with deduction. What would Violet do? he thought. Violet would carry on interviewing until she'd spoken to everyone. Then she would sit down and analyse their responses. But Lawrence had less than twenty-four hours before it was too late. He didn't have time for idle chatter, hoping something would develop from it. No. He would have to use his default position, his tried and tested instinct. What was it telling him? That everything centred around the Creeper, and he must find him. But how? He could speak to Bill Wright if he could get within a yard of him, but that was unlikely with reporters milling around the village. Who else had had direct contact with the Creeper? Ellen Blowers, of course. And she wasn't a witness and had been nowhere near the Gardiner case.

He could get to her with ease, as long as she was at home, wherever home was.

Lawrence jumped to his feet and walked straight to George Whiting's cottage, knowing he could quickly provide an address. Whiting was toiling over a last in the workshop when Lawrence arrived. He pushed the half-open door and strode through without knocking.

George Whiting looked up and raised a sandy eyebrow. "Happy with your lodgings?" he asked.

"Yes. More than satisfactory. I need your help."

"Go on?"

"Where does Ellen Blowers live?"

"Why?"

"I want to talk to her."

George did not press the matter. "Church Lane," he said. "Blue door halfway down with a boot scraper in the shape of a rooster outside. You can't miss it."

"Thank you," said Lawrence, turning on his heel before he had even finished speaking.

#

Contrary to Lawrence's expectations of a dowdy middle-aged harridan, Ellen Blowers was a relatively young woman, only thirty years old, with high cheekbones and soft hazel eyes. Had she remained silent, Lawrence would have considered her beautiful. But the moment she opened her mouth, a torrent of ill-considered words revealed her as an inveterate gossipmonger who enjoyed speaking ill of her neighbours. Lawrence employed no skill in encouraging her to talk to him. He didn't need to. She relished the opportunity to spew information unguardedly in the guise of being helpful, and seconds after Lawrence announced himself, she took him to the kitchen, where they sat by the fire.

"The children are at school," said Ellen, "and Benjamin is working. It's a good thing too. My husband disapproves of honest opinion, but he's wrong. What's the point in pretending? If you've got something to say, just say it and never mind the consequences."

"Then I'm sure you'll be invaluable," said Lawrence.

"I'm sure I will. That's what the reporter said last night."

"Oh. I didn't think they would bother you, not being a witness to the crime."

"He didn't come here if that's what you mean. But I heard him speaking to Mrs Pepper, and the silly woman was talking about William Gardiner as if he was a perfect angel. Well, he wasn't. I can't say that he killed Rose Harsent, but he wasn't innocent by any means. Bill Wright saw them together, you know. And I believe Bill. Why would he lie? Just because Gardiner was his foreman. That's all the more reason for frankness, don't you think?"

Lawrence opened his mouth to speak, but Ellen was already answering her own question.

"Fonso agrees with Bill. They saw Gardiner at it," she continued. "In the doctor's chapel, no less. Well, there was a big Methodist meeting, and they cleared Gardiner of any wrongdoing. He's one of them, and Bill Wright isn't. It wasn't fair. I mean, really. What sort of justice is that?"

Lawrence seized the opportunity to speak. "How well did you know the Gardiners?" he asked.

"Him, not at all. I didn't like the look of the man, all swarthy and bad-tempered. And as for that simpering little wife of his, she's not worth the bother. We were friendly once, but she took umbrage at a bit of well-meant advice and hasn't spoken since. Well, it's her loss. I have lots of friends, and the few old biddies she had are deserting her in droves. Serves her right for being a doormat."

"Why do you say that?"

"If my husband brought disgrace to my door, I'd make him pay. Not let him go about his business as if he was the victim."

"But what if he was? They've acquitted him twice."

"I don't care. Gardiner's lucky. But it doesn't matter, anyway. If a man gets himself into such a pickle that he's arrested and charged, it doesn't matter if he committed the crime or not. He's stupid, and stupidity comes at a price. Mrs Georgiana Gardiner will suffer rumours and innuendo for the rest of her life. She's a fool to tolerate him. I told her that, and she didn't like it."

"Is that why you stopped speaking to each other?"

"No. That was the other thing."

"What other thing?"

"The thing Rose's mother said."

Lawrence raised an eyebrow and waited for her to continue. Ellen took the hint and leaned forward conspiratorially.

"Rose's mother told Sarah Self that she thought Rose might be in the family way. Well, Sarah is a nurse, and she let it slip to Bridget, who told a few others."

"I thought nobody knew."

"Nobody knew for certain," said Ellen. "But Rose's mother suspected. Anyway, naturally, I told a few people. I think it's important for folk to know the truth about their neighbours. The girl had fallen into bad ways, whether or not by Gardiner."

"Ah," said Lawrence. "So, you told Mrs Gardiner."

"I thought she should know. After all, Rose was a family friend. But I didn't expect her to get so protective over the girl. Mrs Gardiner didn't believe a word of the gossip, you see. She thought that careless talk had cost her husband his reputation, and she said she didn't want the same thing happening to Rose. She told me to stop spreading unfounded rumours and said she didn't believe Rose was pregnant. Well, she had to eat her words when Rose died a short time later, and Dr Lay found she was with child after all."

"Have you ever considered that Gardiner is innocent?"

"I told you. It doesn't matter. Perhaps William Gardiner didn't kill Rose, but he got too close for a married man."

"Tell me, what would it take for the gossip to stop? If someone else killed Rose, would that be enough for William Gardiner to return to the village and live a normal life?"

"The gossip, as you call it, will stop when hell freezes over. It's too late. Gardiner was never popular in Peasenhall, and we're as tainted as he is by what has happened. Don't you see that? It doesn't just affect him. We're all judged."

Lawrence considered her words. It was the first sensible and non-malicious sentence Ellen had uttered during her long diatribe. She was right. The Goddards had set him an impossible task. William Gardiner would never be free from speculation if he returned to Peasenhall. And as long as he lived in the village, his life and theirs would remain in limbo. There was no point in continuing with the investigation. He would return the advance to the Goddard brothers and go home in time to collect Daisy from school.

"Thank you," he said, rising to go. "You were most accommodating, and you have helped me to put things into perspective."

"Is that all you want?" asked Ellen disappointedly.

"Yes. I understand the way it works now. Gardiner's situation is untenable, and nothing will make a difference. It's a matter of accepting things as they truly are."

"Exactly," said Ellen. "That's what I said to Phoebe Mullings the other day when she complained about the cost of liniment. Two whole pence more than the previous week, she said. Though goodness only knows how she can have got through two bottles in so short a time. I couldn't see anything wrong with her, but I suppose she has a rash or a bite concealed beneath her clothes. Not that I'm surprised when she lives in such squalid conditions. I mean, the house is big enough, but then she inherited it from her father, and she doesn't keep it very clean. But I wouldn't want a three-storey house with a poky little attic room if someone gave it to me on a plate. I swear Phoebe spies on people. I always feel eyes on me when I walk down The Street. Mind you, it's far from the worst home in Peasenhall. You should see Betty Smith's house. I went inside once and saw a rat sitting on the mantle as bold as you like. And then there's that hut on the Badingham Road. I wouldn't put livestock in it, but old Harold lives there all year round, whatever the weather. It leaks, you know. He must be as hardy as a goat."

Lawrence rose and made for the door while Ellen was still in full flow. Now that he had decided to abandon the case, he didn't need to listen anymore. He would collect his bag from the Fairweather cottage, and with a bit of luck and good driving conditions, he would back in Bury in a few short hours.

"Are you going?" called Ellen as he walked away.

"Yes. Thanks for your help," said Lawrence, closing the door behind him.

CHAPTER TWENTY-EIGHT

Stalking the Stalker

Lawrence whistled as he walked away from the house, glad to be free of the gossip and relieved to be giving up on an unsolvable case. Violet wouldn't be happy when she heard. It would be lean pickings for the business this month, even if Violet solved the Tibenham case, which was looking increasingly unlikely. He would find a way to help her if their cash reserves dropped too low, but he wished with all his heart that she would swallow her pride and allow him to make a fair financial settlement on her and Daisy. Lawrence admired Violet's tenacity and determination. She was an independent woman living in a man's world. Others might judge her harshly, but Lawrence felt only pride at Violet's strength of character. If only he hadn't pursued Loveday, they could be together now. But Lawrence could never regain her trust, and perhaps it was time to stop trying. Violet had made her feelings very clear, and he didn't want to be the type of man who rides roughshod over a woman's wishes in pursuit of selfish happiness. Lawrence was middle-aged and set in his ways. He had always imagined growing old with a loving wife, and he did not want to suffer the boredom of retirement alone. If Violet didn't want him, someone else might. Sadness washed over him as a second wave of clarity hit him hard. He would die alone and unloved if he didn't seek a companion now. As much as he adored Violet, it was time to let her go. He would always stay close, forever a part of Daisy's life. But he would accept things as they were and not try to force change.

Lawrence was about to cross the road when he noticed an automobile parked outside the village store. It looked strikingly familiar, but it took him a few moments to comprehend who it belonged to out of the usual context. The vehicle he was staring at was an Arnold Benz identical to the one Francis Farrow had owned, which meant that Michael must be in Peasenhall for reasons unknown. No sooner had these thoughts crossed his mind than Michael emerged from the shop clutching a brown paper bag.

"What are you doing here?" asked Lawrence.

"Wasting time," said Michael gloomily. "I still can't find Aurora. Violet said you would investigate when you could. I can't face the thought of returning to Netherwood, and so I came to find you. Perhaps I can be of some use?"

"When did you arrive?"

"An hour ago, or thereabouts. I was hungry," Michael said, opening the brown bag to reveal a pasty. "What sort of man worries about his stomach when his friend is alone and afraid?"

"You don't know that," said Lawrence. "We're only surmising."

"I can feel it, Lawrence. My years of counselling parishioners have left me sensitive to distress. Aurora is alone. She's frightened and can't trust anyone, least of all me."

"Wait a moment," said Lawrence before disappearing into the shop. He returned almost immediately with an identical brown paper bag. "Follow me."

"Where are we going?"

"To the churchyard," said Lawrence. "It's frosty, but we can eat and talk before returning to Bury."

"Have you finished?"

"In a manner of speaking. Here, take a seat."

The two men sat side by side, eating their food in companionable silence while ruminating over their various problems. When he had finished, Lawrence crumpled the paper bag and put it in his pocket. "I will do anything I can to find Aurora."

"Thank you. I appreciate it. Violet has offered some useful ideas about where to start."

"Good," Lawrence replied. "She's a far better detective than me."

"What's wrong?" asked Michael.

"Nothing. But it's been a long time since I've given up on a case. Wounded pride, I suppose."

"Given up? Why?"

"Because they've asked me to solve a murder hoping that a man can return home and live a judgement-free life."

"You're referring to William Gardiner?"

Lawrence nodded.

"And you haven't discovered who killed Rose Harsent?"

"No. But more importantly, I've realised that it doesn't matter. Even if I could provide proof positive of someone's guilt, it won't make any difference. Too much has happened. There's no reversing public opinion."

"So, Gardiner is damned whether guilty or innocent?"

"I'm afraid so. The least I can do is return my advance to the Goddards. We'll leave as soon as I've tracked them down."

"I'm surprised at you," said Michael.

"For accepting the inevitable?"

"Not that. You've no choice in the matter. But the old Lawrence would want to know who committed the crime regardless of the outcome. A young girl has died horribly, and she'll never get the justice she deserves."

"I know, and I'm sorry, but perhaps it's time to wave the old Lawrence goodbye. Thinking you can change the world is a young man's game. I am old enough and wise enough to know when to let go."

"You're not only talking about the case, are you?"

Lawrence ignored him. "None of it matters," he said.

"Every life is important," said Michael. "Rose Harsent was a servant girl, and she made mistakes. But she was somebody's daughter and might have been a wife and mother or gained useful employment as a nurse. She could have saved lives, brought happiness, raised a child who invented something important. Who knows what her future might have held? Instead, she is lying dead in the ground, and her family will never know why."

Lawrence stared into the distance, stung by Michael's words. "Don't you believe in accepting the inevitable?" he asked.

Michael shook his head. "I've known Aurora barely any time, but I will never stop looking for her. Perhaps I'll find her, and she will laugh in my face, tell me I'm a fool and ask me to leave her alone. But I must know. Don't give up, not until you've exhausted every possibility. If you truly believe you've done everything in your power, then walk away by all means. But I know you, Lawrence. You will regret abandoning this case if you do it too soon."

Lawrence tilted his head back, stared at the sky, then faced forward, emitting a deep, heartfelt sigh. "I can't get any further without finding the Creeper."

"Ah yes, Violet mentioned him. She's worried about you."

"He's elusive, impossible to find, Michael. If I had more time, then perhaps we could conduct a thorough search, but as it is…"

Michael waited for a moment, and then he rubbed his arms as the cold air infiltrated his greatcoat. "We'd better go."

The two men left the church and soon encountered a crowd of people clustered around Alma Cottage.

"Urgh. Reporters," said Lawrence, watching a wisp of smoke emerge from the chimney pot. "Mrs Gardiner must be back, poor woman. She'll be cowering inside for days if they don't leave her alone. Oh dear, that's unfortunate."

"What?"

"You mean who. The man with his hand on Mrs Gardiner's door is Samuel Goddard. I need to tell him I'm leaving, but not in front of the press. Can you imagine what would happen to our business if they seized upon my failure and published an article?"

"They have bigger fish to fry," said Michael. "I hope the local ministers are helping. This press intrusion must be very distressing."

"Yes," agreed Lawrence. "The cottage is so close to the road that there's nowhere to hide from prying eyes. Even if reporters weren't camping outside, they could get a good eyeful anywhere close." He glanced down The Street towards Providence House, and his eyes settled on a property across the road – a three-storey house with ill-fitting windows in need of repair. But Lawrence's interest did not lie in the property's condition, only the triangular attic window at the end of the eaves. Ellen had spoken of something similar during their earlier conversation.

"Look at that," said Lawrence, pointing to the window.

"What about it?"

"How much do you think you can see from there?"

"Plenty. The shop, most of the houses, the footpath."

"Not Providence House though," said Lawrence. "The tree is in the way. Even so. Let me think for a moment."

"About what?"

"Someone I spoke with this morning said she felt as if someone was watching whenever she passed this house. And," he continued, clicking his fingers, "the liniment. God, I'm such a fool. Who needs cream?"

"Someone with a skin complaint?"

"Exactly. But to use two bottles in as many weeks indicates a significant problem. This is it, Michael. Are you coming?"

"Where?"

"Over there," said Lawrence, pointing to the house again.

"I don't understand."

"You will if you follow me. We're going around the back. I can't afford to be seen by reporters."

Lawrence walked towards the property at the end of the terrace, glanced behind him, and then proceeded towards the garden. He strode to the rear door and loudly rapped, then waited.

"Why are we here?" hissed Michael.

"Because somebody in this house is watching as people pass by. And this person needs regular medication."

"Do you think—" asked Michael, but he did not have time to finish his question before the door opened and a woman in her late thirties appeared. She stood shivering in the doorway, wrapped in a thick, bedraggled shawl covered with animal hair.

"You're letting in the cold," she complained.

"Are you Phoebe Mullings?"

"No, I'm Louisa. Phoebe is my sister."

"Can we come in?"

"No. Phoebe wouldn't like it."

"Very well. Do you and your sister live alone?"

"Mind your own business. Go away. I don't want to talk to you."

"Don't be frightened," said Michael. "We mean no harm."

"The woman pushed her chest out and drew herself to her full height. "I'm not afraid, you nosy blighter. But I don't have to answer your questions unless you're the law. Now, bugger off and leave me alone."

Lawrence put his foot in the door. "The shawl you're wearing has seen better days. Would you like a new one?"

Louisa stared at him, open-mouthed. "I might be poor, but I'm not some dolly mop," she retorted.

"That's not what I meant," Lawrence replied coolly, extracting his wallet.

"What do you want then?"

"Information."

"Alright," she said, eyeing the coins greedily. "But we'll have to talk outside."

"No," said Lawrence. "There are press reporters everywhere."

"Sorry. You can't come in, and that's the end of it."

"Do you and Phoebe live alone?" Lawrence asked again.

Louisa bit her lip and glanced behind her. "Yes," she mumbled. Lawrence watched as her throat speckled red, revealing her nervousness. He was right. She was hiding something here in the house.

"Where do you want to talk?" he asked.

Louisa pointed to a low wall twenty yards farther down the garden.

"Ladies first," said Lawrence, waving ahead.

As Louisa walked away, he gestured to Michael to follow. Neither Michael nor Louisa noticed as Lawrence doubled back to the house until he slammed the door shut and turned the key.

"Get out," shrieked Louisa, hammering on the door, but it was too late. Lawrence was inside.

#

Lawrence swept through the small kitchen and into a dingy parlour, with a mean-looking fire smouldering in the grate. A look around the room revealed only functional items at first glance. Two wooden chairs and a stool were clumped around the fireplace, and a single tattered curtain hung from the window. But despite the evident poverty, two new dresses of differing sizes were hanging from the door recess. Lawrence touched the fabric. It was of good quality and incongruously opulent compared to the living conditions. The sisters, it seemed, were happy to save their money for luxuries at the expense of a good standard of living. At least one of them must be in a well-paying job unless they were getting funds elsewhere. Lawrence took the stairs two at a time and found two bedrooms on the next floor with a narrow set of stairs to what he supposed was the attic. He quietly tiptoed up to find himself in a room running across the width of the house. A straw-filled mattress lay in the highest-ceilinged part of the room, and at the windowless end were several trunks, an old broken bedstead, and a stack of chairs, none of which appeared intact. Lawrence walked towards the window opposite and sat on the three-legged stool nestling in a recess beside it. Then he peered out of the window and watched as the people of Peasenhall went about their business. Lawrence could see the grocer's store and Alma Cottage. As he suspected, Providence House was just out of sight, and the window provided a clear view of anyone walking along The Street. But a large tree obscured Rose Harsent's window, and Lawrence wondered what information the Creeper could provide, even if they had found him.

The Creeper couldn't have witnessed the murder from this room, assuming he was in Peasenhall at the time of the crime. Yet, had he taken to following people, as seemed to be the case, then perhaps he had seen something useful on his travels. Lawrence stood to leave, but as he scraped the stool back, he clipped something which rolled towards the window. It was a brown bottle. Lawrence unscrewed the lid and peered at the chalky viscous liquid inside, then smelled the contents. The bottle contained calamine lotion. Lawrence was right, and the Creeper lived right here in the attic. Filled with a renewed sense of purpose, Lawrence proceeded towards the trunks at the end to see if they contained anything of interest. He was just making his way across the squeaky floorboards when he thought he heard a rustle in the room and stopped for a moment. Silence returned once he was still, and Lawrence set off again, assuming the sound was nothing more than the creaks and groans of an old house. Lawrence knelt beside the trunk in front of the furniture and eased the clasp free, then he opened the lid and stared in surprise at what appeared to be an old uniform. He stood, shook it free, and his eyes settled on a blue sailor's outfit of the kind worn by ratings. As Lawrence examined it, he chanced to catch sight of a recess behind the bedstead and noticed an item looking suspiciously like the tip of a shoe. He quietly returned the uniform to the trunk and stepped right to get a better view. But as he moved, he trod on another loose floorboard, which let out a sharp squeak, immediately marking his presence in that part of the room. Lawrence barely had time to think before a stack of chairs came crashing towards him, hitting him squarely on the chest. He fell backwards, breaking his fall with his elbows and narrowly avoiding bumping his head on the floor just in time to see a man with a bandaged face running out of the attic room at breakneck speed.

Lawrence hurled the chairs aside, jumped to his feet and set off downstairs in hot pursuit. But the Creeper was ahead and ran straight to the locked rear door. Lawrence reached the bottom of the stairs just as the Creeper realised that not only was the door shut, but someone had taken the key. Louisa Mullings was on the other side of the door, and Michael was out of sight. The Creeper gasped and lunged for a drawer, removing a sharp-bladed knife. Waving it in front of his body, he advanced towards Lawrence with a trembling hand. Lawrence raised his arms in a gesture of surrender and backed towards the parlour while the Creeper continued towards the front door, turning as he approached to keep the knife ahead. The Creeper reached behind, clutched the front doorknob, and darted outside, stooping low beneath the hedge as he crossed the neighbouring property. Lawrence bolted through the front door, almost catching up as he spotted him trampling through a vegetable plot, but the Creeper knew the area well, and Lawrence did not.

The Creeper vaulted across a low gate and set off across the fields, running with an odd gait, half stooped yet fleet of foot. At first, Lawrence tracked him easily, running towards him as his bandages made him visible in the flat, frosted fields. But once he headed for the edges, crossing in and out of hedgerows, Lawrence caught only intermittent glimpses as he traversed the fields. Then, just as Lawrence started gaining ground, the Creeper vanished into a densely wooded area at the end of the field. Undaunted,

Lawrence followed, crashing through the undergrowth until he found himself alone. He stopped and listened, hearing nothing but the pitter-patter of rain as a cloud broke above. Lawrence patiently waited. The Creeper was not so far ahead that he could move without Lawrence hearing. And after ten minutes, the sound of movement rewarded his patience. He watched as the Creeper broke free from the cover of a low bush, evidently believing himself to be alone. Lawrence ran towards him, determined to close the gap. The Creeper bolted, running full pelt through the woods, his feet heavy on the leafy floor. Lawrence was getting nearer. He could hear the Creeper panting, his breath short and panicked. He was only ten feet away, then five, and Lawrence lunged forwards, grabbing a coat sleeve. But the coat was unbuttoned, and the Creeper squirmed free, slashing his knife towards Lawrence before turning and running away. Lawrence dropped the garment, took a deep breath, and kept going. The Creeper was slowing again while Lawrence gained ground.

"For God's sake, stop," yelled Lawrence. "I only want to talk to you."

The Creeper did not reply but ran on, his stoop more pronounced than ever. He was no longer panting but made another sound, a strange keening like an outpouring of despair.

"Stop. I won't hurt you." There was barely any distance between them now. "Stop," yelled Lawrence again.

The Creeper turned around, waved the knife, then turned back again. But tiredness made him careless, and he didn't see a large tree root in front. Lawrence was almost level when the Creeper fell to the floor, then groaned as if all the life had left him. Lawrence dropped to his knees and examined the fallen man. A large red stain welled across the Creeper's trousers. He stared at Lawrence in shock, still holding the knife, now bloodied and with a jagged end where the tip had come away.

"Let me help," said Lawrence, removing his scarf. The man offered no resistance.

"What's your name?" Lawrence worked quickly as he joined the ends and tied them tightly around the man's punctured thigh. Then he removed his coat and placed it over the Creeper's shoulders before hauling him up to recline against a tree.

The Creeper's breathing was loud and laboured.

"I'll fetch help," said Lawrence.

"No. Don't leave me." His voice, when it came, was gentle.

"There's a lot of blood. You've nicked an artery," said Lawrence. "You'll die if I don't do something quickly."

The Creeper brushed his hand across his thigh and examined the bright red stain. "It's too late," he said.

Lawrence tightened the rudimentary tourniquet. The bleeding slowed to a trickle but did not stop.

"Is there anything you want to say?"

"Tell my sisters that I died painlessly. I'm not sure they care, but they'll want to know."

"What happened to your face?" asked Lawrence, bluntly.

"Open my shirt."

Lawrence loosened the man's cravat and opened the top two buttons, then stared at his scarred and pitted skin in undisguised horror.

"What happened to you?" he asked.

"There isn't time," said the Creeper.

"Does anyone know?"

"Phoebe and Louisa. They took me in, but they did not want the rest of the village to find out. But for that, I would have sought my old friend."

"I can give him a message. Who is it?"

"It doesn't matter."

"What's your name?"

"Jacob. Jacob Mullings."

"Well, Jacob," said Lawrence gently. "You're right. You've lost a lot of blood, and you may not survive. If you want to pass on a message, now is the time to do it."

Jacob closed his one remaining eyelid, and a tear slid into the bandage.

"I can't," he said.

"Why don't I ask you some questions," said Lawrence. "Perhaps you know something about Rose Harsent's death."

Mullings winced, whether, from his injuries or something else, Lawrence couldn't tell. "I can't talk about that," he said.

"You must."

"No. I've known too much disloyalty to inflict it on another."

"But an innocent man will suffer."

"If you mean Gardiner, nothing I can offer will improve his position."

Lawrence sighed. "So, I keep hearing. It's not fair."

"Life isn't fair," whispered the Creeper. His eyelid was closing, and his face had taken on a deathly parlour.

"Tell me what you know before it is too late."

The Creeper opened his eyelid and stared languidly at Lawrence.

"Will you make a solemn promise to a dying man?"

"I will."

"Promise you will do right by the Gardiners."

Lawrence stared in surprise. "I thought you said you couldn't help Gardiner."

"I can't. You must listen now. I'm growing weaker."

Lawrence touched Mullings's neck, his fingers settling over a welt of scar tissue as he located the carotid pulse. It was feeble and barely perceptible.

He moved next to the man and sat beside him on the forest floor, leaning against him to share his body warmth.

"I lived in Sibton when I was young," Mullings whispered. "Cyril and Georgie were my two best friends. They were good to me when nobody else cared. And I swore I would always protect them. But I returned to Peasenhall looking like this," he continued. "I would not have inflicted myself on public view, even if my sisters had allowed it. But when I saw Georgie, after all these years, I wanted so much to reveal myself. But I couldn't. It wouldn't have been right. I could only watch from a distance and remain a loyal friend. I heard the rumours about Gardiner from my sisters. And having nothing better to do, I followed him and then I followed others besides. But everything changed when Rose died. I could no longer watch people for amusement. Now I needed to find out what they knew and offer my protection."

"Did you kill Rose?"

Mullings sighed, and his head lolled momentarily against the tree. "No. Of course not."

"But you saw what happened?"

"Yes."

"You saw Rose's lover?"

"It was Ludbrook," said Mullings.

"Henry Ludbrook killed Rose?"

"No. Ludbrook was Rose's lover. He lay with her that night, but when he left, she was perfectly well. I know because I saw her."

"Then who?"

"Remember your promise."

"I do. I will not use this information against the Gardiners."

"It was Georgie. My old friend Georgie killed Rose."

I presume you mean George Whiting?" said Lawrence.

Mullings stared at him silently, and his eyes grew glassy. Lawrence took his pale hand and patted it sharply. Mullings continued to stare vacantly ahead and listed towards him. Lawrence turned, knelt directly in front of him, and gently slapped his cheeks. It worked. Jacob Mullings opened his eyes. "What did you say?"

"I was talking about George. How do you know he killed Rose? Did you see him do it?"

Mullings shook his head. "I didn't say that. Listen properly."

"Tell me, then – quickly, man."

"I saw Ludbrook leave, but Rose was still awake, and a candle burned somewhere in the room. She was evidently expecting Ludbrook, but I couldn't help feeling there was still some unfinished business as I walked away. So, I doubled back and waited in the garden of Providence House, as I had done so often before. But at about half past eleven, the heavens opened, and the rain came lashing down. It happened so quickly that I didn't have time to think. The Crisps put a small conservatory on the back of the house, which they rarely locked. I ran towards it, just as thunder crashed across the sky, and it was open, thank God." Mullings shuddered at the memory.

"Go on," said Lawrence.

"I found a blanket on the back of a rocking chair, covered myself and watched the storm. I only intended to stay until the rain stopped, but I was warm and dry, and before long, I dropped off. I woke at about twenty past one. The storm was over, and I was angry with myself for falling asleep, so I opened the door and went on my way. But as I left the garden, I heard the soft sound of footsteps running towards the house. So, I hid by the hedge and watched Georgie approach and open the door."

"Why didn't you tell anyone?"

"I couldn't," said Mullings. "Hush now and listen."

Lawrence nodded and squeezed the man's hand.

"I waited a few moments and peered inside the kitchen window. Rose had come down from her bedroom and didn't look surprised to see Georgie, at least not at first. But then Georgie said something, and Rose stood with her hands on her hips, looking puzzled. I don't know what Rose said, but Georgie's face was a mask of fury, and I suddenly saw the glint of a knife as it plunged into Rose Harsent's neck. Blood spurted from the wound. Rose fell heavily, dislodging a shelf and its contents, which fell to the floor just as she let go of the paraffin lamp. Flames licked around the spilt fuel, and Georgie took one look and ran towards the door. I barely managed to dart into the hedge before it was all over."

"But tell me, man. Where can I find Georgie?"

"Come closer," said Jacob Mullings before whispering in Lawrence's ear.

CHAPTER TWENTY-NINE

Righting a Wrong

Thursday, January 29, 1903

Jacob Mullings expired less than half an hour after uttering his final words. Lawrence had wrapped his arm around the dying man and stayed close until his chest stopped rising and falling, then he had lowered him to the ground and covered his face with a handkerchief. Lawrence had set off for the village at a run but soon stopped, his energy sapped and his thoughts elsewhere. He crunched across the field, returning the same way that he'd come, feeling sick at the idea that Mullings might still be alive if he hadn't chased him until he fell. It was late evening by the time Lawrence had reached The Street, and he'd headed straight for Dr Lays' house, hammering on the door until his housekeeper answered. The doctor had sent for help, and Lawrence directed Alf Grice and a few trusted others to the wood where Mullings' body lay. Then he had returned to the Fairweather cottage, exchanged a few insignificant words, and went upstairs to bed where he spent a restless night, tossing and turning as images of Mullings' broken body infiltrated his dreams. Dr Lay had warned Lawrence that there would have to be an inquest, but as long as Mullings' injuries were consistent with his story, he had nothing to fear. But Lawrence wasn't worrying about legal matters. The dilemma of what he ought to do about the information given by the dead man solely occupied his thoughts. Lawrence had made a promise. A solemn promise and feeling responsible for Mullings' death, he was determined to keep his word.

Lawrence lay in his bed contemplating the matter as dawn slowly rose, and the birds started singing. He was still there two hours later, angsting over his potential actions, when a cheery greeting from Samuel Fairweather followed a knock at the front door. Moments later, he heard the soft tread of feet, and Michael walked in.

"There you are," said Michael, sighing in relief. "I spent half the night looking for you?"

"How did you track me down?"

"I heard there had been an accident, and you found the body, so I visited the doctor hoping he would know where you were."

"Ah. Good old Dr Lay. A man with a fine ear for detail. I barely mentioned the Fairweathers, but he was obviously paying attention."

"Yes. Well, Dr Lay wouldn't tell me very much. He seems to think Mullings' death was accidental."

"It was," said Lawrence.

"Did you tell him you were in pursuit?"

"No. I told the doctor that I saw a man fall, went to investigate and found Mullings lying on the ground with a knife wound."

"But you didn't tell him you think he is the Creeper?"

"No, and I'm not going to. I've thought about it all night. Phoebe and Louisa were ashamed of their brother. I doubt they would welcome publicity, and I'm sure they will remain silent on the matter. But I'll visit them later to be on the safe side."

"I wouldn't get too close to Louisa Mullings. She'll have your guts for garters. She was furious."

"Undoubtedly, but I'll do whatever it takes to keep her quiet."

"Why?"

"Because I would prefer it if talk of the Creeper faded away. There is no reason for anyone to connect Mullings with Rose Harsent, Bill Wright, or Ellen Blowers. If Louisa and Phoebe keep quiet, it will appear as if their long-lost brother returned from sea one night, suffered a tragic accident and expired."

"I don't understand. I thought you needed to find the Creeper to solve the crime?"

"As I told you, Michael. It won't make any difference in the scheme of things. William Gardiner must leave Peasenhall never to return."

"So, you're just going to walk away from the investigation?"

"No. I'm going to visit the Goddard brothers and discuss the matter with them."

"Well, you might be in luck. I've just seen Abraham Goddard running the gauntlet of reporters outside Alma Cottage."

"Excellent timing," said Lawrence. "Let's hope he's still there. Go downstairs for a moment, there's a good chap. I need to change."

Five minutes later, Lawrence was leaving the cottage fully dressed and carrying a small overnight bag. The two men walked briskly towards Alma Cottage, negotiating their way past a small pack of reporters as they approached the front door.

"Let's hope Goddard is still here," muttered Lawrence, knocking loudly. "I don't like our chances of getting inside, if not."

For once, luck was on his side. Abraham Goddard opened the door and raised a bushy eyebrow at the sight of Lawrence.

"Now is not the time," he hissed. "Mrs Gardiner is very distressed, as I'm sure you can imagine."

"Trust me when I tell you that it's exactly the right time," said Lawrence. "I need to tell you something that Mrs Gardiner ought to hear. Please let us in."

"I don't think so," said Goddard. "I'll speak to you when I've finished here."

"No. Now," said Lawrence, pointedly looking towards the reporters.

"This better be good," growled Goddard, opening the door to allow the men access.

Lawrence bent his head and walked through the door, then proceeded towards the parlour. Sitting inside was a small, dark-haired woman dressed neatly in a black gown with a high lace collar which looked likely to be her Sunday best. Beside her sat Amelia Pepper and an older woman with grey hair shaped into a bun around which she had pinned a black veil.

"Who are you?" asked the woman, looking anxiously towards Goddard.

"Mr Harpham, this is Mrs Gardiner. Mrs Gardiner, Mr Harpham and his friend."

"But what does he want?" asked Mrs Gardiner, directing the question back to Goddard.

"He has yet to tell me," muttered Goddard.

"I must speak to you privately," said Lawrence, turning to Mrs Gardiner.

"No," said Goddard firmly before she could answer. "Anything you want to say to Mrs Gardiner, you can say in front of me."

"Agreed," said Lawrence. "It's essential you hear this too. But ladies, please give us some privacy."

"Stay if you wish," said Mrs Gardiner, her eyes round with concern.

"No, dear," said Amelia Pepper. "I need to get back anyway."

"I don't," said her companion.

"It's for the best," said Amelia. "Come along."

"Mrs Pepper, Mrs Dickinson, good day to you," nodded Abraham Goddard, touching his forelock.

He escorted them from the house while Michael and Lawrence waited in silence, watching as Mrs Gardiner glanced anxiously towards Goddard. She let out a sigh of relief when he returned to the room.

"Now, what do you mean by this, Harpham?" asked Goddard, sitting heavily in the chair vacated by Amelia Pepper.

"I mean to tell you who killed Rose Harsent," said Lawrence. "And then you're going to let me know what to do about it."

#

The room fell silent, and then Mrs Gardiner let out a stifled sob.

"What do you know?" asked Abraham Goddard.

Lawrence hesitated. "Before I go any further, I promise I can and will keep this information secret if that is what you decide."

"Why would I want to do that?" asked Goddard, leaning forward with his hands on his knees. "I purposely employed you to locate the murderer so Mr and Mrs Gardiner could live freely among their friends without judgement."

"Hear me out," said Lawrence.

"Nothing you can say will stop me going straight to PC Eli Nunn as soon as you reveal Rose Harsent's killer."

"Very well. Have it your way. But you may feel differently when I tell you that her killer is in this room."

Michael started in shock while Abraham Goddard's face turned florid, his eyes bulging in disbelief. "How dare you make such a foul implication?" he said, thumping his hand on the upholstered armrest. "I'm a man of God."

"Not you," said Lawrence, shaking his head. "Nor Michael, before you make that assumption." Lawrence turned to Mrs Gardiner, who was quietly weeping in the corner. "But we can't say the same for you, now, can we? Why don't you tell us why you murdered Rose Harsent?"

"Don't be a fool," cried Goddard, sitting upright and glaring with unbridled disgust.

Lawrence ignored him. "I'm afraid it's true, isn't it, Mrs Gardiner. Tell me your maiden name?" he continued.

Mrs Gardiner pulled a handkerchief from her sleeve and wiped her eyes but said nothing.

"Your name," said Lawrence firmly.

"Georgiana Cady."

"You were quite a tomboy when you were younger, and your two closest school friends were Cyril and Jacob."

Georgiana Gardiner looked up, her eyes wide with surprise.

"How do you know?" she asked.

"Because Jacob Mullings died last night."

"No. You are wrong. Dear Jacob went to sea many years ago and never returned. I haven't laid eyes on him for fifteen years."

"Yet he has lived only a few yards from your house for some time now."

"What? Here in the village?"

Lawrence nodded.

"Then why didn't he visit me?"

"He couldn't face you or anyone else," said Lawrence. "I don't know how it happened, but he suffered injuries of a most disfiguring nature. He kept out of public sight, but I spoke with him before he died, and he said that he has watched over you since the day he returned."

Georgiana Gardiner closed her eyes as if in pain, then blinked new tears away.

"What has this got to do with Rose Harsent?" asked Goddard.

"Are you going to tell him, or shall I?"

Mrs Gardiner put her head in her hands and sat quietly, hunched over her lap, her breathing shallow as she fought for composure. Goddard stood to go to her aid, glowering at Lawrence as he moved, but before he could reach her, Georgiana raised her head and looked Lawrence straight in the eye. "Did you mean it when you said you could keep my secret?"

Lawrence nodded. "Yes. But Mr Goddard must make the final decision, and I will abide by his choice."

"Then I will tell you everything," said Georgiana. "Abraham, you have been so kind. Please don't be too disappointed in me."

"What are you trying to say? Don't let Harpham force you into well-intentioned lies. You obviously couldn't have hurt anyone."

"Mr Harpham is correct. I killed Rose Harsent. I wish I could say that her death was accidental. But that would be untrue. I killed her quite deliberately, and I did it to save my family."

"But why would you do such a thing?"

"Because William might have left me had Rose borne his child."

"His child? I thought you didn't believe the rumours?"

"I didn't. I firmly believed my husband's denials, especially when the ministers cleared him of all wrongdoing. Months passed, the gossip petered out a little, and I thought we were home and dry. But Ellen Blowers stopped me on the doorstep a few days before Rose died with a story so utterly horrifying that I knew I must act. She told me that Rose Harsent was with child and her source was impeccable. Nobody knew the father, but everyone supposed it to be William. I wanted to scratch her eyes out, the little cat, but for the first time, I seriously considered the prospect that William might have done me wrong. I wasn't in my right mind, Abraham. I had just lost a child, and it seemed so unfair, and the thought of William having fathered Rose's baby sent me reeling. I didn't know what to do. I couldn't eat, and I barely slept. All I could do was think about it. Then, suddenly, it came to me. I would see Rose and have it out with her. I would make her tell me if she carried William's child, but I didn't want to speak in front of anyone. William was at home in the evening, and Rose worked during the day. It wasn't a suitable conversation to have on the street, and I knew I must conduct it privately. But if I asked to see Rose late at night, she would wonder why and might not let me in. So, I copied William's handwriting, wrote her a note and slipped it under the kitchen door while Mrs Crisp was out."

"Ah. So Ludbrook wasn't the letter writer."

"Ludbrook? Why would he write to Rose?"

"No matter," said Lawrence. "What happened next?"

"I should have met Rose at midnight," said Georgiana. But I couldn't get away from Mrs Dickinson. William and I finally left a little after half past one. I checked the children, and William went to the privy. Well, my husband has long suffered from poor intestinal health, and his visits to the outhouse are never quick, so I tucked in my eldest, then hastened to Providence House while William was otherwise occupied. Rose had left the kitchen door open in anticipation of her visitor, so I went inside, turned up the lamp and waited. She must have been on tenterhooks as she was wide awake and heard my arrival from her bedroom. I suppose she must have kept her door open and listened out for movement. Anyway, I was there barely any time before she arrived."

"No doubt thoroughly surprised to see you."

"Yes. But Rose wasn't hostile, not at first, just startled. But I didn't have time to beat about the bush, so I asked her straight out if the child was William's. Rose burst into tears, then became angry and accused me of being a jealous, possessive shrew. She was furious at the accusation but refused to deny it. I lost my temper and pushed her, and she fell against the door. A bottle of paraffin dropped and ignited, burning Rose's dress. I didn't know what to do, so I ran."

"You've missed a bit," said Lawrence coldly.

"I don't think so."

"The knife. You cut Rose Harsent with a knife."

"In the heat of the moment. I didn't mean for it to happen. We were both angry, and before I knew it, her blood was all over my hands."

Abraham Goddard was sitting bolt upright in his chair, pale-faced and open-mouthed, staring at Mrs Gardiner as if he didn't recognise her. "That poor girl," he whispered.

"It was an accident."

Goddard shook his head and stared mutely at Lawrence.

"The question Mr Goddard would ask if he were not reeling in shock, is why you had a knife with you?" said Lawrence, fixing Mrs Gardiner with a steely stare.

Goddard nodded imperceptibly.

Georgiana Gardiner's complexion changed from pale to beetroot in a few short seconds. She licked her lips. "I don't know why I took it with me," she said.

"Did you leave Providence House immediately?"

"Yes."

"Try again."

"No. I used a spill to spread the flame across Rose's dress. Then it would look like an accident."

"Except that the body didn't burn, and the murder and pregnancy were still obvious."

Goddard cleared his throat and spoke. "Do you honestly believe your husband was the father of Rose Harsent's child?"

"Ellen said so, and Rose didn't deny it."

Lawrence flashed her an angry glare. "Ellen Blowers is a shocking gossip. Yes, she had found out that Rose was in the family way. But her theory about the father was plain wrong. And I know this for a fact. Jacob Mullings told me everything as he lay dying. And hear this, Mrs Gardiner – Mullings watched Providence House for several hours on the night of the murder. He saw everything, including a visit from Rose's lover. You don't need to know who that was, but your husband was and remains innocent of that charge."

"Oh, no." Tears fell freely down Georgina Gardiner's face, and she did not try to cover her eyes. "What have I done? William has gone through hell, and none of it was necessary."

"I saw you at the trial," said Lawrence, "and the depth of your grief struck me as sincere. You were inconsolable, and I suppose you were finally feeling guilty for your husband's suffering. And mark my words, he has suffered as no man should, facing two trials and coming within a whisker of being charged again with the risk of a capital sentence. Yes, he has gone through hell. But you put him there. At what point did you think you'd punished him enough?"

Georgiana bit her lip. "At first, I thought it served him right for putting Rose in the family way. But as time went on and William grew gaunt and frail, I wondered if he might be innocent after all. And then it didn't seem to matter anyway. Men are weak in the ways of the flesh. If William had succumbed once, I could overlook it if there were no long-term consequences."

"Like Rose's child," said Lawrence drily. "Didn't you consider telling the truth for the sake of your husband?"

"He wouldn't let me," said Georgiana.

"You mean he knows?"

"I didn't confess, but whenever I tried to speak of it, he stopped me. Somehow, he knew. He's always known."

"What are you going to do?" asked Michael. He had been sitting so quietly that Lawrence had almost forgotten he was there.

"This," said Lawrence. "Mr Goddard. Here is a woman who is directly responsible for one death and influential in another. Jacob Mullings, who you knew as the Creeper, watched over Mrs Gardiner, striking Billy Wright and frightening Ellen Blowers and Fred Davies for their parts in her distress. She has knowingly allowed her husband to suffer the indignities of jail, potentially ending his life on the gallows. She killed not out of love but from jealousy. Yet, the man you have sworn to protect from public opinion will endure even worse distress if they charge his wife with murder. Either way, William Gardiner can never return to Peasenhall."

Abraham Goddard stood and walked to the window, then placed his hands on the sill, staring towards the reporters while heaving an audible sigh. "I don't know," he said, "I just don't know what I should do. *Assuredly the wicked will not go unpunished*."

"According to the book of Proverbs," said Michael. "But God is compassionate and does not seek to punish the righteous."

Abraham nodded. "And as I suspected, William Gardiner is a righteous man."

"Rose Harsent's murder was premeditated," said Lawrence. "In that regard, it is unforgivable. But this crime was borne of a particular set of unique circumstances."

Abraham strode towards Georgiana Gardiner, who looked up at him, clutching her handkerchief tightly. "Will you accept my judgement?"

"Yes," she whispered.

"You will leave tonight, never to return proceeding straight to Southall in London. I have kin there. They will house you in the short term, and when they release your husband, he will join you. Neither you nor your children shall set foot in Peasenhall again, and you will spend the rest of your life atoning for your sins and making your husband happy."

"I will. Thank you, and please forgive me."

"Do not ask it. I cannot forgive you."

Goddard turned to Lawrence. "I'll make the arrangements immediately. Stay here until I return, and I will consider your commission completed."

Lawrence let him out and locked the door behind him. When he returned to the parlour, Michael and Georgiana Gardiner were kneeling on the floor in prayer.

CHAPTER THIRTY

Epilogue

Saturday, February 14, 1903

"Daddy, Daddy," Daisy squealed as Lawrence walked through his office door for the first time in two weeks. He knelt and put his arms around the little girl before hugging her tightly.

"I missed you, little flower," he said, nuzzling her hair.

She wriggled from his grasp. "Don't go away again, Daddy."

Lawrence smiled sadly, not willing to make a promise he knew he would soon be breaking. He reached into his briefcase and removed a rag doll with a porcelain face. "Here. This is for you. Her name is Isabel."

"Ooh. Can we play outside?"

"Of course," said Lawrence.

Violet smiled as she watched Daisy take the doll and rock it gently in her arms before heading into the rear yard through the kitchen. "That was kind," she said.

"I've missed her," replied Lawrence. "It's been a long two weeks."

"Yes, it has. Thank you for your letter. How is Isabel?"

"Much the same," said Lawrence. "Still working relentlessly to protect London's children. I don't know how she does it. I couldn't do her job if my life depended on it."

"Neither could I. Does Isabel still eschew men and marriage?"

"Completely. Isabel's job is her vocation, and she has little time for anything else. But I took her out a few times. Isabel loves the theatre. I say, you will never guess who we saw?"

Lawrence's eyes sparkled while Violet's heart plummeted. There was only one woman who made him that animated.

"Loveday Melchett," said Lawrence.

"Was she alone?"

"No. She was with Tom, of course. I waved, but they were on the other side of the hall, and neither saw me."

"So, you didn't speak?"

"No. Tom is still feeling awkward about the broken engagement. God knows why. I couldn't care less."

Violet grinned. "Good. Well, as long as Isabel enjoyed herself, that's all that matters. Are the Gardiners settled?"

"Yes. And unbothered by reporters, so far. They are living anonymously in quite a busy area. I doubt anyone will find them."

"It seems so unfair," said Violet.

"I know. The situation doesn't sit well with me either. Rose Harsent was full of life. She deserved so much better than to die because of another woman's jealousy. And a woman who she looked upon as a mother figure."

"I wonder why Georgiana Gardiner snapped after such a long time of believing and supporting her husband."

"My best guess is that she was not in her right mind after her child died. She wasn't thinking clearly, and a piece of careless gossip sealed Rose's fate. I have clung to this theory so I can sleep at night. Otherwise, I have to live with the fact that I conspired to let a guilty woman free to escape justice."

Violet pulled her chair across the room, placed it next to Lawrence's, then patted his hand.

"For what it's worth, I think you are right. You won't regret your decision, Lawrence. Everyone would have suffered if the truth came out, the Gardiners, their children, friends, and family. The village would never have known peace."

"But what about Rose's kin?"

"Georgiana Gardiner was always friendly with Rose. Her poor parents would have felt hurt and betrayed. Justice is important, Lawrence, but it's not paramount."

Lawrence smiled. "How did you get on with your investigation? You haven't mentioned it in our correspondence."

"That's because it turned out to be rather complex. Not the mystery, but the ending."

"Let me guess," said Lawrence. "Eliza Sage did it, but young Gracie isn't marrying her young man."

"Well done," said Violet. "You are half right. Hannah Everett poisoned the kettle out of spite. She fell out with Eliza Sage and wanted to punish her."

"By killing her employers?"

"Goodness me, no. That wasn't the plan at all. Hannah thought it would make them sick, and Eliza would get the blame. Their deaths horrified her, and, years later, she confessed her crime to her dying mother who wrote a letter to Mary Leverett."

"So, Gracie's grandmother knew all along?"

Violet nodded.

"They're a pair of witches, those two."

"Who?"

"Mary Leverett and Beth Briggs. Wise old women, bordering on sinister. Mary couldn't have liked her granddaughter much."

"Why would you say that? She loves Gracie?"

"Yet she gave her information that could only harm her marriage prospects."

"She thought it was the right thing to do under the circumstances and didn't approve of Phillip's family's interference. Anyway, how did you know that the marriage wouldn't take place?"

"Michael said they were mismatched, and that young Edward was a far surer bet if only he would speak up."

"He did, eventually."

"And Miss Francis was receptive?"

"More like relieved and delighted. The longer it took, the more the scales fell from her eyes. She loved Phillip, but his mind was always on his inheritance, which came with conditions. She soon realised that she would never live up to his parents' expectations. I was both shocked and delighted when they came to tell me, but Michael wasn't the least bit surprised."

"How is Michael?" asked Lawrence.

"Still at Netherwood and likely to be there for some time. He can't face going back to his parish, and they've extended his sabbatical for another six months."

"Good. He will need it."

"Did you make any progress while you were in London?"

"I didn't have time, and I needed to consult with you first. Do you think we could manage a trip to Knightsbridge? We could take Daisy and leave her with Ann."

"Michael's sister? Daisy doesn't know her very well."

"Or perhaps she could stay here with Michael. Either way, we must help him. I understand if you want to stay behind, but I'm going to drop all my outstanding cases and commit to helping my old friend. Finding Aurora will be my next investigation."

"Won't Michael want to come?"

"Yes. But he can't. He's too emotionally attached."

"How long will you be away?"

"As long as it takes. Look, Violet. I understand your reluctance to join me. It's not just Daisy, is it? I doubt you want to spend time alone with me. You mustn't fret. I've done a lot of thinking these last two weeks, and I can't change the past. I am resigned to our lives as they are. Perhaps a break is best for both of us, but please don't worry. We will always be partners and friends."

"That's not it," said Violet. "I don't want you to go. But this is my livelihood and leaving the office unattended is bad for business."

"Oh, I see. What's the ledger looking like?"

"Healthy," said Violet, moving back to her desk. "But only because our last two cases have paid. Next month, the bills will pile up again."

"Right. Then it looks like you'll stay here, and I'll go to London."

"Do you remember our walks along the embankment?" asked Violet, her eyes misting over. "It must be a decade ago now."

"Yes. I'll be walking there alone this time," said Lawrence. "I must see Frank Podmore at the Society for Psychic Research."

"Please don't. It isn't safe."

"I have friends in the Metropolitan Police. I'll be fine."

"I couldn't bear it if anything happened to you." Tears welled in Violet's eyes and spilt down her face.

Lawrence watched her, perplexed. "Nothing will happen," he whispered. This time he moved his chair towards her, took her hand and stroked the tear away.

"You nearly died."

"But I didn't," smiled Lawrence. "And you did me proud looking after this business alone. I will never forget your loyalty."

"Life was so much easier back then," said Violet.

"I know. I spoiled it. I was foolish."

"And I've been too proud to let you forget it."

"Don't say that. Violet – you are a wonderful woman, brave, sensible, loyal, and wise. You should be proud. It is more than justified."

259

"Do you know what today is?"

"Saturday."

"The date, I mean."

"Oh, St Valentine's Day. I've never bothered with it."

"Nor have I. But Lawrence, I do love you, despite what you think, and today is a good day to say it."

"As a friend, or something more?"

"If you asked me again, I would say yes."

Lawrence felt his heart thumping through his chest as he stared at Violet, looking for signs of doubt. But Violet perched uncertainly, licking her lips, and staring at the ground as if she had made a catastrophic error of judgement. Still holding her hand, Lawrence dropped to his knee.

"Will you marry me? he asked breathlessly.

"Yes, with all my heart."

THE END

Thank you for reading The Maleficent Maid. I hope you liked it. If you want to find out more about my books, here are some ways to stay updated:

Join my mailing list or visit my website
https://jacquelinebeardwriter.com/

Like my Facebook page
https://www.facebook.com/LawrenceHarpham/

If you have a moment, I would be grateful if you could leave a quick review of The Maleficent Maid online. Honest reviews are very much appreciated and are useful to other readers.

The Maleficent Maid

Lawrence Harpham Murder Mysteries:

The Fressingfield Witch
The Ripper Deception
The Scole Confession
The Felsham Affair
The Moving Stone

Short Stories featuring Lawrence Harpham:

The Montpellier Mystery

The Constance Maxwell Dreamwalker Mysteries

The Cornish Widow
The Croydon Enigma

**Book 3 in The Constance Maxwell Dreamwalker series will
follow soon**

Also, by this author:

Novels:

Vote for Murder

Printed in Great Britain
by Amazon